DREAMS OF EMPIRE

JEANNE MACKIN

DREAMS OF EMPIRE

KENSINGTON BOOKS

KENSINGTON BOOKS are published by

Kensington Publishing Corp.
850 Third Avenue
New York, NY 10022

Library of Congress Card Catalog Number: 95-081481
ISBN 1-57566-020-2

First Printing: April 1996
10 9 8 7 6 5 4 3 2 1

Printed in the United States of America

ACKNOWLEDGMENTS

This novel would not have come into being without the help of many people. My thanks to Steve Poleskie, my husband, who stays calm even at three o'clock in the morning; to Diane Ackerman, for her helpful comments on the manuscript; to my agent Victoria Pryor, my editors at Zebra/Kensington, and to the patient staff of Olin Library.

Thanks especially to Brian M. Fagan, for permission to quote a passage from his invaluable book, *The Rape of the Nile*.

For my father

We are never further from our wishes than when we imagine that we possess what we have desired.

—Goethe

The tombs and great monuments of Ancient Egypt have been under siege ever since they were built. . . . Napoleon Bonaparte came to the Nile in search of an empire and left with the first record of Ancient Egypt, a record that caused a sensation in Europe. By 1833 the monk Father Geramb was able to re-mark to Pasha Mohammed Ali that "It would be hardly respectable, on one's return from Egypt, to present oneself in Europe without a mummy in one hand and a crocodile in the other."

—Brian M. Fagan

Europe is a molehill. Everything here wears out. My glory is already past. This tiny Europe does not offer enough of it. We must go to the Orient. All great glory has always been acquired there.

—Napoleon Bonaparte

It is a bad plan that admits no modification.

—Pubilius Syrus

INTRODUCTION

In 1798 General Napoleon Bonaparte, a sallow, brooding Corsican of twenty-eight who had just conquered Italy for France, decided to add Egypt to the French Empire.

The military plan was to conquer and colonize Egypt, make a peace of sorts with the ruling Turks so that they would not enter the fray, then capture the overland route to India, thus destroying the English empire.

And so on a misty May morning in 1798, as a hysterical England awaited invasion by Bonaparte, the French fleet, an armada of four hundred ships carrying 34,000 troops, instead sailed south from Toulon, heading for Egypt.

Josephine, whom Bonaparte had hoped would join him during this venture, was not part of the traveling host. She had decided to stay in France. For her health, she said.

Little was known of Egypt at that time. Bonaparte, in addition to his military goals, planned to make a recorded history of the entirety of Egyptian history and civilization. One hundred and forty of France's intelligentsia, known to the world as savants but to the French army as donkeys because of the back-breaking number of boxes, crates, and trunks with which they traveled, arrived in Egypt with Bonaparte. They were to find and bring back to France bits of this and that, a mummy or two, or some statuettes, with which to amuse the populace and fill the Louvre, making the general a cultural as well as military hero.

This was some many thousands of years after the Pharaoh Shepseskaf learned that self-will and destiny often differ.

The success Bonaparte had known in Italy was not as easily repeated in Egypt. Lord Nelson, not so distracted by Lady Hamilton's charms that he could not smell a fox when it trotted, or more accurately, sailed under his nose, found and destroyed the French fleet as soon as the invaders disembarked on the hot shores of Alexandria, stranding the French invaders in a distant and dusty land. The young Corsican made the most of a difficult situation: he brought Cairo and much of Egypt under control of the French army with little help from his allies in France, who were effectively cut-off from him. It cannot be said that the other members of the Directory were grieved to have audacious Bonaparte thus amputated from the body of their own ambition.

Sultan Selim III, ruler of the ancient and now disintegrating Ottoman Empire, was loathe to relinquish his richest province, Egypt, to his supposed friends, the French. He slyly invited the English to come rid Egypt of the French.

And even as Bonaparte dreamed of the countries and monuments he would collect for the glory of France, another man of ambition, Lord Elgin, suggested to his English government that he should be made ambassador to Constantinople, to help direct the humbling and vanquishing of Bonaparte. While he was in the East, he would, of course, wish to collect some artifacts for the greater glory of England and himself. The latter half of the eighteenth century was a time of great collectors and great collections, which is to say it was a time of greed.

And so this story begins on a hot August night in Cairo, 1799. Ten thousand stars glitter in the indigo sky. Below them, in a *hareem* room shut off from the sky and the night with thick wooden screens, a woman stands, one hand on hip, the other on her forehead, in a posture older than the pyramids. She sees . . .

1

White sand, dark sky, and a shadow crossing the base of the great pyramid, made of the black silhouettes of a caravan pausing before it.

Even at this distance the ill-tempered camels could be heard snorting and complaining as the caravan leaders made their evening fires. Palm trees, solitary as widows, rustled in the breeze.

Marguerite watched them from the cloistered rooms of an Oriental palace built by a bey of Egypt and now inhabited by heavy-footed French savants. Her expression of discontent and regret had no nationality. Her eyes were pale, foreigner's eyes, *farengi* eyes, the Arabs called them. Michel once said they were the clean color of the Seine, north of Paris.

Closer at hand the gardens of Ezbekiah Square, Bonaparte's Cairo headquarters, shone muddy silver, the invading waters of the Nile having made of its courtyards and garden paths a gurgling, still-rising lake.

The Nile, then, before the age of great dams, had three seasons. In September came the Time of Sufficiency, when the resurrected river filled ancient flood basins and irrigation canals, ready to quench the thirst of crops, of cattle, of people. This was a time of great richness and festivity, when the red land turned golden with wheat and wildflowers sprang underfoot.

The Time of Insufficiency began in March. The water inched down the sides of the irrigation canals and basins, and the lakes slowly turned into dusty basins. Sun baked and crackled the land and the *khamsin*, the poison wind, blew misfortune and dust for fifty days.

The Inundation, when the Nile was brought back to life from waters flowing north (it never rains in Egypt) began in summer. The sluggish river turned quick and brown with silt, fertile and fragrant. It carried lime and potash, iron and magnesia, aluminum and silesia, all dissolved into a rich sludge that fed the soil, the crops, the people. Sometimes it brought larger gifts: pebbles of Chrysoberl, chalcedony and jasper, to adorn the proud necks or ankles of pretty young women. Sometimes the waters carried a body along, making the women gathered at the edge of the river with their washing throw up their arms and wail and make signs against the evil eye.

The water carried mystery and ancient troubles still un-resolved. The season of Inundation was a season of charms and spells to encourage the river if it rose too slowly, or placate the river, if it rose too quickly. The people of Cairo looked often over their shoulders at this time.

This was the time of Inundation. Where, just weeks before, people had walked or ridden, little white-sailed boats glided. Cairo, a city of minarets and souks, narrow streets and secret pathways, was turned into a city of canals and bridges, dry hills lapped by marsh and pond. The water was rising quickly this year. The strong-voiced *Munadee*, who cried out the measure of the daily rise through the city, was growing rich with bribes from nervous Cairenes who hoped he would have a private word or two with the river god that they, of course, no longer believed in.

The river was angry. It carried many bodies. Three of them had been the bloated, nibbled remains of antiquity dealers known to the French savants and collectors. Marguerite had looked out one night onto the river and saw one of them float by, naked and white in the moonlight, a kind of horrible fish with little to suggest it had once been human. She had felt curiosity, not repulsion. She had seen worse in France, during the Terror.

The pale-eyed woman looked out the window now, at the brown water, ochre houses, and distant pyramids, and wondered if the river carried bodies this night.

"Come back to bed," a man's impatient voice called to her.

Marguerite Verdier, illustrator attached to the atelier of artist Dominique Vivant Denon, and one of the few women who had boarded ship with the Egyptian expedition, turned and saw her lover's sunburned arm beckoning her back to the rumpled bed.

"In a moment," she said. "There is a breeze here, by the window."

In fact, she was hoping he would dress and leave. His conversation bored her and he liked to converse after lovemaking. She preferred silence. Aristide was her first lover after ten years of marriage and fidelity. She hoped subsequent lovers would not be as garrulous.

"Where are your thoughts? In Paris?" Aristide was jealous.

"Not in Paris. On the river."

Aha. A lie, she accused herself. She had been thinking of Michel, her husband, who was in Switzerland. She hoped to never see him again. She missed him desperately. She returned to bed, to Aristide.

He put his arms too tightly around her, reminding her that she was, for all practical purposes, a prisoner in Cairo. The English navy had isolated the French army and the savants, from the rest of the world; while they ruled Cairo, it wasn't wise to wander the narrow, crowded streets outside the French compounds. Devout Muslims believed themselves polluted by the mere sight of a heathen Frank. It was considered sport to beat them.

Marguerite dared not leave her quarters even to go to the *souks* or baths. Her situation at the Institute, as a foreigner, as a woman, was quite similar to what was called "house arrest" in France.

There were consolations. There was her hookah, which could be filled with tobacco or hashish as her mood demanded. There was her sketch pad and paint box. There was the tiled and marbled, silken-draped luxury of her quarters in the *hareem*. There was Aristide who at that moment was tracing arcane and lovely designs on her bare back, secret symbols that brought the gooseflesh and roused her slumbering lust.

And, there was the knowledge that she could avoid an unpleasant confrontation with General Bonaparte and an equally unpleasant lecture, long and pompous, by Berthollet, who was presenting a paper at the Institute that evening. She had already sent word to the committee that a headache would force her, alas, to keep to her room this evening. With luck, no one would remark on the fact that Lt. Aristide Roux was also missing.

The wind began to moan at the same time that Aristide's cunning fingers made her begin to sigh anew. Grains of sand rained through the apartment. They made a rasping, scratching sound as they hit brass and marble and wood. They grew louder and merged with the hollow sound of hand beating against wood.

"Someone is at the door," Marguerite whispered to Aristide.

"They will go away eventually," he whispered back, continuing.

The knocking grew more insistent. Marguerite pushed Aristide away and adjusted her own clothing just as she heard a key turning in the lock and the door creaking open. Madame Beaucaire rushed in, her heels clicking with self-importance, and Aristide dove under the linens.

"I've asked you before to return that key to me," Marguerite complained, piling books and notebooks beside her on the bed, camouflaging the lumps that were her hidden lover.

Marguerite did not like Adelaide Beaucaire, the rug merchant's wife. Years of exile in this foreign land with only a few too-close friends and her husband for company had rendered Adelaide a bore and a busybody. Marguerite, daughter of a royalist opera dancer with dangerous attachments, knew the value of privacy and discretion. Adelaide Beaucaire allowed her newly arrived acquaintances little of either. Alas, Adelaide was so provincial, so behind-the-times, she still called her women friends madame, not citizeness, as if the revolution had never happened.

"It is best I keep the key for emergency. You can come out of there, monsieur. I would not want you to suffocate." Madame Beaucaire sat gingerly on the edge of the bed and patted the lumps. Aristide groaned and pushed his head and chest out of the bedcoverings.

"We are women of the world, are we not?" Madame said, winking. "Besides. I have important news for you. A surprise. You cannot guess!" Madame Beaucaire rolled her eyes and clasped her hands in theatrical manner.

"General Puss-in-Boots will be at the meeting of the institute this evening," Marguerite stated flatly. There had been a time when she could call Bonaparte Puss-in-Boots to his face, and the general would laugh and pinch her cheek. That was before Josephine's infidelities had been discovered. Now, women rarely made him laugh and coyness irritated him. "Close the door, citizeness, if you please. On your way out."

Marguerite picked up a heavy folio and pretended to study one of Vivant Denon's sketches of French soldiers on parade in the desert. He'd used all his skills as a pornographer—they were considerable—to make the drawing lascivious and comical, with each soldier sporting a huge erection. A group of naked dancing girls cavorted off to the side of the parade. Marguerite's task would be to redraw it *sans* erections, *sans* dancing girls, so that it could become part of the official portfolio documenting the Egyptian campaign.

"Foolish child. The whole world has known for days that Bonaparte will be here. Probably Nelson himself knows, may he go to the devil, and quickly," Adelaide exclaimed. "Can't see why Bonaparte stirs such interest. That sour little general from Corsica will never amount to anything. No, that's not the news."

"I would be careful about deprecating that little general so loudly," Marguerite warned, picking up a thick pencil and beginning to sketch. Aristide, struggling into his shirt, watched over her shoulder, eyes narrowed with amusement as he picked out faces of comrades in Denon's sketch. "Bonaparte has ears everywhere. And now, leave me to my work. I am not going to the lecture and have no interest in whatever is going to happen there."

Adelaide, not so easily put off, pulled the pencil out of the younger woman's hand, and put her face close to Marguerite's.

"Voilà. The surprise will not take place at the meeting, but here, in your quarters. Monsieur Verdier has arrived! Your husband is here!"

On the other side of Cairo, in a house overlooking the Mokattam Hills, Sheik Hamid al Shackoui grimaced and ran his hands over his newly washed and anointed head. The shaved part felt smooth; the long lock he let grow—it was the lock by which the angel would pull him from the grave—was still damp. He put the skull cap on his head, then wound a white turban around it.

He did not wish to attend this dinner. He did not like the company of the infidel French, the unmanly, shaven faces of the men and the brazen, uncovered faces of the women. But his nephew, Ibrahim, wished to go and it would be unwise to let Ibrahim go alone. The young man had a penchant for trouble.

Sighing, hands behind his back, Hamid walked onto his courtyard, into the warm night air and sniffed. He smelled the perfumed rosewater of his fountain, and the dust from the desert, and the earthy, fertile smell of Nile water, rising, rising. Today the water had risen ten digits. That was too much for one day. It augured trouble.

A dangerous time, the flooding of the Nile. A time when things often went badly. The *fellaheen* had many superstitions about this time, charms and spells to keep trouble at bay. He had only his prayers and faith and tonight they seemed not enough.

Hamid plunged his hands into the fountain and rubbed the sweet rosewater into his beard. The water slipped between his fingers, cool and fragrant and as unholdable as the dreams of youth.

Hamid al Schackoui, twenty years before, had been famous for his love poems and his horsemanship. He'd married two women, as the law allowed, one who was young and beautiful and strong, and another who was plain and not young. But instead of getting children from his strong wife and companionship from the plain one, his beautiful wife proved barren and his old wife gave him only girl children, no sons. Blessings on them.

His house buzzed like a hive with the high voices of women. They were obedient and he had no complaints of them. But he had no son to come with him to the mosque, no son to ride with him, to discuss the poets with him and the words of the Prophet. For many years that place in the heart which can only be filled with the love of a son was empty and dry.

Then, his widowed sister sent Ibrahim to him. His sister was rich with sons and this one, the youngest, troubled her beyond her meager store of patience. He climbed down the sycamore tree and stayed out all night. He went to the bazaar and talked to strange women. He drank wine in the taverns where the foreigners drank. And so he had been sent to sonless Hamid, to be instructed, to be made into a man of righteousness, not a lawless youth.

But six months ago Ibrahim had unexpectedly come home with a wife. Her red hair curled out from under her veil and her green eyes assessed the house and its furnishings with a rug merchant's greediness. She spoke with a strange, Turkish accent in a too-loud voice.

"Uncle, meet Atiyah. She is my wife." Just like that.

Where did you meet her? Who is her family? Is she a divorced woman? What about the ceremonies?

Young men did not wish to hear such questions, much less answer them. Hamid could have disowned Ibrahim and shamed him before the entire community and his family. Instead, because he loved Ibrahim, he welcomed Atiyah, the Gallatian woman, into his home.

Trouble. The Nile was rising too quickly this year. There would be flooding and disaster.

There would be trouble tonight. She felt it coming. Marguerite, hurriedly dressed in evening clothes, descended one of the many small staircases that led from the upstairs *hareem* rooms to the larger, public rooms below. If there was to be a reunion with her husband, it had better be in public, rather than private. The last time she had seen him he had been embracing Josette in the stables, during one of their visits to Madame Junot's country house. After he had promised—how many times now?—that his philandering was over. Hence, Marguerite's precipitous flight to Egypt, a land as far from Michel as she could conceive of. Hence, her new foray into the pleasures of adultery, the sweetest pleasure of which seemed to be simple revenge.

The evening would have been troubling even without Michel's arrival, since Bonaparte was back in Cairo. He had not had a civil word for her since he had learned of Josephine's infidelities, as if Marguerite were responsible for the other woman's behavior. It was true that Josephine had stupidly used Marguerite's rooms for some of her rendezvous, but Marguerite, unstylishly prudish in such matters before Aristide had taken her in hand, had neither known nor approved. Yet now she shared Josephine's guilt and Bonaparte's condemnation. This newer guilt had reminded Bonaparte, who felt surrounded by royalist conspiracy, that Marguerite's mother had been a royalist.

The reception room was already crowded when Marguerite arrived. Music, the fluting, sensual notes of pipes, rose up in the dusty air. They had hired musicians. To please Bonaparte. Her searching eyes quickly found Denon, her patron, who was newly returned from a year of marching with the army, sunburned and thin except for his red-cheeked, deceptively cherubic face. He was in good humor and his booming laughter filled the large room.

Bonaparte stood, feet apart, right hand stuffed into his jacket front, in the middle of the room. He had not yet cut his unfashionable but dashing long hair; he had not yet acquired that middle-aged heaviness that would eventually make him look as much like a banker as an emperor. He was surrounded by a large coterie of enthusiastic savants, all talking at once, asking about the expedition to Syria, the battles, the war, and the ruins and monuments they had discovered.

The general's blue uniform was faded to a dusty grey by the strong desert sun; his nose was blistered and peeling. At his side was his new mistress, little Pauline Foures, sometimes called Cleopatra Foures, in honor of the setting of this particular love story.

Poor Josephine. Bonaparte, learning of his wife's infidelities, had lost no time in taking his revenge. A Lieutenant Foures, newly married to a pretty, vivacious blonde who had donned uniform and accompanied her husband to Egypt, was dispatched back to France. His wife, Pauline, remained behind. Days later, little Pauline was Bonaparte's mistress. Within weeks she was divorced from her lieutenant and ensconced in Bonaparte's private rooms. It was rumored that he had promised to divorce Josephine and wed her.

Josephine, of course, would know of all this from Eugene, her son, who was one of Puss-in-Boots aides-de-camp, and wrote regularly to his mother. Josephine, Marguerite imagined, must be tearing her hair in consternation. And Lieutenant Foures had been overheard to say he hoped one day to be alone with Bonaparte, pistol in hand.

Marguerite studiously avoided catching Bonaparte's eye, and glanced over the rest of the gathering.

Michel was there, just as Madame Beaucaire said. Her heart skipped a beat when she saw him, but this, she reassured herself, was due to no finer sentiment than irritation. She studied him coolly, forcing herself to find him lacking and unworthy of the love she had once felt. He looked tired and dusty. His jaw was heavier than she remembered, his nose longer, his expression haughtier. At least he had given up wigs and now wore his hair in a republican manner, trimmed neatly to his ears and unpowdered.

He had been cornered by Adelaide Beaucaire, who was talking quickly, in a loud voice, explaining some marvel she had bought in the bazaar and gesturing grandly with beringed hands.

Feeling someone staring at him, Michel looked up. His eyes met his wife's. Marguerite smiled coldly, snapped open her fan, and turned away, directly into her lover's extended arm. His champagne spilled. Aristide Roux went on his knees and swiped at her skirts with a napkin.

"Get up!" she hissed, smiling. "You are making a scene and it will dry quickly enough in this heat!" Aristide blushed and crossed the room in six coltish strides to refill his glass.

Marguerite felt the night disintegrate into a nightmare. She moved to where Dr. Morello, a dark, quiet Tuscan, shared a divan with Sheikh Hamid al Shackoui, who was obviously ill-at-ease and wishing to be elsewhere. The sheikh's nephew, Ibrahim, stood at his back.

"How is Atiyah?" Marguerite asked the sheikh, pausing before him. She liked this man with the black beard and dark, sad eyes, although she suspected Sheikh al Shackoui thought her a harlot because she went about unveiled.

Hamid pulled at his beard and smiled. "Well," he said. "She is well. Thank you for asking." In truth, he did not know how Atiyah was. The woman kept too many secrets, singing one day, weeping the next, putting the women's quarters in an uproar, for no apparent reason.

The younger man, Ibrahim, spoke up. "She sends greetings and gratitude for the gift of the perfume you have sent. She will come herself, tomorrow, if you will receive her, to repay your kindness."

"She is always welcome, but there is no need for gratitude," Marguerite protested. The last time Atiyah had wanted to do her a favor, she had brought her box of henna paste and insisted on dyeing Marguerite's feet and hands. It had been amusing for a day or so, but it required a week of scrubbing to remove the orange stains from her skin. Marguerite much preferred the amulet Atiyah had given her, a silver crocodile on a long chain, guaranteed to bring long life and good luck in love.

Hamid frowned. French perfume? Was that the stench he smelled last night? Why could Atiyah not be content with oil of roses, as the other women were?

"My dear, we were just speaking of the stone they found in Rosetta . . ." Dr. Morello began. He moved deeper into the corner of the divan to make room for her. A polite man was Dr. Morello, with a forehead always creased in concern, and solicitude mixed with humor in his warm brown eyes. The solicitude was a learned skill, part of his science of healing, but the humor that never found expression beyond the eyes could not be traced to any known source. He made Marguerite uncomfortable. Outside, she could hear the wind rustling the palms and wished she was alone with the night and the wind.

"Who is that new man, in the corner, with our Madame Beaucaire?" Sheikh Hamid al Shackoui asked her now, pointing to Michel. "He does not look like an artist or a man of science."

"What does he look like?" she asked, curious to know how a stranger would see Michel.

The sheikh narrowed his eyes, studying him. "A man of secrets who has learned to be at home everywhere, I would say. A diplomat. No, a spy."

Dr. Morello laughed. "Sorry to disappoint you, my friend. To me, he appears to be just another Frenchman eager to see the mysterious Orient and take home a mummified cat or carnelian scarab. Not artist nor scientist nor soldier nor spy. A mere hanger-on."

"He is my husband," Marguerite said quietly.

Both men cleared their throats and quickly resumed discussion of the stone found in Rosetta. The young man, Ibrahim, said not a word, but leaned closer, eager for details. Marguerite half-listened for a few minutes, then prepared to face the inevitable.

The tight circle around Bonaparte was thinning. The general had ignored her so far, and she knew she could not let that continue. A pretence of civility was required. Anything less would be dangerous. She must find a way to placate him. She rose and made her way towards the general, still ignoring Michel. Bonaparte looked fatigued. He was thinner than he had been a year before—who wasn't?—and there were deep shadows under his eyes. His complexion, beneath the sunburn, was greenish.

"Ah! Citizeness Verdier!" he acknowledged. His voice was cold, his eyes metallic. Pauline Foures, sensing trouble, moved protectively closer to her general.

Marguerite smiled, moved closer, and extended her hand, though she would have as soon thrust that hand into one of the cobra baskets in the *souk*.

"It is good to see you, my friend. Cairo has missed you. I hear the campaign was a great success." Even she heard the insincerity in her voice. She was glad that, being only a woman, she would not be required to define a military success.

Two thousand French soldiers lay mummifying in the sands outside of Acre. Thousands more were dying of plague and starvation. Kleber, Bonaparte's chief aid, had been heard to remark that Bonaparte was the kind of general who needed a monthly income of ten thousand men. Morale was low among the thin, dysentery-ridden soldiers, and among the members of the scientific institute. There was more grumbling going on than was good for a campaign. And back home Austria had declared war on France.

The Orient was no longer the place for an ambitious general to be. Rumors were spreading that Bonaparte planned to leave Egypt, soon. And alone. In fact, some speculated that this evening's honored appearance would be Puss-in-Boots's last at the institute.

This made things a little tricky for the orientalist Marcel, who had yet to finish his Arabic translation of the ode on the conquest of Egypt by the French. He had scowled for days, trying to think of a suitable way to end the ode.

"A death would do nicely," he had concluded the day before. "A death full of glory and honor."

Bonaparte nodded at Marguerite without smiling and studied her with cold, opaque eyes.

"I warned you not to come. This climate is not kind to women," he finally answered.

Marguerite forced the tight, about-to-crack smile to remain on her face till this painful exchange could be ended. Then, she would return to her quarters, lock the door, and stay there till she could find transport to France. She would swim if she had to, damn Nelson.

"I think Citizeness Verdier looks splendid. Like a tall, brown Bedouin queen," said a familiar voice. Michel, standing now at her side, took her elbow in a familiar, protective gesture.

"May I introduce myself, General? I am Citizen Verdier." Michel bowed to Bonaparte.

"I ordered that no more civilians were to come to Cairo. How and why are you here? Why aren't you in the army?"

"I am a member of Talleyrand's staff. I am here, General, to visit my wife. And I arrived on the same ship that returned Lieutenant Foures to you."

Bonaparte turned white under his tan. Pauline blushed. No one dared mention Pauline's husband to her lover's face. Bonaparte turned on his heel, pulling little Pauline Foures with him.

"That was not well done, Michel," Marguerite whispered furiously.

"It was a gamble. A man of humor and sophistication would have said 'touche!' and laughed." Michel, unabashed, took his snuff box from his vest pocket, inhaled a pinch in each nostril, and sneezed heartily into his handkerchief.

"Bonaparte does not laugh at anything these days. Especially reminders of his mistress's husband. Speaking of mistresses, husband, why are you here?"

"For you, my dear," Michel said smoothly, tucking the snuff box back into his pocket. "After all the hardships of travel I have endured to be at your side, have you no kind word of greeting? Didn't you miss me just a little?"

"Not at all, my dear," she lied for the second time that night. Dream of a thorn, and someone will lie to you,

Atiyah had told her. Outside, the wind whispered and the playful notes of a fellaheen's pipe danced through the dusty night. Water gurgled and rustled as the Nile continued to rise.

Madame Beaucaire glided by, surprisingly light on her small feet for a woman of such girth. She paused in front of Marguerite.

"My dear! You didn't tell me monsieur, your husband, was so very attractive," she cooed. "What a pleasant addition to our community! I must arrange a little entertainment for him!"

Marguerite smiled at madame's *faux pas*. That was how some aristocrats, weary of death and dying, had referred to the guillotine: as a little entertainment.

2

Egypt: The Red Land
3737 BC

R ed sand, pale purple sky, the brown, foaming river flooding closer, closer . . .

On the other side of the river, a dark line of bent-backed laborers moved on the horizon, dividing earth and sky. Watching from the shelter of his lion-guarded balcony was a man who, though surrounded by courtiers and retainers, was alone. He wore the double crown of upper and lower Egypt. He was a god. It was his tomb they built, and the god-man frowned with worry.

It was the twenty-sixth day of the first month of *akhit,* the Inundation, the anniversary of the great struggle between Seth and Horus. It was a dangerous day. A day for caution.

Shepseskaf, Pharaoh of Upper and Lower Egypt, stepped further out onto his balcony, close enough to the chained lion that it sniffed his hem. Pharaoh, ignoring the tamed beast, turned slightly, making the new sun reflect off his headpiece and send glints of gold into the eyes of the laborers. He lifted his head to better display his gem-heavy pectoral and then clapped his hands twice. A stream of slaves appeared, carrying baskets of new wheat and caskets of beer; they moved towards the workers' encampment.

Pharaoh would have liked to cross the river and distribute the bread himself. But this was a hostile day, one in which it was forbidden to embark in a boat. The gifts must wait till tomorrow. He hoped it would not be too late.

There had been fresh rumors in the necropolis workers' camp that he could not pay their wages, that the royal treasury was emptied.

Let the tomb builders see the gold of my headpiece, Pharaoh thought. Let them see the lapis and garnet of my necklaces and bracelets and the white ibis feathers woven into my pleated skirt. Let them eat my bread and drink my beer. Let them see and believe that I, Pharaoh, am still the mightiest in Egypt. I, Shepseskaf, not the priests, rule.

Hathor, little goddess, protect me and let them see a lie.

The treasury was growing bare. Great Egypt, and the Pharaoh, was crippled with debt. Foreign wars and the building of the great pyramids had bled the land. And now the priests, greedy as kings, were draining off the remains. Worse than the greed of the priests was their heresy: they said that Pharaoh was a man, not the god incarnate. And the people began to believe.

The pyramids cast shadows large as cities. His tomb would cast no such shadow. His tomb, his home for eternity, was but a simple mastaba, a flat, squat brick rectangle such as courtiers used to be buried in, not divine Pharaoh. There was no apex pointing to the path of the Sun chariot for Shepseskaf, no miles of secret and false paths to deter grave robbers, no chambers filled with wealth enough for the ages. Shepseskaf, penurious in life, would be so throughout his eternity. His cartonnage would be of thin wood and despite all the embalmers' arts his dust would mingle with the dust of the desert.

The priests had seen to that. They and their greedy god, Ra, had stolen Pharaoh's wealth and power.

Pharaoh's hands, hanging at his side, clenched and then relaxed. Useless. He turned away from the sight of the flat, squat tomb, from the long line of tomb-builders that had slowed and was now studying him, Pharaoh. He would go into his curtained chamber and rest, though he was not tired.

There was a movement behind him; a shadow fell between Shepseskaf and the royal pavilion, blocking his way. It was his daughter's husband, Ptahshepses. His son-in-law fell to the ground before Pharaoh and lowered his forehead to the ground.

Shepseskaf could remember brighter yesterdays when the sight of this man had gladdened him. They had grown up together, like brothers, taking their lessons from the same tutors, sharing the same bath. His father had treated Ptahshepses like a son. Better. Now that only truth was left to him, Shepseskaf saw that there never had been a time when he had not been jealous of Ptahshepses, the boy-child found in the desert, half-buried like a statue coming to life by the sculpturing wind. Ptahshepses had always received the best hunting dogs, the largest jewels, and the sweetest perfumes as his share. His father had loved him and Shepseskaf had loved him, as his father wished.

When Shepseskaf took the royal scepter into his hands after his father died, he had rejoiced that his daughter, Ma'tcha', wanted Ptahshepses for her husband. That was before Ptahshepses became high priest and wore the robes of power and performed the rituals for his all-powerful, his singular Ra. Before Ptahshepses turned against the royal family, his benefactors. Now there was only hatred between them.

"You block my way, priest," Pharaoh said.

"I ask your forgiveness, Great One." Ptahshepses, on his knees, did not move aside.

Shepseskaf stared down at the freshly shaven and perfumed head of the man who was both brother and son-in-law to him. Forgiveness? Shepseskaf didn't think so. This was another trick. He could have the man cut down on the spot. He could release the lion which was not so tame that it did not enjoy a bloody game. Pharaoh still yielded that much power. But that would displease the other priests and he dare not do that.

His daughter, he thought ruefully, would not be displeased if this husband no longer returned to her in the evening. Love, for her, had long since turned to hatred. She saw, too late, that for Ptahshepses she had not been a woman to love, but a means to power. Ptahshepses's greatest pleasure was to humiliate the daughter of Pharaoh, his wife. And there was nothing Pharaoh could do. There was nothing Ma'tcha' could do. Her heart withered in her chest and the light fled her eyes.

The laborers' singing had ceased. Heads were turned this way, waiting and watching.

"What do you want of me?"

"To kiss your feet, so that the people may see I love you," said Ptahshepses, keeping his face pressed to the white sand, but speaking loudly.

The courtiers standing at Shepseskaf's side shifted uneasily and made as if to speak, but Pharaoh raised his staff, commanding silence. He kept his face immobile, but anger and bitterness flooded his eyes.

"You have no right to touch Pharaoh," he answered.

"Your humble servant begs to kiss your foot," Ptahshepses repeated.

"Pharaoh cannot be sullied by mortal touch. Only my wife and child may touch me. You know this, priest."

"I am also your son-in-law and father of your grandchild. Let me kiss your foot, father-in-law."

Ptahshepses stayed on his knees, but he lifted his shoulders and head. With a shrug he threw back the coarsely spun mantel covering his robes. His chest blazed with gold and jewels. Sapphires and rubies flashed in his breastplate and armbands. The green glass that was more precious than diamonds glittered in his belt and huge gold discs dangled from his ears. A panther skin, draped over his shoulders, was adorned with pearl stars, to show he was chief of the secrets of heaven.

Ptahshepses smelled of myrrh and roses and was clad in the wealth of Egypt. Wealth. Power. More wealth, more power than Pharaoh had, and this priest was threatening to stand and reveal his riches to all who watched. Pharaoh knew now the origin of the rumors that Pharaoh was unable to give the tomb-builders their allotted bread, beer, and linen. The priests, with their lies and their cunning and their greed, had won the loyalty of the laborers.

Pharaoh looked about helplessly. The laborers watched. And on a dune lined with tents, the priests watched, too, and waited. Birds ceased flying, the wind was stillborn.

This had been planned by the priests. He had been out-maneuvered. If he refused the priest's wish, the laborers might strike, and the tomb would not be completed. If he granted the wish, he would be defiled for eternity.

Shepseskaf felt his heavy heart, torn by this choice, break in two. It was over. The old gods had lost. The priests and their ascending, power-jealous Ra would win.

Pharaoh, his face a frozen mask, already looking as if the master carver had sculpted it for his mummy case, lifted his left foot a handspan from the dust, where his footprint remained only for the briefest moment before the wind obliterated it. Ptahshepses crept forward and took the proffered foot in his hands. He put his rouged lips on the high arch of Pharaoh's divine foot.

Shepseskaf ground his teeth. The watching priests and tomb builders stirred with satisfaction.

Then, there was a roar from the river. A dike had broken and the flooding waters washed through the workers' camp, dousing fires and carrying away baskets. As Pharaoh and the terrified workers watched, the water seemed to swell and rage like a living thing, a monster, until it washed up to the very balcony on which Pharaoh stood.

Ptahshepses, still on his knees before Pharaoh, began to

tremble. Some men feared the desert scorpion, others feared poisoned wine. Ptahshepses feared the river. When he was a small boy crossing the river with his family, their little boat had overturned and his mother, father, and sister disappeared into the hungry water. The boatman had saved him by grasping his uncut hair. Each night in his sleep he still felt the embrace of the river, driving the breath out of his lungs.

Ptahshepses, thinking that the jealous river had again come for him, put his hands over his ears, and fell into twitching, choking convulsions. The priests, their robes lashing at their ankles, came and carried him away.

Pharaoh watched and his heart grew lighter. Hathor had done this for him.

Later, after the purification ritual had been performed and his feet massaged with scented oil to obliterate the evil touch, Pharaoh opened the chest that contained his funerary statues. The statues of the gods had been his comfort and pleasure, and his concern, for he lived in perpetual fear that they would be stolen from him.

He brought out and caressed statues of Pharaoh as a young man and of his wife, young and beautiful as she had once been, and his daughter, smiling as she once had.

Under the other statues, wrapped thickly in clean, snow-white linen, was the stela for the secret door to the burial room, carved with protecting incantations and the form of his favorite goddess, Hathor, goddess of joy, goddess of the Morning Star.

The goddess was clothed in a thin linen robe that clung to the curves of her belly and thighs; a heavy collar rested on her delicate throat and shoulders. Her arms were raised as if in protest or to defend herself. Her open mouth, carved in profile, was a half moon. She faced Anubis, the jackal headed god of death. Behind the two figures, wavy lines indicated the flooding Nile, the river of death and resurrection.

Hathor, representation of nature, of the world in which gods dwell, commanded Anubis, god of death.

It was as it should be. Anubis would take her with him, to the other world, and each time Hathor would arise again, young and renewed and eternal. It was a fight for power, and Hathor would be repeatedly defeated, and always win.

Just as he, Pharaoh, defeated by the priests in life, could yet win in death. Hathor promised him immortality.

Pharaoh, consoled, wrapped his funerary statues and set them back into the chest. Hathor he put aside. It was time for the engraver to set Pharaoh's name on the stela.

3

Broomhall, Scotland
August 1799

Yellow gorse, grey sky. A deep silence, suddenly broken by a fluttering of wings, a loud report, and the controlled exuberance of a hunting dog plowing through the gorse and heather. What had once been living, shimmering beauty was now a bloodied, lifeless mass of feathers.

"A fine specimen. I'll have it mounted." Thomas Bruce, Seventh Earl of Elgin and newly appointed Minister Plenipotentiary of His Britannic Majesty to the Sublime Porte of Selim the Third of Turkey, pried the pheasant from Bonnie Charlie's pink-gummed mouth. He expertly examined the lapis sheen of the perfect, long tail feathers. "Always room for another trophy, 'eh, Pol?"

Pol did not think so. Eggy was a little prodigal in his collecting of specimens. The hall was filled with the glass-eyed, sawdust-filled forms of deer, pheasant, and other assorted dead animals. Eggy was, well, immoderate, it seemed to her. His enthusiasms verged on obsession. It reminded her of the old pagan kings who had had their wealth buried with them, as if heaven could be purchased. And she had dreamed once that a case of his bric-a-brac fell on her, suffocating her, so that she became as dead and dull as one of the birds mounted in the great hall. He had pointed her out to visitors, along with the glass-eyed eagle and hawk.

Her husband extended the drooping, limp bird toward his bride of four months, the handsome and steady-eyed nineteen-year-old Mary.

"Eggy, do be careful. It's dripping," she protested in a fluting, girlish voice, backing away. Her riding habit was new, part of the large and practical trousseau she and her womenfolk had barely completed in time for the wedding. It was fashionable, but not unduly so, not in a way that would date. With care, the habit would last for decades. Mary intended it should do so.

Lord Elgin, frowning, put the bird in his hunt bag. A bit too fastidious, his Pol. Fine in the drawing room but he resented the way she rose immediately after each night-time marital encounter and scrubbed herself till she glowed pinkly moist and clean. "Never get a son that way," he reprimanded her often. "Jumping up like that. Let it be, Pol."

She ignored the warnings, following instead some ancient counsel or inclination probably passed on by her mother. Let her not be like her mother, he feverishly prayed each night. Pol was an only child. And he wanted to fill the nursery of Broomhall with brown-eyed, light-haired sons made in his image.

Despite her fastidiousness she had proved a passionate girl, and that was all to the good. It was very good. It reminded him of something he had once written to his mother, half in jest. "It is my ill fortune rather than my fault that I have only to show myself to excite tender passions. Veni, vidi, vici." He'd been younger then, traveling abroad for the first time, and his mother had had the usual motherish fears of secret filial weddings to opera dancers, clandestine visits to unfashionable doctors to be treated for unmentionable diseases. The boast had been meant to lighten her fears. In vain, those fears. He had neither wed secretly and unwisely nor needed doses of mercury. The chancre, just a little one, had disappeared all by itself. (It would return, sooner rather than later, but on this fine late summer morning neither the earl nor his bride had reason to suspect the incipient disaster of syphilis.)

But something had to be done about Pol's squeamishness. It was caused, undoubtedly, by too much time spent in the drawings rooms of Edinburgh, not enough time in the fields of Archerfield or Biel. Or Belhaven, for that matter, though the hunting was not so good there, Elgin suspected. He smiled as he mentally listed Mary's estates, and placed the lifeless pheasant into the game bag, being careful not to spoil the tail feathers. He had married well. The girl was both rich and beautiful, an heiress of a wealthy, landowning family, with dark hair and eyes and a matchless figure. A Greek goddess with an Edinburgh accent.

A Greek fertility goddess, with wide hips and full breasts and a new swell to her belly that indicated his warnings had been a waste: despite all her jumping up after the marital embrace, he was certain that Pol was already with child.

As for the wincing squeamishness, his new embassy to Constantinople should take care of that. She needed to see a bit of the world.

Beaming and possessive, he took Pol's little hand in his.

"Time to get some breakfast in you," he said. "Kidneys and eggs. A kipper or two."

Mary nodded, wondering if she could get the cook to bring her some of last night's apple pie, instead.

It was a longish ride back to Broomhall, near Dunfermline on the Fife side of the Firth. They passed the lime quarry, the harbor, the collieries, all land and operations owned by Elgin, all part of his grand scheme to develop the family estate, to make it an archetype of modern productivity. This was, after all, almost the nineteenth century. The millennia was around the corner. Time to bring Broomhall into the modern world. In years to come they would talk not of Fourier's utopia, but of all that Lord Elgin had accomplished, or so Lord Elgin hoped.

But it was when they came in sight of Broomhall itself that he felt his proudest. Despite his mother's warnings and protestations about cost and emptying bank accounts, he had pulled down the old family home and from its ashes rose, phoenix-like, a new, timeless splendor.

He had found a kindred spirit in his architect, Thomas Harrison. Someone who appreciated the attic style, the glory of ancient Greece, the sublime lines of an architecture that showed, in line and form, that man, improved by education and industry and honor, was closer to the angels than the devils. Someone who appreciated him, Lord Elgin, and could design a living temple to enshrine him and his deeds.

"Eggy, don't you think the windows might be just a little too large? Think of the expense in winter and the drafts." Mary's voice was cajoling, reminding him that she was a girl used to having her way, a beloved only child. Spoiled. Well, he would take her in hand and do his husbandly duty, molding and forming her every thought till she was the perfect vessel for his children and his dream.

"They are the perfect size, Pol," he said, thin-lipped with irritation. "Have you not yet studied Pearsal's Illustrations of Attica? I gave you the volume some weeks ago."

"There has been so very much to do, Thomas." She pouted. "I cannot trust the maids to pack properly. I'm sure Pearsal is very informative but the book is so very, very thick."

Elgin chuckled. He shouldn't make intellectual demands on her. Mary's appointed role in life was maternal. He could be content with that. If he wanted to talk about architecture or politics there was always the smoking room after dinner and the companionship of other men.

At tea, served before a roaring fire in the great hall under the reproachful, glassy-eyed stares of several mounted birds and deer heads, they opened the day's post. A servant brought in a salver loaded with correspondence and Mary buttered scones while Elgin sorted through the envelopes. He balanced them on his palms, judging the weight and quality of the paper, looking for familiar handwriting. Notices from creditors were put back on the salver, unopened, to go to the estate manager who would also ignore them until the addressing handwriting indicated a certain level of fury, impatience, and even legal threat.

The first letter opened was from his old classics tutor, George Hill. Elgin, holding the unopened letter, leaned back in his chair, eyes closed, remembering. Sixteen he'd been. An important age for a youth, one when dreams are being formed. Late nights. Oil lamps blazing. Red wine in two plated goblets set next to a bowl of grapes, bread, cheese, and olives, the latter procured at no little expense. Food of the Gods. Hill, talking, talking, talking . . . silver, winged words pouring from him as he recited Ovid, discussed the Histories, recited the ancient laws.

All he knew of the Greeks he'd learned from George Hill. On some occasions they'd even undressed and wrapped themselves in bed linen, reclining on the pillowed floor, both pretending to feel no self-consciousness as they tried to enjoy the pure sensation of the body, modestly covered but unencumbered by belts, garters, ties, laces, and the other artificial contrivances of post-classical civilization.

He blushed to think of that. But what he'd give to do it again. Would Pol . . . ? No. He carefully opened the letter and smiled at the familiar handwriting.

Congratulations, dearest Thomas. I have heard of your appointment and must say it could not go to a worthier man. Of course, young Jenks was a better Byzantine scholar, but that's water under the bridge, I'll not quibble with the minister's choice. This post should suit you. And you, it, of course. It is not Athens, but remember that Constantinople is, largely, a Greek city. Enjoy. Learn. Be a leader of men, an *anax androm*. Do not, as Virgil, once self-accused, waste time in the lap of sweet Parthenope, enjoying the studies of inglorious ease. Practice *ataraxia* preserving the health of both body and mind and be disposed to neither idleness or excess. There is important work ahead of you. And when you have a chance, give a thought to an old friend, and send me news of your affairs and discoveries. Keep an eye out for my old friend, The Woman Carried Away.

How I envy you this opportunity to follow in the footsteps of Winckelmann and Jandolo! keep your copy of "History of the Art of Antiquity" close at hand, my boy!

The Woman Carried Away. Hill, an avid student of the Ptolemic period, had discovered a brief and unique reference to a stela removed from a pharaoh's tomb and given to Mark Antony by Cleopatra, last of the Ptolemies. He had, at the time, concluded the reference to be one more piece of romanticism charged to the material of Cleopatra. Had Hill changed his mind?

Well, he would keep his eyes open. If he made a present of the stela to Hill, perhaps his old professor would finally forget, or at least cease referring to, the time Jenks had bested him in the essay on the life of Theodora.

"What do you say, Pol? Hill wants me to keep an eye out for a stela for him. Think we might do some digging around?"

"Whatever you say, Eggy," Pol replied, distracted by her own correspondence.

"We'll bring back an antiquitiy or two. Why not? Bonaparte is certainly helping himself to anything that captures his fancy. He's had the Vatican marbles carted back to Paris and forced the Duke of Parma to pay his taxes in pictures and spoils. Paris is flooded with da Vincis and Vermeers and he's probably planning to bring the Sphinx itself back from Egypt. If he returns from Egypt, that is. I'll trump him to a few artifacts, including this stela for old Hill."

"Yes, Eggy." Mary, engrossed in a letter full of London gossip, did not look up.

"Did I ever tell you, Pol? I saw the collections of M. Bonnier de la Mosson in Paris? Strange lot of knicknacks and novelties. Even a room of cadavers."

Mary, frowning, lifted her eyes from the letter to her husband.

"Why," she asked, "would anyone desire to possess a room of cadavers? It's ghoulish, Eggy." She looked at her husband with a new wariness. Would he take up collecting cadavers, since it seemed the continental thing to do?

"Stunk like hell, despite all the preserving chemicals. Most bizarre. But the man had the true instincts of the collector. Indeed. I'll find that stela for Hill."

But as soon as he said it, Elgin knew that if he discovered the stela, he would keep it for himself. He liked possessing what others desired. Hence, his avid and successful courtship of the wealthy, lovely, and very popular Mary Hamilton Nisbet, his shelves of first editions in the library, the hall wall of ancient weapons, and the sealed case of Roman coins.

A copy could be made for Hill. Just as he intended to make copies of the frieze of the Parthenon to adorn the completed Broomhall. Ah, but to return to Broomhall with the originals!

"More tea, Eggy?" Mary poured without waiting for his answer. "Eggy, do you think it will be difficult to get decent tea in Constantinople?"

The glass of tea had grown cold. Dr. Morello did not notice. Nor did he notice the others milling about in this Cairene palace, French mostly, in clothes unsuitable for the climate and brave, easily transparent smiles. There was a handful of Egyptians, sunburned with turbans wrapped about their heads, who were less at ease than the French. Years ago, as a child, traveling from town to town, country to country with his mother and father, he had learned to sleep anytime he could, and to concentrate his thoughts anywhere. Now, he simply did not notice what was going on about him, and turned his thoughts inward.

He thought of her, the blue-eyed Turkish girl, and his concentration was so intense that his own eyes had gone blind, unfocused, though they remained open. She had fled him. She had tried to flee him. She had come to Cairo. And so had he.

Just as well, really. The Sublime Porte had jailed most of the foreigners in Constantinople, thanks to General Bonaparte's little expedition into the Orient. It had been a good time to move on. Business was better here, in Cairo. It became tedious at times, all those orders for mummies. Fools. Spooning mummy powder down their throats, just to get a good hard-on. When all they really needed was the right woman. A blue-eyed Turkish woman. But the mummy trade paid well. And sometimes there were more exciting offers, commissions that stimulated him, elated him. Catherine of Russia, for instance, as rich as she was capricious, had voiced a desire to obtain some Roman funeral masks of good-looking centurions. At this very moment, his workmen were digging through an old cemetery collecting masks.

He sipped the cold tea, still ignoring the polite conversations buzzing about him and smiled. Catherine would undoubtedly make good and perverse use of the masks. And she would pay well.

Well enough to make it possible for him, the collector, to obtain a few items for himself. He was tired of obtaining masks and coins, murderers and eloped daughters, stolen art works, dragons' teeth and Roman swords, Dutch bulbs, doll houses, silver plate used by Voltaire, coats of arms, sea-

shells, six-legged dogs and two-headed calves, and all the
other assorted objects that others had hired him to find
over the years. He had found something he wanted for
himself. Two things. A blue-eyed Turkish girl and a stela
stolen from a pharaoh.

The glass of cold tea was empty before him. He didn't
remember drinking it. He must have. The glass was empty.
And he had work to do. He rose, a tall man, much taller
than average and thin, as if he never had enough to eat.
Collectors, he had noticed, invariably grew fat with time, as
if the objects purchased at great expense and then locked
into cabinets and rooms fed them secret manna. He
pressed his bony hands into the thin, sinewy muscles of his
thighs, trying to will his legs to engorge themselves, to
flesh out. He'd had the unpleasant sensation, recently,
that every object he discovered and then turned over to
another, diminished him. He was wasting away while others grew fat. One last commission, one last reward, a large
one, and he, too, would become a keeper and grow fat.

4

Marguerite stood alone thinking in the darkening salon, surrounded by the buzz of conversation. Atiyah, the Turkish woman, had taught her a remedy to cure bewitchment: take a beetle, remove its head and wings, put it into fat. After the full moon, place the beetle over the heart. She had tried every other remedy, it seemed. Why not a beetle soaked in lard?

There was a year, anger, a string of mistresses, and now her own lover between them, but her heart, which had grown small and hard, had expanded and softened when she saw Michel. He was not to know this, she determined. Passion for one's husband leads to many follies, but she was resolved to preserve what was left of her dignity.

A bell rang and the savants, with a great show of hunger, sat down to dinner. As lack of appetite was the first sign of plague, none of the French in Egypt would admit to even the slightest ailment, lest they be sent to one of the plague houses in Cairo. But when the steaming platters of camel meat were carried in, Marguerite saw Michel twitch his nose in distaste.

"You should have stayed in France," she whispered to him.

She took possession of a place at a small table far from Bonaparte, her lover, and her husband, wishing to avoid all of them. But when the shuffling for chairs was over, she unhappily found herself seated between the frowning Bonaparte and her too-obviously pleased husband. Aristide was at the next table.

The impromptu seating was a social disaster: Pauline and Eugene, Sheik Hamid al Schackoui, Bonaparte, Denon, Morello, Michel, and Marguerite, all at one table. Atiyah had instructed her in the way of *afreets*, Egyptian devils, and Marguerite wondered if an *afreet* had joined the *soirée* and arranged this seating.

Pauline and Eugene coldly avoided looking at each other. They broke their bread into angry little pills as they competed for the attention of Bonaparte. The sheik looked longingly over his shoulder at the table where the other sheiks sat. His nephew and guard, Ibrahim, stood tensely behind him, hand gripping the sword jutting from his belt, as though assassins were about to leap out of the curtains. Dr. Morello seemed preoccupied and not in a mood for conversation.

Vivant Denon, cherub-faced beneath the sunburn, smiled in quixotic amusement.

Small quantities—very small, thanks to Nelson's blockade—of French wine were poured into waiting glasses. Those who wished to ingratiate themselves with Citizen Bonaparte drank the omnipresent lemonade instead, as did the general. When in Rome, he jested, lifting his glass. The tables were heavy with flat breads, fruits, and roasted meats piled over mountains of rice.

Bonaparte removed his gloves and encouraged them to eat with their fingers, Egyptian style. (He had even, at one occasion, indicated they should consider converting to Islam, as he himself considered. Nothing came of that suggestion.) Half-heartedly, the members of the Institute pulled off their gloves and waited as servants carrying basins and water pitchers moved around tables to perform the ritual handwashing. That done, they curved their

French fingers ineptly into the common platters of food, imitating their general, and sighed for knives and forks.

Dr. Morello made the first attempt at conversation.

"Have you had a copy made of the script on the stone from Rosetta?"

"No," said Bonaparte.

"You should. Just in case. England is greatly interested in the stone."

"England will never have it," said the young general. "It belongs to France."

Sheik Hamid al Shackoui cleared his throat. "We may be willing to lend it to France for a short while," he clarified. "The future here at the moment does not bode well for fragile objects."

The table grew silent again. There had been an insurrection in Cairo last year, centered on the Mosque El Azhar. When it was over, three hundred French were dead and three thousand Cairenes. The mosque, with all its ancient books, students' desks, lamps, and other objects, had been nearly destroyed. It had been difficult, after that, to convince the Cairenes of Bonaparte's benevolence and good will towards them.

"I returned their sacred books," Bonaparte protested.

"Could you return life to the corpses that floated down the Nile?" Hamid al Shackoui asked mildly. "You are a great man, truly. But not that great, Sultan El Kabir," he mocked, using Bonaparte's self-given Arabic title. Behind him, Ibrahim's black eyes narrowed with pleasure at the French general's discomposure.

"The rebels deserved to die," protested young Eugene, eyes blazing in his rosy, unbearded face.

Marguerite wished herself very far away, in Paris, in her apartment near the Opera, dressing for the theatre or having a late dinner with friends. It was hot here, claustrophobic. She felt Michel's eyes on her and looked up. Husband and wife exchanged an open glance of longing, regret, and hope. Then Marguerite remembered Josette, naked, tangled in bedclothes, with Michel posed over her, and the wife's eyes grew opaque with bitterness, obscuring the hope.

As archeology and military strategy proved to be failures as dinner topics, Pauline next tried the subject of homesickness.

"I, myself, am quite frantic to be back in Paris," she revealed in her high, girlish voice as she picked over the pieces of meat on the common platter. "Except, of course, I would never leave my darling general behind. As I am sure . . . ," her voice took on a stronger edge, ". . . as I am sure he will never desert me."

Bonaparte patted her hand and sipped his lemon sherbet.

"On the contrary. My stepfather is most eager to return to France, when the moment is right. He has, after all, a wife waiting for him," said young Eugene, looking at Pauline.

"Why all this talk of France, when Egypt is so fascinating?" suggested Bonaparte, looking at no one.

Marguerite began to talk, too loudly and too brightly, of last month's expedition (well armed, well guarded) to Mastabat Far'un, a desolate place in the western desert where ancient tombs had once stood. Now there was only sand and the occasional charred circle of a dead fire from a passing caravan, but she'd made some fine sketches nonetheless, at least she thought they were fine, certainly the Academy would be interested in them. . . .

Vivant Denon gave her ankle a gentle, but judicious kick. Marguerite grew quiet, realizing that Bonaparte had been glowering at the ceiling all the while she spoke.

"Citizeness Verdier has made some fine sketches, indeed, General Bonaparte," Denon declared on her behalf. "She has been an invaluable aid to me. It was wise of you to suggest she accompany the mission." Bonaparte had refused permission for Marguerite to travel with them until the very last moment, when Denon had insisted, but it seemed judicious to re-invent the facts at this juncture of time.

Denon's thick, sensual lips curled in a cynical smile and his eyes glistened with pleasure. Discomfort aroused him. It awoke the imagination and at that moment, the table's occupants were very uncomfortable, providing him with a splendid and unexpected vision of Marguerite and Pauline, naked and slick with oil, bathing each other in a harem bath and . . .

"Yes?" Bonaparte asked, unconvinced. He respected Denon's opinion, though. The artist was one of the few savants who had dared make the Syrian expedition with the army, and the man was almost foolhardy in his bravery and possessed incredible strength and stamina. Hard to believe that this artist, this fop dressed in silk and lace and with that unattractive, almost feminine pout to his mouth, could march uncomplaining alongside his hardened soldiers.

"Very fine sketching," Denon repeated, called back from his imaginary romp with the two women. "And so dedicated to her work! Just this evening she was adding some finishing touches to an earlier sketch of mine, that large drawing of your soldiers on parade outside of Luxor . . ."

Denon glanced mischievously at Marguerite. "Put all to right, have we?" he asked her.

The long, Egyptian summer day faded and died. One by one the oil lamps were lighted and the room became a study of light and dark. Flickering lamps cast checkered, ornate shadow through carved grills. Marguerite longed for pencil and paper as white-robed servants removed the platters of rice and meat. Bonaparte took advantage of the commotion to make a hasty and discrete exit, one hand clutching his stomach.

"Parasites. Nothing to worry about," said Dr. Morello. "The worms grow quite large in this climate. I've started a purge regime for him, he'll be well enough in a month or so if he eats sparingly and of bland foods."

Marguerite pushed away her dish of sherbet and figs, no longer hungry.

By the time Bonaparte reappeared, coffee had been brought out, four large brass and porcelain services, one for each table. At her table, the service was placed in front of Marguerite. She was, Pauline sweetly pointed out, the oldest woman at the table, and so should have the honor. Marguerite, wearing the same frozen smile with which she had begun this evening, poured thick coffee into the small, egg-thin cups and passed them around. One cup was different from the others, European in design rather than Oriental, and larger, with a pastel design of centaurs chasing nymphs circling it.

"This is my stepfather's, General Bonaparte," said Eugene, carefully cradling it in both hands. "It was a gift from my mother."

He put the filled cup in front of Bonaparte, who stared at it as if it were a poisonous serpent. Pauline turned red, then white.

Marguerite, fascinated, watched the play of emotions on Bonaparte's face as he pondered the situation his stepson had purposely created. If he drank from the cup, he would insult Pauline, who did not like to be reminded of Josephine. If he did not drink, he would wound Eugene, his only heir so far, and builders of empires did not like to alienate their heirs.

Eugene, seeking in this boyish manner to protect his mother's interests, had played his card well. But not well enough. Bonaparte, ever the strategist, gently pushed the cup away.

"Coffee, at the moment, does not agree with me," he

said. "In fact, Dr. Morello has recommended I not partake
of it."

At that moment Kleber, sitting at the next table, swallowed his entire cup of coffee in one mouthful, not notic-
ing that a moth had flown into it. He choked and
staggered to his feet, while a servant came and pounded
his back. When the commotion was over, and Marguerite
turned back to the coffee set, Bonaparte's rejected cup of
coffee was in Ibrahim's hand. "With permission," the
young Arab said, nodding at the general.

"Of course, of course," said Bonaparte.

Ibrahim drank the coffee in one long sip and returned
the cup to the table.

Eugene stood abruptly, made a curt little salute to his
stepfather, and stalked from the hall.

"Well," said Denon blithely. "Shall we begin? Tonight's
lecture will be an interesting one." Though not as interesting as the meal had been, he added mentally to himself.
"Monsieur Berthollet is going to discuss his findings on an
old legend of Egypt, a bas-relief sculpture of a woman
being carried away by death. Ah, death. The last seducer!"
He rubbed his hands together with glee.

There was a clattering of spoons and glasses being set
down as the Scientific Institute of Cairo hastily rose;
Sheikh Hamid al Shackoui summoned his servants with a
clap of his hands.

"I will leave you now," he said. "Neither my command
of French nor my knowledge of science allows me to enjoy
these esteemed scientific evenings." He turned to Bonaparte and made a perfunctory *temennah*, his hand flying
hastily over chest, mouth, and forehead. The food had
been ill-prepared. The conversation had been unenlight-
ened. Let Ibrahim come alone, if he must come to this
place. He, Hamid, would come no more. He walked out, a
tall, sad-eyed man dressed in flowing robes, followed by his
nephew, Ibrahim.

The members of the Institute formed a desultory line and walked through a walled garden where fountains splashed and birds sang. Yellow sand whirled through the garden, stinging hands and eyes. They passed wooden-latticed windows and mosaic rooms furnished with silk pillows, brass tables and the omnipresent, gleaming waterpipes, rooms within which the fourteen generations from Abraham to David might have been begotten, rooms where David might have first looked upon the married woman, Urias, and known he must have her for himself, so that his son, Solomon, would be born.

Just as Bonaparte hoped for a son from Pauline Foures, Marguerite mused. And in the surrounding desert were the great ancient idols and temples, half-buried in the sand, silent, waiting, mocking the ultimately futile efforts of the living.

"Dare I hope that sigh is for me?" Michel asked, newly close at her elbow. He was panting slightly.

"It was not. Where were you, Michel? You have been running to catch up with us. A man of your years should not run." Her voice was taunting.

"With Eugene. He is an earnest young man."

"A rather choleric young man. With reason, I admit. Tell me, how is Josephine?" She lowered her voice to a furtive whisper.

"She would like a letter from you. A long letter," he whispered back.

"The post arrangements are somewhat difficult these days. Does she know?"

"About Pauline Foures? Who doesn't? Packing the husband back to France so that the little madame could move into Bonaparte's own apartments here was not an action meant to keep the affair secret."

"It was part of his revenge."

"Marguerite, about Madame Barbe . . ."

"Yes. How is Josette?"

"In Switzerland. With her husband."

"Ah. I wondered why you were here. Now I understand. The husband arrived. It grew crowded."

"It grew tedious. I left well before Monsier Barbe made his appearance. I returned to Paris, to find you gone. . . ."

"You should not have been surprised, Michel. How is Paris?"

"In need of repair, from top to bottom, but the Directory is busy with other matters, mostly mistresses and extortion. The Royalists are still plotting a restoration, and Talleyrand is still putting people in power or toppling them, as the occasion demands. In other words, all is the same, only the faces change. And you? How have you been, Marguerite?"

She did not like it when he called her Marguerite, rather than dear, darling, or wife. It reeked of sincerity, a quality she had long since ceased to expect from him.

"Very well, thank you," she replied stiffly.

"Why did you run away?"

"I did not run away."

"You did. You fled. You are becoming cowardly, Marguerite."

Marguerite thought of what she could say. That it had been painful enough four years before, when he had taken her friend, Delphine, as a mistress. But Josette had been her enemy. Josette hated her. And to bed Josette had been Michel's ultimate betrayal. Instead, she smiled and said, "Your trunk will be put in the servants' closet. There is a divan there on which you may sleep, till arrangements are made for your return to France. Or maybe you would prefer Constantinople. That is far enough away to suit me."

"Dearest, they are slaughtering French in Constantinople. Nobody is taking holidays there this year."

"Ah, well. I see the point. France it is, then. And pray that one of Nelson's ships does not take you. I hear he demands ransom, and then sells his unclaimed prisoners to the slave traders."

"Then you do care. I always suspected as much."

"No, I do not care. But I would detest being bothered with ransom arrangements. Especially for a husband I detest."

"You do not. You say that only to wound."

"Try me."

"I have. I am here to bring you home with me. I care for you. More than Aristide Roux does, you will discover."

"What a strange thing to say," she protested.

"Don't be coy. It does not suit you. As your husband, I have every right to call him out at dawn tomorrow, considering the way he has been looking at you all evening."

"Is that why you came? To accuse me of your crimes and fetch me back to Paris? Then you have made the trip for nothing."

"Ah, well. Two birds with one stone. Talleyrand also wished me to spend some time here. He is getting nervous, having the Corsican general so far and so long out of touch."

"That is not what I have heard. Bonaparte has written repeatedly, and Talleyrand does not answer his letters. Strange, isn't it? Soldiers and politicians always claim to detest each other. Yet the one would not exist without the other."

For a moment their mutual hostility was replaced by a shared silent musing. Their mouths formed the same, thin line of concentration, they both frowned and clasped their hands behind their backs as they walked. They looked startlingly similar.

They had not married for love. Michel, the youngest son of the Marechal de Verdier and a devotee of the opera, had met Marguerite backstage, where she had been helping to dress her mother. She was seventeen and still in convent school. She was wealthy, thanks to her mother's talents and cunning and judicious choice of protectors. Michel, almost thirty at the time, had been handsome, furious with his father, and broke. The match was quickly made: Marguerite's wealth bought a titled husband. No one had thought to ask Marguerite what she thought of this, but it seemed sensible enough to her that she did not protest. Marriage suited her. Michel pleased her.

Then came the revolution. It had taken all of her fortune, all of his wits, to simply survive. And somewhere along that way of survival, Marguerite had allowed herself to depend on Michel and trust him . . . until she learned that Michel was unfaithful. Repeatedly.

"Think nothing of it. All husbands are unfaithful. How boring if they weren't!" her friends said. They had laughed about silly little Madame Sauzet, who had pounded at her husband's mistress's door until the two had come down in their nightclothes, begging her to go away. Paris jested about it for weeks! Marguerite, afraid of being laughed at, pretended not to care.

Now, she was tired of pretence.

"Go back to Paris, Michel," she said. "Without me. I am your wife no longer." She had not rehearsed those words, nor even known she would say them. Yet they brought a sense of finality she enjoyed. It was over.

They had overtaken the group ahead of them. They could hear isolated words from a conversation as whispered as their own. Kleber, Bonaparte's chief aid, was speaking softly to a man she could not identify. ". . . a blood bath." "the soldiers are ready to . . ." "too much grumbling for the general's purpose and safety . . ."

She could guess the rest of the conversation. The Egyptian campaign had been costly and not as successful as one could have wished, though no one dared say it aloud. Certainly, when Bonaparte returned to France he would not be hailed as the Hero of Egypt, as he had earlier been hailed as the Hero of Italy.

At the doorway of the lecture hall, which last year had been a sheik's *ka'ah* where learned *imams* had debated points of theology, Michel took her aside. He held her slender wrists in his hands and pushed her shoulders against the wall, imprisoning her.

"When I leave, you will leave with me," he repeated.

"No. I will not. You collect women's reputations the way other men collect statuary and engravings. I will have none of it. I am finished."

5

Shepseskaf, dying, tried to remind himself that Anubis was a friendly god. It was Anubis who would carry his *ka* up to the father, Osiris, for eternal reward and joy.

But strapped on his bed, covered with useless poultices and charms and with the air of his room poisoned with the smell of his own decay, it was difficult to welcome the jackal-headed god.

The silent land beckoned and Shepseskaf was not ready. It was too soon. He had dreamed many times that he had pricked himself with a thorn and so knew that his death was not distant. But this was too soon.

It was dusk. A solitary lamp had been lighted in his chamber and he could not see into the shadowed corners, where demons waited.

Arise, Pharaoh, he commanded himself. Arise and finish the work of the day, before even the day abandons you. He could not. A simple lifting of the head exhausted him.

Failure. Every meal of this life had been spiced with failure, his gut had rotted from it, and now there was the last and worst failure of all to face. It pressed on his chest, squeezing the life out of him.

He was being poisoned. Slowly. And there was nothing he could do, no slave he could trust, no taster who could save him. He would die. But the tomb was not finished. He had not been able to outwit the priests of Amon-Ra. He could imagine them, sitting at their tables, laughing and feasting and boasting of how they had robbed the royal treasury, how they had cheated Pharaoh, how they were greater than Pharaoh, who was not god they said, but simply a man who will rot and die and then lie in an unfinished tomb, his immortality stolen as easily as his life and power had been stolen. One of them would soon boast of how he had poisoned Pharaoh.

Shepseskaf groaned. His daughter, Ma'tcha' rose from the shadows and came close to him. He smelled her perfume of myrrh and rose, the same perfume her mother had worn. How many years ago?

"Father. Beloved one." Her soft hand touched his forehead.

Shepseskaf forced his eyes open. The light of the lamp sent shafts of pain through him.

"Promise," he said.

She bowed her head, helpless before him, knowing already his final request.

"Promise the tomb will be finished in time." The words came from deep inside him, from a place of jagged knife edges and broken glass, a destroyed temple fallen into darkness. "Promise in the name of Hathor."

She raised her head and looked at him, the glass beads in her hair clinking and making sweet music. But Shepseskaf saw only destruction in her face. This, too, was the work of the priests.

"I promise, Beloved One."

Though his racked body was still confined to the bed, he felt himself slipping away from the lamplight, the stench, the sound of the wind. He no longer felt her hand on his forehead. His closed eyes saw a distant landscape rich with palm and fig trees, with calm pools of precious water shining like emeralds set in red gold. He glided towards it, propelled by a force that was both within and without himself, and as he moved towards it he felt the things of this world slip away. The love of gold and power, the love of women and of one's children, the various joys and deceits of the flesh, and the wealth that bought them, were as nothing. This surprised him. He had not thought death would be so kind and, at the same time, so severe. Must he give up everything?

On that horizon towards which he moved, the jackal-headed god, his beaded wig making sweet, clinking music, rose in greeting.

Shepseskaf felt a jab of joy. It pulsed within him as he balanced between the sickness chamber and the silent land, his *ka* hesitating, wondering. It was not yet right. But what was wrong?

Hathor. She had not promised in the name of Hathor. Too late. His feet were touching the silent land. He was home.

Ma'tcha' kept vigil over the empty vessel that had once been her father. She poured ashes on her head and rent her garments and tore from her throat the gold and silver necklaces her father had bestowed upon her, scattering glinting pieces of metal about her bare feet. She smeared mud on her beautiful face and her shrieks drowned out the noise of the jackals that bayed each sunset.

She watched through narrow, unfocused eyes as the embalmers removed her father's heart and other organs and placed them in the four canopic jars that would be protected by Emset, Hape, Duamutf, and Qebhsneuf, Osiris's sons, and when the linen-wrapped vessel was taken on its last journey, she was first in line behind the coffin bearers. Her sorrow shamed the priests.

Her husband though, unmoved, chastised her for her grief.

"It was time. Do you question the will of Amon-Ra?" he

asked. He towered over her in their bed chamber, angry, dominating, untouched by the mysteries of death.

"It was not his time. The tomb is unfinished. The stela is not in place."

She would no longer look at him. Once, when he had come to her, he had been gentle, cooling her fever with love words and tenderness, his hands had turned her body into a shrine, a perfumed oasis.

That was before he became high priest, when in the spring of his life he had cherished love before power. His spring was past and he had the aging man's craving for ascendancy and command above all else. And that was before their years of marriage would end in barrenness. She had given him no children. He hated her for that more than for being the daughter of Shepseskaf, the charity giver.

"That, too, is Amon-Ra's will," he said.

"No. It was your will."

He pushed her onto the bed, where she lay passive and indifferent, ready to be mounted as animals are mounted. Instead, he studied her ash-tainted face streaked with tears, her unkempt hair and clothing. He turned away in disgust.

"Shepseskaf told me once that his father raised me from the dust. Without him, I would have been a stonecutter's slave. It would have been better if the river had taken me." Ptahshepses spoke to himself, musing over the old wound. "He wanted my gratitude. He made me show my gratitude with every meal I shared with them, with every pet I was given, with every garment they threw my way. And everything he gave me was flawed. The birds in the aviary he gave me sickened and died. The villages he gave me were poor. And you, the wife he gave me, are barren."

Ma'tcha' moved on the bed behind him, reaching for his sleeve. He pulled away.

"I was not grateful. Not for gifts so miserly bestowed.

The giver should be light-hearted so that the receiver may be light-hearted. Shepseskaf counted the value of each item and recorded it, and the value was little." His eyes glinted like cold pieces of silver cast on a bare floor.

"Do not compare me with the rest of the entombed. Search the bottom of the river with a scoop and see what clay is brought up. Such is the clay that has made my house of death, as you behold it."

Ptahshepses, made larger than life by the ceremonial robes and headpiece, read the inscription aloud as the stone was slid into place, sealing Shepseskaf into his mastaba. Stones ground and roared against each other as ropes were cut and levers pulled. From deep inside the earth came a cracking noise of slabs dropping into place, the noise that announces the shutting off of the dead from the living, the living from the dead.

Clay. A monument of clay. That was Pharaoh's eternity. Ptahshepses smiled. Let the wind come. And the summer floods. And the passing years that steal as they flee. Let them wash away all trace of the charity-giver.

Ma'tcha' stood in the western portal of the tomb, facing the sunset. She prayed to Osiris of the True Words, asking for leniency and for forgiveness for her father, who must appear in the hall of the two truths before the forty-two animal-headed demons. Eater of Blood, Eater of Shadows, Eye of Flame, and Bone-Breaker would judge Shepseskaf. If he was found innocent, Thoth, the scribe of the gods, inscribed his acquittal. If not . . .

She stared fiercely into the setting sun. Of what was he guilty? Resignation to his fate. He had not fought the priests. Is weakness a sin? The clamoring dead, with their clutching empty hands, the Bone-Breaker and Eye of Flame struggled behind her unmoving eyes, yelling and screaming so that she put her hands over her ears, but the noise grew stronger, not weaker.

She knelt and touched the stone sealing her father's tomb. "Thou who didst love to walk freely are now held fast, a prisoner swathed in thy bands," she intoned. "Thou who had a great store of fine things now sleeps in the linen of yesterday." She tried to recite the sacred formula which would guarantee her father comfort and wealth for eternity. The words were stopped in her throat.

There was a hollow indent in the wall, where Shepseskaf's panel, giving his name and titles and accomplishments, the panel adorned with the little goddess Hathor confronting Anubis, was to have been. The tomb was unmarked, unnamed. She had failed him.

She turned away and followed her husband, back across the river, back to the land of the living.

By what shall I be judged? What measure, what standard will be used?

The question haunted Ma'tcha'. She had failed in many things. She had been unable to win her husband's love. She was barren. She had not been able to comfort her father's last years. And now, she could not even pray. The heaviness of her heart was unendurable.

Outside her curtained room, frogs croaked from the marsh. So many frogs, she could not remember a time when their noise had been this strong. They mocked her.

A white ibis appeared on the stone terrace outside her door with a great fluttering of ivory wings beating against a black, moonless night. The bird watched her with its amber eyes, and this she took for a good sign. When it flew away, it left behind one large, perfect, white feather. Ma'tcha' picked up the feather and walked down the path, to Ptahshepses.

He was alone, stretched on his bed, arms stiffly at his side, staring up at nothing. For a moment she thought he was dead and her heart lurched with joy. Then he moved ever so slightly. He turned and watched her, his eyes as

cool and indifferent as the eyes of the ibis. She had
donned her wig, and painted her eyelids green again.

"Do you hear the river? It is breaking the dikes again,"
he said. His lips were thin, the whites of his eyes large. She
listened. There was no sound of water or of flooding.
Akhit, this year, was tame, Hapi, the god of the Nile, was
being gentle. She smiled.

"My husband. My beloved." The words slid smoothly
from her mouth, like thin poison being poured into a cup.
Dream of a thorn. I am lying to you. But I will have two
things of you: a child and my father's stela.

When she kissed him, his mouth was cold and inflexible.
But he responded, pushing her down onto the couch,
turning her over onto her hands and knees. She whim-
pered and pleaded, to increase his pleasure. She lay still,
letting the seed inside her float to fertile ground and take
root.

"Give me a gift," she asked later, resting stiffly by his
side. Her body hurt from his use of it, but she felt light,
almost floating.

"What do you want?" His voice was sleepy, relaxed.

"The door panel. Hathor and Anubis. That which will
finish the tomb."

Wary now, he laughed and pushed her away.

"Daughter of Shepseskaf, here is your price." He tore a
ring off his finger and flung it at her. "Consider it charity.
Taste charity. And ask nothing more of me."

He put his foot on her back and pushed. She fell to the
floor, next to where he had thrown the ring.

She picked it up. It was of gold, with green glass insets.

Green glass could be prised out and ground to powder.
Green glass could be ground fine enough to put in a drink
of new spring mead, and be tasteless, textureless, unno-
ticed, until the glass, cutting, infiltrating, mortally wound-
ing the secret inner rivers and chasms carrying it along,

found its way deep into the body. And then it would be too late.

She would clothe her husband in the dress of yesterday and send him to the silent land. She would stand over his body and say the words of farewell: "When time has become eternity then shall we see each other again, for you go away to that land where all are equal."

His suffering would last an eternity. That would be her reward. She closed the precious ring tightly in her palm and thanked him.

Her gratitude pleased him so much he smiled at her as he walked out.

6

". . . and so we have yet to deduce exactly why this particular tomb went unmarked, and why the funerary door panel was never put in place. . . ." Berthollet's voice droned on. "You understand, of course, *mes amis,* that the existence of the stela is a matter of speculation. Even those few historians who write of it do not admit to having actually seen it. . . ."

Marguerite, yawning, supported her chin in her hands and studied the ormolu clock on the side table. It was just past midnight. Berthollet, bright-eyed and impassioned by the crate of notes he had accumulated, had been lecturing for two hours. The entire assembly was restive and the shuffling of feet, coughs smothered into handkerchiefs and cracking of fans provided background music to the first violin of Berthollet's voice.

Denon had gone to sleep, chin on chest, and peaceful snores occasionally lifted the lace at this throat. Michel, seated beside her, shifted constantly, throwing one leg over another and polishing his nails against his waistcoat.

Pauline, her blonde curls drooping from heat, fanned herself vigorously. But whenever Bonaparte turned to her, she smiled and nodded with forced enthusiasm, eager to please and mindful of the fact that Berthollet was one of the general's favorites.

Bonaparte himself sat stiffly at attention, alert always but now especially so. With that uncanny sense that made others around him so nervous, he knew that something of great importance to himself was about to be said.

". . . and one of Alexander's secretaries recorded that the legendary panel was once beheld in the conqueror's hands, before it disappeared again. . . ."

Alexander had possessed this stela.

Bonaparate, jealous of the fame attached to the earlier conqueror, decided at that moment that the stela would be his. The certainty of it made him smile and Marguerite, spying that little, secretive smile felt suddenly quite uneasy. It was remarkably similar to one of Michel's expressions, the one which indicated a pretty mouth or rounded arm had caught his eye.

She turned her attention back to Berthollet. His vest buttons were ancient Roman coins, polished but with enough of the tarnish of centuries left on them to indicate their antiquity. It was Berthollet who had headed Bonaparte's so-called "Commission for the Research of Artistic and Scientific Objects in Conquered Countries." The commission and its members had jubilantly returned from Rome with the Vatican's treasures bundled into saddlebags—and more secretive places. Jewels worn by Ann of Cleves. Louis II's carved ruby ring. Murano glass. Altar tryptychs. Portraits by Rembrandt. The Madonna paintings by Fra Angelica. Byzantine goblets. Vials containing the blood of St. Helen, the sweat of St. Peter. The Duke of Modena, impoverished from the war with Bonaparte, paid his taxes with his private art collection. Now, there was talk of a private museum newly opened only to the most discreet of guests, in Berthollet's country house.

And, of course, there was the Louvre itself, that ancient rehabilitated hunting lodge which now awaited the glories of the ages to fill its echoing bowels. Just weeks after Bonaparte and his savants had sailed to Egypt, there had been a grand opening of the new museum complete with a parade of giraffes and camels and chained lions, a true victory march, similar to Caesar's, when he paraded the effigy of Cleopatra and the spoils of Egypt through the streets of Rome.

". . . said to have been carved into grey granite, with space left at the top, sides and bottom for inscriptions which were never completed. Or started, for that matter," Berthollet droned. "Indeed, Zenobia, once said to be in possession of this panel, attempted to have her name and title imposed onto the panel but for some reason the stonecutter did not honor her command. Many superstitions had already attached themselves to the panel by this time, the most extravagant one claiming that the panel brought unlimited power to the one who managed to keep it. . . ."

Bonaparte leaned forward. He exchanged a quick glance with Denon, who was now fully awake. Denon nodded. Bonaparte had already asked him to find two other rumored, legendary objects—a statue of William the Conqueror and the marble columns from Charlemagne's tomb. If they existed Bonaparte must possess them.

Marguerite, spying these glances, wondered what drove men to fill rooms and palaces and towns and countries with objects that could not, in the long run, either delay death or prolong pleasure.

A phrase, unbidden, sounded in her thoughts. By what will we be judged?

Berthollet, his face wet with perspiration, finally finished with a slight flourish of his large hands, cleared his throat and stepped aside of the podium, ready to receive accolades for his paper and subject matter.

Just then, the wide double doors were flung open and an Arab unknown to them, tall, dark, and stormy-faced, strode into the room.

"I come from the house of Sheik Hamid al Shackoui,"

he announced. There was menace in his voice and glinting black eyes. A dagger and sword were tucked into his belt, although arms were forbidden inside the institute. "You are to know that Sheik al Shacoui's private guard and nephew, Ibrahim, has been poisoned this evening."

The room grew so silent Marguerite could hear the gentle coursing of water in the flooding Ezbekiah square. Poison. A common enough recourse in peace time, of course, when princes desired to quietly do away with other princes. But in wartime? And who would poison Ibrahim? Why?

The messenger stood, feet wide apart, arms folded across his chest. He stared longest at Berthollet, who still stood next to the podium but was newly speechless. Berthollet's eyes were fixed on the messenger's swordhilt, encrusted with jewels.

"If Ibrahim dies, the old law will be obeyed." An eye for an eye. A tooth for a tooth. A death for a death. The messenger turned his back on them and left.

Little Pauline Foures shrieked. Madame Beaucaire swooned. Marguerite, still with her hand in Michel's, remembered that the *fellahin* called the time of the flooding a dangerous time. They made sacrifices and said prayers to ward off the devils it brought. But she couldn't think of any prayers to say. Something had begun and, like the Nile, it would go its course, undeterred by them.

Bonaparte, ashen under his sunburn, called an immediate reconvening of the group, requiring the presence of all the savants and guests who had been present at the dinner. He pulled Pauline, who begged leave to go home to bed, sternly beside him, and walked angrily on his heels, making the tile floors ring with the riding spurs he had not thought to remove.

They gathered, all except Sheik al Shackoui and Ibrahim, and sat at the same places, feeling more than a little foolish because servants had long since cleared the room of everything but tables and chairs. They had the lost and desolate air, Marguerite thought, of children kept after school for misbehaving.

Bonaparte, wringing his hands behind his back, moved from table to table. "Of course it is impossible," he finally spoke. "We all ate from the same dishes. If one were poisoned, we would all be poisoned. Sheik al Schackoui will agree that is true."

Michel, relaxing a little, took out his snuff box and went through the comforting ritual of opening, pinching, sniffing, and sneezing. His mundane pantomine somehow made the shadows less menacing. There was nervous laughter and a snapping open of fans.

But relief was evasive. At the same moment the same thought occurred to a handful of people. Michel looked at Marguerite. Eugene watched Bonaparte. Bonaparte studied Dr. Morello's face. Across the room, Vivant Denon struck his forehead with the palm of his hand. Aristide Roux glanced briefly at Marguerite. Their eyes met. He looked away first. He was ambitious, Aristide, and fate or something even worse had just removed Marguerite from the brief list of things and people for whom he could care. She was suspect.

Coffee had been served separately. Ibrahim had taken Bonaparte's coffee, set apart from the others by his unique cup. Eugene had produced the special cup for his stepfather which now, it seemed, had poisoned the drinker.

But Marguerite had poured the coffee.

Michel gripped her shoulder, steadying her, as Bonaparte, deeply frowning, turned and stared. Eugene was an innocent in the general's eyes. She was not.

Marguerite grew light-headed with fear. She was glad for the familiar feel of Michel's hand on her shoulder. She no longer wished to be alone.

A breeze rippled the midnight-silvered waters of the Nile. It passed over the gardens of Ezbekiah, where Bonaparte ran his fingers through his unfashionably long hair and wondered what cryptic knowledge Alexander the Great had used to avoid assassination. Because this wind carried an *afreet*, a devil, it stopped and played with the general's hair, and while it was there it planted in the general's mind the thought that he, a general in a faded and frayed uniform, was a fool and would never compare to Alexander the Great or even his groom.

Bonaparte, trembling with anger, pointed his finger at a thin, black-haired woman and roared a command.

Pleased, the *afreet* moved with the wind over the city and rattled the wooden screen of a sheik's house, making the women inside wail even louder. The *afreet* discovered a sheik sitting by the bedside of a young man. The sheik wept and pulled at his black beard. The young man on the rumpled bed writhed in pain.

The *afreet* paused, making a sound like an old woman sucking in her breath. There was much room here for mischief. It played with the fringes on a curtain; it stirred a piece of paper on a small table; it tickled the older man's nose and then crept under his white turban.

It is written, Hamid thought. He is a disobedient boy. He wed without my permission. He spends too much time with the Franks, getting into who knows what trouble.

Hamid's eyes glittered. That thought is beneath me, he reprimanded himself. He does not deserve this pain.

"Is the pain lessened?" he asked.

"No, uncle, it is not." Ibrahim tried to smile, but could only grimace. A wave of pain seized him and carried him away, to a shore where the human voices around him were blurred by the roaring in his head as the pain tossed him under and over.

Hamid reached under his robe and took out his *mus-bat*, a tiny copy of the Koran enclosed in gold. His father had given it to him on the day of his circumcision thirty years ago, and he had worn it ever since. He unfastened its gold

chain. He put the charm around Ibrahim's hot, da
neck. Ibrahim quieted for a moment, than another wa
seized him and tossed him on the ocean of pain.

"Do something!" Hamid roared. Four physicians scurried about the bedside, muttering, feeling for the pulse at Ibrahim's neck and wrists, wiping the sweat from his forehead, holding thick and yellowish potions to his lips.

"There is nothing they can do." A tall, pale-eyed woman with red hair hanging in long plaits down her back separated herself from the chorus of weeping women stationed at the foot of Ibrahim's bed. The conviction in her voice had more to do with despair than certain knowledge. Ibrahim had been good. He had been kind. Like all good and kind beings, he would be taken from her.

"There is nothing," she repeated.

The devil-carrying wind, hearing these words, rejoiced. The robes of the men and the full trousers of the women filled with the playful breeze, like sails on the ocean of Ibrahim's dying.

Marguerite heard waves washing onto a shore. Eyes closed, more asleep than awake, she listened to them contentedly for several moments, remembering the golden seashore of Menton and a holiday she'd had there once with her mother.

Then she remembered that the Nile, even during the height of the Inundation, does not make the sound of waves. Under the sound of the waves was a newly discovered hostile silence. No birds sang. No vendors called beneath a window grill. No servants padded up and down stairs.

She opened her eyes and sat up. She saw Michel curled next to her on a pile of straw. She jabbed him with her elbow.

The sound of the waves stopped instantly as her husband's breathing changed from that of deep sleep to alertness. The trousers and satin vest he had slept in were rumpled but he had, the night before, thought to drape his new and costly waistcoat over a large, nail-studded metal object whose original function Marguerite now quickly decided not to think about.

The dungeon. At least that was what it would be called in Europe. What did they call it in Egypt? Never having seen this one before, she hadn't even known that Quassim Bey had kept such a large and formidable one in the bowels of his palace.

Frightened, she tried to smooth down her bristling black hair. The familiar action brought some semblance of normality to a morning that was proving to be a continuation of last night's nightmare. She wanted her brushes and her cologne. She wanted a fresh change of clothes. She wanted the little porcelain shepherdess that sat on her dressing table and which Marguerite greeted silently each morning. She wanted the freedom of her rooms, remembering that the day before those rooms had felt like a prison.

"Is breakfast served?" Michel asked, trying to make her smile.

"This is no time to play the fool, Michel."

"On the contrary. I think it is the perfect time."

He stood and stamped the numbness from his feet.

"I slept well. And you?" he asked amiably, as if they were meeting in one of their favorite cafés for a quick *petite dejeuner*. This was the old Michel, the one who had bluffed his way through border crossings with forged papers, the one who had marched brazenly into the meeting of the Central Safety Committee of Paris, demanding the release of his wife, claiming her detention was a hardship no married man should have to endure.

"You slept well because the walls appear to be ten feet thick, I'd say. This place is like a tomb."

"Wretched choice of words, Marguerite. Let us just agree we have had better accommodations."

"What are we going to do?"

"Make much noise, for a beginning. We need to talk, and I will not face this on an empty stomach. We are French citizens. We are entitled to *café au lait* and bread. They brought breakfast to Marie Antoinette before she went to the guillotine, didn't they?"

"Wretched thought, Michel. Please."

He moved slowly, stumbling his way through the semi-darkness and pounded on what he assumed was the door. After too long of a while, one of Bonaparte's soldiers opened it.

"Coffee. Rolls. And some fruit, if you can find it," Michel commanded.

"I have no orders to . . ."

Michel produced a handful of dinars from his pocket. The soldier grinned, accepted the coins, and returned an hour later with a tray.

"Service is execrable, too," Michel commented. "He has spilled most of the coffee. But we must be lenient with the serving class, especially when they are also our soldiery." He handed a cup to Marguerite. She was shivering.

"Drink. I need you to be clear-witted."

"I've lost my taste for coffee, thank you."

He took her cup, sipped, then handed it back. "No one will want to poison us. We are scapegoats, and scapegoats are more useful alive than dead. For a while at least. Don't look so surprised, Marguerite. Last night was carefully arranged by someone. Unless, of course, you did poison the coffee. No? I thought not. Drink your coffee, it's quite safe."

She drank.

"Better?" he asked.

"Someone has tried to assassinate Bonaparte."

"So it would seem."

The coffee sharpened the edges of her thoughts. She let Michel pour her a second cup and sat on a wooden crate, thinking. Several times she opened her mouth to say something then, peering at Michel, changed her mind. Finally, when the second cup was finished, she pointed her finger at her husband.

"You knew of this. That is why you came. Not to see me."

"Suspected. Talleyrand received a letter . . . unsigned of course, stating that dire things might happen to Bonaparte if he stayed in Egypt. Probably a disgruntled soldier, or even Pauline's former husband, but we thought it should be looked into. Though I was not adverse to a reunion with my wife."

"Yes. We must do something about that."

"About what?"

"Wife. Michel, I want a divorce."

"I protest, Marguerite. I have been accused of trying to assassinate a general, locked in a dungeon in a foreign land, and now my wife says she wants a divorce! Enough, Marguerite! I have had enough blows for one day! Besides, I don't want a divorce. And in my way, I have made you an excellent husband. We French have not yet sunk to the point where we must, like the backward Americans, have only one bedroom and sleep with one's spouse every night in order to enjoy a good reputation. . . ."

"Do not quote Talleyrand to me," Marguerite snapped.

"I will talk no more of divorce. My wife you are and my wife you will remain. Let us think of the matter closer at hand. Who poisoned Bonaparte's coffee?"

"You are changing the subject."

"Yes. I'm glad you noticed. Now think."

Michel sat on the crate next to Marguerite. He put his coat over her shoulders and smoothed her hair back from her face.

"Lt. Foures. Though he is not in the immediate vicinity," Marguerite speculated, flinching at her husband's touch and shrugging his coat off her shoulders. She remembered that last night, when the nightmare began, she had found comfort from the pressure of Michel's hand on her shoulder. But this morning she had awoken filled with anger and the old pain. Josette, disheveled and narrow-eyed with satisfaction, haunted her thoughts.

"His proximity, or lack of it, is of no consequence. This is the Orient. Poisoners to do the job for you abound. He remains a possibility." Michel, rebuffed, studied his wife. He had never known her anger to last so long. There was a cold knot in his stomach that had nothing to do with Bonaparte and the dungeon. Until this moment, it had never occurred to him that Marguerite would not return with him to Paris and resume their life together.

Later. There would be time to think of that later. He hoped. Now, he must take his own advice and deal with the more urgent matter.

"Eugene?" he suggested.

"Or someone sent by Josephine. She would rather be a widow than a divorcée, I think."

"Kleber. He has heard that Bonaparte is returning to France and leaving him in charge of the Egyptian campaign. I believe he is not enthused about this plan."

"Or one of the sheiks," Michel said. "They are even less enthused about the campaign. Some Parisians are equally unenthused. There is talk of a royalist plot to be rid of the Directory. I assume that would mean ridding France of Bonaparte, as well."

"The list is getting long."

"The first thing we must do is secure our own release," said Michel, a long moment later. "As pleasant as it is to sit here in the dark with you, it will not provide opportunity to point an accusing finger at someone other than ourselves. And I do not wish General Bonaparte to labor long under the illusion that I . . . or my wife . . . desire him dead.

Such an error is definitely not propitious for one's social position or longevity."

"And you can work this miracle, our release?"

"Marguerite. You never used to doubt me so. It ill becomes you. First we will try good sense and negotiation. Surely they will see the error in this. I am new to this part of the world and, moreover, have no complaint with the general. You are his personal friend."

"His wife's friend," she corrected.

"Yes. I see the point. We will try good sense and negotiation anyway."

He pounded again at the door. The same soldier opened it, no longer looking frightened.

"See. He, for one, does not believe us to be assassins," Michel said.

"Makes no difference what I think," said the guard, grinning. "More coffee, Citizen?" He held out his hand, palm up.

"An interview if you please. With General Bonaparte."

"He's gone back to his quarters." The guard's smile disappeared. If there was no money to be made, he was eager to return to his card game.

"Could he be sent for?" Michel asked patiently.

"Not by me."

"Monsieur Berthollet, then . . ."

"He's gone, too. Off to the desert looking for some new ruins. As if there weren't plenty all over the place."

"General Kleber . . . but of course he will be at the opera."

The guard looked confused. "No, he's in a staff meeting and left word not to be disturbed."

"Who is in charge, then? The cook?" The whites of Michel's eyes flashed in the semi-darkness and Marguerite heard the grinding of teeth.

"Orders. Here you stay." The guard turned and left.

7

freets are not benign. They are bitter and troublesome. They remember that once they were gods and they ruled heaven, earth, and the places of the dead. Once, they wore jackal masks as Anubis or cows' ears as Hathor, and guided trembling humanity through life and death.

But when the new religions came, as they always do, the old gods were reduced to mere *afreets*. They were no more pleased with this demotion than was their northern companion, Lucifer. But work is work.

While it is not easy for an Egyptian *afreet* to fly all the way to the moors of Scotland, it sometimes happens. On a particularly damp summer evening, the same *afreet* who had lingered in Ibrahim's death-room, blew the heady smell of sand and heat into a Scot's bulbously pink nose and peered over his tweedy shoulder as he penned a letter.

Lord Elgin, still dressed in his shooting clothes, paused and sniffed the smell of adventure and acquisition. It was past sunset. His study was dark and beyond the warm circles of lamplight where shadows played, he imagined glimpses of pale villages and fields, hot with the southern sun, poor and abandoned, half-buried in sand and dust, waiting. For him. Where others might anticipate a language to be learned, foods to be tasted, vistas to enrich the eyes, he saw treasures, buried and not, waiting to be plucked from indifference by him.

A half-smile played under the pink, slightly moist nose. He thought of Roman statuary in his garden, Greek death masks in his study. His heart beat faster. He dipped his pen in the ink stand and wrote. The *afreet,* wondering how these northerners could stand the cold and damp, the acrid smell of hound that emanated from carpet and sofa, balanced on the tip of Elgin's pen and blew the ink dry as quickly as the Scot wrote.

BROOMHALL, AUGUST 2ND, 1799
FROM THOMAS BRUCE, LORD ELGIN,
TO PROFESSOR GEORGE HILL:

How vexatious to have missed your grandiloquent lecture to the Ladies' Society whilst you were in Edinburgh! I hope the members of the audience of that gentler sex paid the rapturous attention which is your due, though, of course, they could not have been expected to understand all that your lofty mind would be desirous of conveying to them! I am, as you can imagine, in the throes of chaos, making all the preparations which are needed for a mission such as the one I am about to undertake. Pol and I have not a moment to ourselves, nor a free moment to enjoy the loftier pursuits of life (and few moments of less lofty pursuits, I assure you!).

Your letter of August 8th, informing me of the lecture, was safely received, opened and read with sincere delight. Good of you to think of me, old friend and mentor, *ab imo pectore*[1].

Indeed, I anticipate the voyage and the embassy to Constantinople with the greatest enthusiasm! It presents an opportunity to assist my country, show Pol a bit of the

---

[1] from the bottom of my heart

world before she settles down to raise a brood here at Broomhall, and, of course, add a few little mementoes to the collections here at Broomhall. Perhaps a suggestion of kudos will be earned by your former student during this expedition? Perhaps history will sit up and take notice of this scion of an ancient and illustrious family? I must remain modest in hope and demeanor, however, so we will not talk of glory. It will enough to be so near to my beloved Greece!

Oh, ancient lands of poetry and reason! To tread her holy soil and ancient steps! To stand, in reverential awe, on the sacred steps of the Parthenon! To touch, with trembling finger, her antique, venerable walls!

Mater has bottled up an entire case of tincture of rhubarb to keep my bowels conditioned. Do you know of a good traveling medicine for adenoids? Pol, I'm sorry to say, suffers the same choking fits that sometimes beset me.

As for this "Woman Carried Away." It is not just legend? I remember bringing up the subject with Professor Bouchaud of the Ecole de Droit, and the way he sniggered for days over my presumption that the object was real, not myth. You know, my dear Professor Hill, how condescending those French can be.

One more missive, I beg of you, and then your eternally grateful student departs for lands unknown. Well, at least for lands exotic and probably quite injurious to the health, though a man of courage never considers the sacrifice. How long do you think I must attend to duties in Constantinople before making a foray to beloved, sacred Athens?

The *afreet*, light-headed from blowing on the ink and pleased that the job was well done, took shelter in Maisie, a bitch of sweet disposition who, before that night, had never done anything as naughty, as forbidden, as chewing her mistress's slippers.

Holding the sodden, frayed pink remnants before Elgin
the next morning, Pol frowned prettily and defended
Maisie.

"She knows we're leaving her, Eggy."

The *afreet*, bored with its gurgling, padding, drooling
dog-shape, followed the letter off the silver salver, into the
courier's bag, into the fetid, book-strewn, dark study of
Professor Hill.

Professor George Hill to Thomas Bruce, Seventh Earl of
Elgin:

Don't be a nitwit. Of course it's genuine. When did I
squander time teaching you about fantasy or superstition? *Absit invidia.*[2]

Confirm sources of one Helios, scribe to Octavia, wife
of Marcus Antony. Finally, I have been commissioned to
do a decent translation of this scroll and discovered,
upon minute examination, that the phrase translated as
"the stolen girl," thought to refer to Cleopatra's daughter, is actually "the woman carried away." Different matter altogether, indeed, the words echo, repeat the
legend known to have survived to us from the mysterious, catastrophic reign of High-Priest Ptahshepses, favorite of Shepseskaf, a pharaoh of no reputation
whatsoever. If only we could translate those pictographs
and make more sense of Egyptian history than Mane-
thos provides! To the matter: Cleopatra's daughter, Selene Cleopatra, was taken to Rome as a captive after her
mother's death, and whilst there, a prisoner but a prisoner of royal blood and appropriately treated we must
assume, had opportunity to converse with the poet Ovid.
She spoke often about a stela, an ancient funeral panel
left over from the time of the Pyramids, that had passed
from hand to hand through the centuries, and ended up

[2] No offence intended.

in the vast art collections of the Ptolemies. It was a carving of the cow-goddess, Hathor. Ovid recognized this primal female figure as one of the ancient love goddesses, a prototype of Aphrodite and Venus, and worked her into some of his love poems. Ah, but then Ovid never was your best subject. Did you ever finish that translation I ordered as a tutorial assignment?

The stela, the missing funeral panel, is real. I feel quite certain of it. As for the legends carbuncled over it, they are mere superstition. No stone can grant immortality and supreme power, as Alexander's secretary, Media, wrote of the panel, though possessing the stela seemed to confer a certain fame and reputation: think of its reputed possessors and those who have aspired to possess it: Cambyses, Alexander, Ptolemy Lagus, Herodotus, Cleopatra, Ovid, Zenobia, Queen of Palmyra. . . . I'm surprised that Corsican devil, Napoleon Bonaparte, hasn't already called a search for it. It would certainly make a stronger impression of victory than those fusty mummies circulating in the lecture halls of Europe! Perhaps it has something to do with why he sent his fleet south, rather than invading England? But the greatest mystification is this: if it is a funeral stela, as all sources state and as I believe, why is no name carved on it? Why was it never put in place?

Pleasant journey. Limit yourself to Cypriot wines, which are of the highest quality, and you need not fear for your bowels. *Actum ne agas.*[3]

Edinburgh
23 August 1799

From Thomas Bruce, Seventh Earl of Elgin and Envoy Extraordinaire, to Selim III, Lord of the Sublime Porte and Ruler of the Ottoman Empire:

Greetings to our dear friend and ally, from the Envoy

---

[3] Get on with it.

Extraordinaire and The King and peoples of Britain. We are pleased that you have approved our mission to the Sublime Porte and eagerly await the moment that our mutual amity, and that between our two empires, may be celebrated in person. The embassy will embark from Britain in early September, weather permitting, and we hope to sail to your fair and welcoming shores by the end of that month. Particulars will be supplied as our expedition progresses. Lady Elgin will be accompanying me, and she is most avid to see the harem, should such a slight favor be granted.

I shall be content to simply serve, asking no favors, no considerations, no gain, except that someday history may unite our two names and reputations. We shall drive the invader, Bonaparte, from your lands, the lands he so barbarously and iniquitously usurped.

Should I also chance to catch a fleeting glimpse of that ancient artifact known as "The Woman Carried Away," I will know that the Divine Lord, in his graciousness, and Selim III, in his generosity, has looked kindly upon my efforts on behalf of the Sublime Porte.

Broomhall
August 25, 1799

The *afreet* much preferred Constantinople. It was dry and warm, and the air smelled of roses, not hounds. He knew the city and its limitless resources for mischievousness well. If only this sultan, this skinny Selim, had more imagination. It was a long while since interesting events, such as sewing virgins into bags and throwing them in the bay, had occurred. The *afreet* sighed and kicked a jar of perfume into a marble basin of water.

A servant, clucking his tongue, retrieved the jar and dried it on his sleeve as Selim III, Sultan of the Osmans, rose wet and steaming from his marble bath. Circassian eunuchs, the sultan's favorite because of their beauty and gentleness, scurried forward to dry his divine body with cashmere towels, and cover his nakedness with silk and sable robes.

Inside the towels Selim shivered, remembering his dream of the night before. His body had been of wood, his feet were roots digging into the earth, clinging. But his hands and arms, his limbs, were withered and dying. Birds of prey, Russian, English, French birds, nested in the withered limbs, waiting for the tree to fall. Huseyin Kuchuk Pasha, Ottoman Grand Admiral and boyhood friend of Selim, lounged against a white marble wall, smoking and sniffing at the vials of perfumed oil lined up on a small table. He replaced the still damp vial of sandlewood that had, by itself it seemed, jumped off the table into the bath. Then, he leaned forward and adjusted the yellow sash being tied around Selim's thin waist. It was an intimate gesture, one that spoke of years of trust and shared confidences.

"So the English are already requesting favors," Huseyin Kuchuk said. "Let us hope we can satisfy them easily. Before they, too, decide to set up a foreign government in Egypt."

"The letter is from a place called Broomhall. The envoy must be a man of very low stature to have his home named after a scullery closet. Huseyin Kuchuk, should I be insulted?"

The sultan sometimes asked questions of such naiveté they stole Huseyin Kuchuk's breath. Selim knew only what people reported to him. He had lived all his life within the Sublime Porte, within a handful of rooms which, no matter how rich with gold and silk those rooms, were still rooms nonetheless, small and confined and shuttered away from the larger world.

Selim knew of broom closets and of kitchens and dark corridors and the smell of cheap tallow candles, from the Valide, the queen mother of the Sublime Porte. She had been a Creole raised by nuns in Martinique, before being brought as a slave to Constantinople and raised to favorite.

"His dwelling is most likely named after a plant which grows in great abundance in Scotland, not a scullery closet. There is no cause for insult," Huseyin Kuchuk reassured him, picking up a different vial of perfume and sniffing. He shifted his long legs, and his black military boots left a scuff mark against the white marble wall. A slave hurried forward to wipe it away, lest the ugliness of it distress the sultan. Kuchuk, bored with the long ritual of the Sultan's bath, put a foot on the slave's backside and pushed, sending the slave sprawling. The Sultan laughed, revealing strong, white teeth, then grew serious again.

"I treasure your opinion, Kuchuk. Let us not fear it has been a great mistake to allow this Scotsman to come to us. And who is this wife he speaks of, who wants to see the royal *hareem*? Do they not know the *hareem* is for my pleasure only?"

"It is a fad in the non-believers' lands, to visit and then write a monogram about a *hareem*. This desire to see the wives of the sultan is, I think, a weakness of mind resulting from forcing men to live with one wife all their lives. It gives the men, and their over-used wives, a prurient curiosity about our ways. This perfume is excellent. What is it?"

"They are an uncivilized people. The perfume is from Alexandria. Lotus blossom and orange. Put it down, I am trying to have a conversation with you." Selim slapped his hand lightly. The two were no longer youths. Selim was thirty-eight. Yet in privacy, in the baths and sleeping rooms and small coffee rooms of the seraglio, they reverted to the intimacy of earlier years, when the darkness of a just-growing beard and love poetry took precedence over affairs of state. They had been young together.

"Backward in many ways, yes. But they have perfected the art of war, and it is for that knowledge we welcome them to the Sublime Porte. We must not lose sight of that.

As for visiting the *hareem*, remember that Louis of France allowed the unwashed masses to witness his Sunday breakfast, to satisfy their curiosity.''

"And lost his head.'' Selim had been in his thirtieth year and the third year of his reign when the French king and his Austrian wife, Marie Antoinette, were beheaded. He had grieved, because Aimee, the Valide, the Creole who had become a Sultan's favorite, grieved. And, because all kings grieved, seeing in Louis's violent death the possibility of their own.

Through the latticed window Selim heard birdsong and the high voice of the muezzin calling the faithful to prayer. The afternoon heat was dissipating, bringing Topkapi, the royal city, back to life.

Selim bowed his head and a tall, feathered headdress, heavy with pearls and rubies, was fitted onto his head. His thin brows arched higher. Tendons in his long, slender neck bulged from the weight of the headdress. He adjusted his robes to cover more of his neck. It was too thin. The neck was a man's most vulnerable spot, the death spot. In France, they killed with the guillotine, severing the head from the body. In England, they hung men by their necks. In Turkey, men were dispatched by a bowstring around the neck, twisted by deaf mutes, the professional assassins of the Sublime Porte. Someday a silken bowstring would end his days. It was written.

Fully dressed now, Selim turned carefully and looked at Huseyin Kuchuk and a second man who had watched the bath ritual silently, unsmilingly.

Ishak Bey was an impatient man. Food never arrived quickly enough, women never surrendered soon enough, when the sun shone, the day was too long, and when the moon rose, the night seemed to last forever.

It was his bright impatience, his hummingbird brilliance that first made him beloved of Selim, and then brought him to ruin. Years before, when Selim's uncle had ascended the throne and Selim had been confined to the Cage (that golden imprisonment of heirs to the Ottoman throne, with only eunuchs and women to occupy the long years of waiting for the Sultan to die so that he could take his turn to rule), it was Ishak Bey who had been Selim's eyes, ears, and mouth in the outside world beyond the Cage. Ishak Bey had gone to France as Selim's representative. Ishak Bey liked France very much. Of course, it was expensive. And all his brilliance, all his promise, was soon tarnished by the crime not of accepting bribes from those who wished Selim's favor, but of being too greedy, of getting caught. Ishak Bey's greed was such that even the corrupt ministers of Versailles complained of him.

Now, in disgrace, he still had Selim's heart, but was trusted with no duties greater than translating for the foreigners. Ishak Bey would be sent to greet Elgin.

Selim, dressed now, looked at Ishak Bey and at Huseyin Kuchuk and his black eyes grew soft and liquid. He loved them with all his heart. But he did not trust them.

"Ishak Bey, you are very quiet today. Has someone given you offence? Has a pretty woman turned you down . . . or betrayed you to her husband?"

Beyond the window, a muezzin called louder. Prayers would start soon. Selim moved impatiently, hurrying his slaves to finish the last bucklings, lacings, and adjustments of his robes and jewels.

Ishak Bey was not quick to answer. He loved France, despite having been sent home from it in disgrace. This war between the Sublime Porte and France did not please him.

"I wish with all my heart it was simply a woman or gambling debt that troubled me. You know the question in my heart."

"Once we have invited the English to our lands, how will we rid ourselves of them?" The Sultan spoke quickly, impatiently, then answered his own question. "The same way we will get rid of the French. We will go to war and drive them away. After they have taught us the new warfare."

Ishak Bey smiled politely, but the crease between his eyebrows did not disappear.

"Acre," Selim whispered. "Acre. Remember. The French are not invincible. We defeated them there. They are not invincible."

"With the help of the English," Ishak Bey whispered back. "The French were defeated at Acre with the help of the English. Who will help us defeat the English in Cairo, after they remove the French? The Russians?"

Selim's thin, long-nosed face grew stormy. He hated the Russians more than any other people on the face of the earth.

Outside in the gardens of the seraglio, songbirds fluttered in the ancient cypresses and roses sweetened the air. They heard fountains splaying and somewhere, behind one of the many walls, a woman sang a love lament.

"There must be a splendid exchange of gifts," said Huseyin Kuchuk. "The English do not impress easily, and it is vital that we impress them. They must not see us as weak, as inferior, in any way." Though of course, they will, Kuchuk thought.

"What do you know of this man from Broomhall? What does he crave? What is his weakness?" Selim asked.

"Antiquities. He is a student of the past and wishes to possess pieces of it."

"And this 'Woman Carried Away' he writes of?"

"A fable for children, a story of a stela stolen from a pharaoh's tomb. There is no such stela," Ishak Bey said.

"The man from Broomhall seems to think there is. Find it. We will present it to him. When he has finished his work for us, it will make him that much more eager to return home with his gift. And send a hundred roses to the Queen Mother tonight. I will visit her for another chess match, and to see if she has heard from her country-woman, Josephine."

Sultan Mahmud's pretty French slave, when still a schoolgirl in Martinique, had been friends with another Creole, a petite brunette named Josephine, the same Josephine now married to Bonaparte. Never had Selim wished to widow a woman as much as he wished to widow this Josephine.

The *afreet*, who feared the imams and muezzins, did not follow the three men to the mosque, but instead played in the gardens of the *hareem*, planting lustful thoughts into the minds of the unused virgins cloistered there, so that the eunuchs had much trouble keeping order that night.

8

Ibrahim, over the next two days, worsened. Fever and pain radiated from his belly and the young man writhed in his bed and grew delirious. Desperate, Hamid sent for the Frank doctor, to see if his skills were any greater than those of the Cairo doctors.

Dr. Morello, leaning over Ibrahim's bed, put an arm under Ibrahim's limp head and brought their two faces close together.

"Where is it?" Morello whispered. Ibrahim's lips did not move. His eyes did not open. A pink bubble of blood frothed at the corner of his mouth.

Hamid, watching, tilted his head. He could not hear what the doctor was saying. Had he done wrong, asking this *farengi* to attend his dying nephew? For surely Ibrahim was dying. That much could be seen in the glazed eyes, the ashen skin. But why? This was not a natural death. Ibrahim had been strong and lively one hour, the next he lay dying. No, it was not a natural death.

Soon, this would be a matter of vengeance. But now Hamid could think only of the son of his heart who was to have said the prayers over his own grave someday. Now, Hamid would have to pray over Ibrahim's grave. The old mourning the young. It was not natural. It was not right.

"Where?" Morello whispered again.

"What are you asking him?" Hamid asked, moving protectively closer to Ibrahim's bed.

"Where the pain seems to be centered."

"Can you help him?"

"I do not know. Keep him warm. Force liquid down his throat every half hour. Wait. Pray."

"Yes, yes, the women of the house know that much," Hamid said impatiently.

Morello rose to leave. There was nothing he could do here. Ibrahim had slipped into unconsciousness. There seemed to be extensive internal damage. The young man was bleeding to death, and the only blood that showed was that little bubble at the corner of the mouth. What a strange machine the body was, so vulnerable and so filled with secrets.

"Payment," Hamid muttered, clapping his hands. A servant stepped forward and extended a purse towards Morello.

"I would dishonor myself to take your money, my friend. It is my pleasure to do what little can be done for your nephew." Morello eyed the purse impassively, then turned back to the little table near Ibrahim's bed.

Hamid, watching his eyes, said, "If it pleases you, take it."

Morello picked up a small lion carved from camel bone and pocketed it. From the style of the workmanship, he guessed it to be a good example of fifteenth-century Coptic art. The lion of Christ. How many strange forms we have given god, he thought. And the foolish priests would have us believe that god invented us.

The carving was not to everyone's taste, but Baron Vivant Denon collected bones and he would certainly pay well for this trinket.

"I am sorry I cannot do more," Dr. Morello said.

"I am sorry, too," said Hamid.

————————

By afternoon, the cold politeness which had reigned in the dungeon gave way to blatant anger and recriminations.

Marguerite: "If you hadn't come, I never would have been suspected. A woman alone, unprotected, a gentlewoman, would have been immune to suspicion."

Michel: "Alone? I do not think so. There was that young lieutenant. A gentlewoman? Marguerite, really, my dear, your mother was an opera dancer. Ah, yes. The gentle sex. Lucrezia Borgia. Messalina. Zenobia. Cleopatra. Gentle. Hah!"

Marguerite: "I never wanted to see you again. I detest you. Why did you come?"

Michel: "You are my wife. I never give up what is mine."

She sat as far from him as possible, surrounded by darkness and anger. During the course of the afternoon Michel was able to purchase from the guard his own travel trunks, some of Marguerite's clothing, clean sheets to cover their straw beds and several basins of hot water, but she continued to disdain him, while accepting his largesse.

When he attempted to sit next to her, she removed herself to the other side of the room, to another place of darkness and anger.

"I do not even want to look at you," she said, when he lit a lamp and offered it to her.

He placed the lamp in the middle of their dungeon and sat opposite her, musing. He would have to win her all over again. Woo and court and win her. His wife. It would be more difficult this time. She was no longer seventeen. She was no longer easy to impress.

Or, he could do as she wished. Let her go. He thought of their rooms in Paris, emptied of Marguerite and Marguerite's things, the boxes of powder and wire skirt frames, her shelf of books and cabinet of china, the dancing slippers and whale-bone corsets thrown over boudoir chairs the color of burgundy wine. Marguerite at her little writing table, attending to her correspondence, Marguerite at her pianoforte, practicing an aria by Mozart, Marguerite in bed, her hair soft and dark against the white pillow.

Lose Marguerite? He could not. He would not.

If only he could make her understand. This matter of other women, she took it far too seriously. If you hung every man who took a mistress the continent would soon look like a large convent. It was not as though he diminished her with these games. And they were just games. Other wives understood. Why couldn't she?

"You must understand . . ." he began.

"No. I must not," she cut him off.

"You did pour the coffee, after all," Michel said on the second day.

"And that means . . . ?"

"Only that you poured the coffee. I am trying to make some sense of this, Marguerite. You could stop pining for your lieutenant and give this matter some thought yourself."

"Oh! The beast dares show jealousy! I, the wronged wife in all your sordid affairs, am accused of pining! I will not tolerate this!" Secretly, she was pleased. Michel was jealous. Michel was suffering the pangs. She turned away to hide her smile of satisfaction.

"I would not have come under suspicion, had not my wife been one of Josephine's wanton associates."

"You would not have come under suspicion had you stayed in Switzerland, with your mistress. Oh, but I forget. She had tired of you. So sorry."

"Why did you cut your hair?" Michel asked on the third day, hoping to begin a neutral conversation.

"I was ill, when first I arrived in Cairo."

"The nature of the illness?"

"A private matter."

"Private from your own husband?"

"Especially from my husband, since he had abandoned me several months before."

"I went to the spa in Geneva. That is not abandonment."

"It is when you journey with your mistress."

"You lost no time finding someone to console you. But a lieutenant, Marguerite? Surely at your age you deserve a general at the least."

"I almost died from the fever," she said suddenly, springing to the attack, wanting to wound.

Michel squeezed his eyes shut against the image of Marguerite, small and deathly white except for that black hair, lying alone and dying in a foreign place.

He wanted to fold her in his arms and comfort her. But he dare not. He felt like a fool. She had been alone at a time when she most needed him. Had Lt. Foures been there? "I am sorry," he said. "I am truly sorry. I will find a way to make this up to you."

"You cannot," she said, turning away to hide her pleasure. The lie had found its target.

There were no windows in the storeroom, so night merely brought deeper darkness. On the fourth night of their imprisonment they had reached a state of fear and exhaustion that allowed, indeed required, courteous discourse. They avoided certain topics of conversation so that they might better concentrate on the current predicament.

The door between them and freedom was of thick wood latched with an Egyptian wooden puzzle lock the size of a hatbox from Madame Gerard's. Neither Marguerite nor Michel had hopes of opening that lock, but Michel thought that, with the proper tool, he might be able to loosen the door's side hinges. They spoke of escape, realizing that this very conversation made them the criminals that others already believed them to be, and then set about searching the storeroom for instruments with which to accomplish their escape.

This was no easy feat. The storeroom was actually a series of small, low-ceilinged rooms that led in and out of each other in dizzying manner, especially when illuminated by a single oil lamp. It was there, in those dark, subterranean rooms, that the members of the institute stored the great quantities of items they intended to bring back to France, items garnered from sandy ruins, abandoned temples, riverbanks and field, river bed and marsh. Marguerite and Michel moved from room to room, their footsteps echoing on the worn stone floor, their lamp illuminating each corner at a time.

They discovered huge vats filled with preserving fluid and entire carcasses of ostriches, crocodiles, ibis and hyena, storks and purple geese, the Egyptian vulture known as Pharaoh's hen, which broods over the ruined monuments, and the bon-bon colored flamingo. Next to the vats and jars were long rows of wooden presses between which were dried specimens of yellow-blossoming cotton, poppy, millet, and maize, mimosa, tobacco, indigo, and papyrus. In two separate rooms were coffers in which still rested the mummified bodies of cats, dogs, birds, and a court scribe or two, and shelves and shelves supporting stone carvings of jackal-headed gods and cow-eared goddesses scoured from old tombs, headdresses, small sphinxes, figurines, amulets, and ornaments, a giant foot carved in stone, an equally giant head, open-eyed and benignly smiling, scrolls, and sarcophagi painted with the face of the mummy inside and symbols of the moon and the lotus.

There was, in fact, enough to begin a small museum of Egyptology gathered in those storerooms. But there was neither lever nor pry with which they might free themselves.

"How old the world is," Marguerite said, wiping her brow and hating the silence that surrounded them. She sat on a sarcophagus and shook dust webs from her fingertips. Michel sat next to her and put his arm around her shoulders.

"We are not going to be able to open that door. Say something, Michel. Anything," she ordered, fighting back panic.

He tightened his grip on her shoulders. How thin she felt, how fragile. Protectiveness surged in him, strong as the appetite to eat, to gamble. No other woman called forth this particular quality in Michel.

"Will you come back to Paris with me, Marguerite?" he asked. "I will be a better husband than I have been."

"Oh, leave me in peace. I am truly afraid."

He looked down at her little bent head and patted the thick, bristling black hair. It made him think of his mistress's hair, which was soft and blonde. He thought of Josette, waiting to feel the emotions he had felt a year before: passion, adventure, a sense of danger and adventure that men found only in battle or in the mistress's bedroom. He felt nothing. Indeed, he had been glad to leave Josette and Switzerland.

In the airier spaces of Quassim Bey's palace, the institute was attempting to go about its normal routine. In fact, the more immediate matter of Bonaparte's travel plans and intentions occupied the thoughts of the savants. The general was about to abandon them. Gloom was the predominate mood among the savants, except for Vivant Denon, who was restless.

Marguerite, that little chit, had left him high and dry. Disappeared somewhere with that husband of hers. And just when he was on the brink of greatness, and fame. The Great Man had come personally, secretly, to see him, Denon. Actually, he had called him Vivant, by his Christian name, as if he and the general were closest of friends. The Great Man was impressed with Denon's work in Egypt, with his bravery and fortitude. He would be well remembered, and rewarded, when they were back in Paris, the Great Man had pointedly said. A post was what he meant, of course. An important post that would involve a wood-paneled office, a large staff of lackeys, and access to the art of the ages.

Denon was all but dancing with joy. His middle age was secured. He had found a patron, and that patron was the most powerful man in the world. Or soon would be.

So where was Marguerite? There was work to be finished!

He hadn't seen them since the night of the coffee cup incident, when Bonaparte's guard had led them away for questioning. Marguerite, then, had looked charmingly frightened. But was that reason enough to abscond with a husband, when there was work to do?

His drawing of the Battle of the Pyramid—the good copy, *sans* phalluses, *sans* dancing girls, the copy being tidied by Marguerite—was unfinished, and Bonaparte would be leaving any day now. Denon had hoped Bonaparte would take the drawing back with him, for safe-keeping. Denon was starting to suspect its safety in Cairo was a highly debatable point.

There was a tension in the air, a sullenness on the faces of the Turks and Arabs he met, that reminded him of last year's uprising. It did not frighten him. He was a man who did not easily succumb to fear. The entire army still talked of the Syrian expedition when Denon had brought out paper and crayon and drawn the scene of battle whilst bullets and sabres flew about him. But this new tension, this waiting for something to happen, made him uneasy. It upset his day and his work schedule, and the artist in him resented that more than the threat of bodily harm.

Sighing, wringing his hands behind his back, Denon

paced in his studio, trying to formulate a plan for the day, the week, the month. In Egypt, one did not think beyond a month. It was impossible.

Fully dressed in a blue linen suit except for his high-arched bare feet, he shuffled over the canvas covering the floor. A lover of beautiful objects, he had dutifully protected this room, with its marbled mosaics and carved pilasters, from any harm he might cause it.

He could complete the drawing himself. But then who would finish the new one he had begun? Marguerite, where are you? he screamed in his thoughts.

He would forgive her only if it turned out she had been with little Pauline, engaging in some of the caresses he had imagined passing between them during the last meeting of the Institute. And if she told him every last detail, every emotion. Perhaps they had even contrived a way to force Bonaparte to watch their loveplay, as punishment for this rumor that he was leaving them, including Pauline, behind, while he returned to France, to glory.

Smiling again, humming to himself, Denon picked up a charcoal crayon and made sinuous, curving motions with it in the air. He pointed his fine, small foot and danced to the easel holding his new drawing. It was a still-life of some various objects they had acquired during desert expeditions. The little statue of Seket was not right. On paper, copied, she looked stiff, like the stone thing she was. In reality, when held in the hand, the little goddess seemed to brim with life.

Denon sat on a stool and pulled on his boots. Next door was a small workroom that Dr. Morello kept stocked with medicine, should any of the Institute fall ill or be wounded. In a drawer of the cabinet was a key he was not supposed to know about. It unlocked the storeroom layered deep in the ground, under the palace, where the little statue of Seket was being stored. He would fetch it forth.

It was dark, cool, surprisingly quiet in the dungeon. He couldn't even hear the wind blow. It was haunted. Redolent of pain and torture. Denon had read vivid accounts of some of the practices of the Turkish inquisitors and found them excessive. The custom of bundling unfaithful women into burlap bags and drowning them was, he had decided, an absolute waste of womenflesh. But the fear in their eyes, their tears and pleading as the bag was pulled over them, must have been delicious. Past tense. This latest Sultan, Selim, was not interested in women, he'd heard. And that thought sent Denon on a whole new stream of fantasy. The wasted harem. The bored harem. Rooms and rooms of exotic creatures, languishing for want of male attention. For want of him, Vivant Denon. By now he was singing outright, his unpracticed, unreliable voice rising and falling precipitously in Figaro's jubilant song about the delights of the wedding night.

He stumbled through the dark, dank rooms, preoccupied with Suzanne's—a new, never-staged Suzanne, with black hair tumbling loose to her hips, clothed only in a spangled veil—trepidations of what would be done to her. He stumbled over something soft. It moved. It sat up.

"Who the hell are you?" Denon asked, more shocked than frightened. People ought not to be sleeping in the storeroom.

"We have met only briefly and I know my face is not a memorable one, but there is no need to curse," said Michel irritably. Marguerite, sleeping next to him, sat up and pushed a curl out of her eye, yawning.

Denon was speechless for a moment, then his eyes twinkled, his full mouth curved into a lecherous smile.

"The reunion between husband and wife, especially after a long separation, sometimes requires . . . what should we call it? Novelty? The suggestion of danger? . . . to rekindle passion," he purred. "Have you enjoyed the dungeon, monsieur? Marguerite, I will forgive your abandonment of duties if you will explain this to me more fully. Very fully."

Marguerite rose stiffly and adjusted her loosened clothing. Denon pretended to look away for modesty's sake, but while his face turned, his eyes stayed glued on Marguerite's becoming dishevelment.

"We are not here by choice. And certainly not to enjoy any sort of reunion," she murmured.

"We have been relocated to these rooms for confinement," Michel said. He looked from Vivant Denon to his wife with increasing interest. Apparently, Denon was her sponsor during the Egyptian expedition. Were they lovers? Marguerite and Denon? His wife bedding the most notorious pornographer of France, next to de Sade? Jealousy knotted his stomach.

Marguerite, watching Denon's face and Michel's, read them both.

"Fools, both of you," she said. "Where will we go, now that you have come to release us?"

Denon set his candle on a shipping crate and sat down next to Michel. He scratched his head and considered.

"I will assume this has something to do with the attempted assassination of Bonaparte. Most certainly. I haven't seen you, Marguerite, since that night."

She nodded, appalled that a matter of life and death to her seemed to be a trivial detail forgotten by the others of the Institute.

"We have been held here since then. Most unjustly. Why has no one come to defend us?"

"There has been more pressing business, my dear. Bonaparte is leaving us, as you know," Denon said.

Marguerite lunged forward to take the dangling keys from his hand. Denon, quicker, hid them behind his back.

"I must think," he said.

"Think quickly. There is a guard around here somewhere," muttered Michel.

"I think it would be wiser to wait," Denon said slowly. "Until Bonaparte leaves the immediate area, this is probably the safest place for you to be. He will not want to be reminded of the attempted assassination."

"I . . . we . . . did not try to assassinate him," said Marguerite, careful for the first time in many years to include her husband in a statement about her life and actions. She did not want to be alone in this.

"Of course not, my dear. But you must admit it looks as if you did. To release you prematurely and provide the means for flight would add to your appearance of guilt."

Marguerite looked from Michel, who was slightly red in the face with anger, to Denon, who grinned sheepishly and shrugged. She could probably convince Denon to release her, but not both of them. Although newly arrived to the status of adulteress, she was certainly not innocent of the ways of the world and of certain men. She could take Denon by the arm, kiss his strangely cherubic face and voilà! imprisonment for her would be ended.

But would she? Denon's bedroom fantasies were far too wicked for her taste. And, there was Michel, the cad. Abandoning him at this moment, in this place, seemed especially cruel. In the past few days he had tried to make amends, to ingratiate, to apologize even, for his many sins. He had not won her over, but she was starting to appreciate the efforts. Once this was over, she would turn her back on him forever, but right now, well . . . she would not desert a comrade-in-arms.

"How long?" she asked miserably.

"A matter of days, I surmise. His sea chest is already packed."

9

The burial could be undone. The tomb dwellers of
the necropolis who slept in the sacrificial alcoves
whispered to her of prayers unsaid, rituals undone.
Anubis, guardian of the dead, could be bribed. The dead
could return to take their revenge.

Ptahshepses refused to put the funeral stela in place. He
refused to tell her where he had hidden it. Ptahshepses
must be punished.

And so Ma'tcha' decided to unseal her father's tomb.

It was not an easy thing. She could not go to the priests,
for they reported every stolen grain, every fallen bird, every
rumor, every frown, back to Ptahshepses. She could not go
to the tomb builders for they hated all who claimed immortality, knowing as they did that their own bodies and souls
would be consigned to dust. Injustice lasts for eternity.

She could not go to the courtiers who had once been
ruled by her father, because now the fear of Ptahshepses
ruled them.

Ptahshepses told all who would listen that his wife was in
the hand of god, she was crazed. All her reason, goodness,
and beauty had been stolen away from her. He could not
name the culprit. It had happened one night in darkness,
when the demon's face could not be seen.

He grieved openly for his wife, but in their private

rooms he kicked her away and would not listen to her pleas to put the stela in place on her father's tomb, so it could be completed, so her father's spirit could finish its appointed journey to eternity. Nor would he bed his wife any more. He wanted no children from the daughter of Shepseskaf, his enemy.

Once, knowing that she spied upon him, Ptahshepses lay with his wife's own maid and made noises that filled the night with lechery. Ma'tcha', listening, saw fronds copulate with the palm trunks, alligators mate with swans, dogs cavort with monkeys, the moon rape the anchor star, till finally she could stand it no more. She ran away from light, into darkness, chased by laughing devils. She ran until she reached the necropolis. She slept in the city of the dead, pillowing her head on a sharp corner of her father's incomplete tomb.

She dreamed of the goddess Hathor being carried away by Anubis. Hathor wept and pleaded. Better for the dead to walk among the living than to rest in an incomplete tomb, waiting an eternity, dissolving into nothingness, Hathor said.

That night Ma'tcha' met the necropolis dwellers who melt in and out of darkness, seen only by the creatures of the night. Plague-bearers, lepers, untouchables, they cohabited with the already-dead because the living would not have them.

A stench woke her when the moon was high in the sky. It smelled of blood and rotten meat and hopelessness. She did not move, knowing that the wild thing would run and hide, should she stir, and she wanted to see the creature that gave off this reek of decay.

A black shadow took form, stole its outline from the night sky, and crept near. She watched from one narrowly opened eye. A hand, black with dirt, reached out and touched the whiteness of her linen skirt. The hand had only three fingers; the others had been eaten away by disease. From the wrist up to the shoulder it was wrapped in coarsely woven linen caked with dirt. A living mummy.

Ma'tcha' forced herself to stay still. Another shadow appeared, and another and another. They lined up before her like the demons of the Hall of Truth. They watched, and poked her, and laughed, showing gapping black holes for mouths, and after a while they left.

The next night, Ma'tcha' brought them bread and cheese, cold meats, sweet dates. She laid these before the tomb, on a piece of clean white linen, and retreated back into the shadows. She slept with the dead, and when she awoke the offerings to the almost-dead were gone.

This became her nightly ritual. No one questioned her night-long absences from the high-priest's palace. She came and went like an invisible creature, a spirit woman.

Ptahshepses, who had felt only scorn for his wife, began to fear her. He would not enter a room if she was in it, would not sit at a table with her. He turned white if she looked at him, seeing in her gaze something that no one else saw. It was Shepseskaf staring at him, accusing. Shepseskaf in woman's form.

One evening, when he was surrounded by his favorite women of the house and listening to a flute player, Ma'tcha' went into the room and approached him. She walked with her head down, and when she was an arm-length from him, she knelt.

"Husband, tell me how I have offended you," she asked. The courtiers in the room blushed with pity for her, her voice was so sweet and sad. Only Ptahshepses heard the dead pharaoh's voice come out of the woman's mouth.

"Leave me in peace, woman," he roared. He jumped up, spilling a young girl and plates of sweetmeats from his huge lap. He, the high priest who had once been slender as a palm, had grown monstrous since Shepseskaf's burial. He could not stop eating: the food he swallowed had its nourishment stolen from it and could not satisfy him.

"I wish only to sit at your side, in my rightful place. You need not change other things." Gently, she helped the sprawling girl to her feet and led her back to Ptahshepses, as an offering. The girl giggled nervously as Ma'tcha' pushed her back onto the high priest's knees.

How could he refuse? He saw the way the others watched. He saw Shepseskaf staring at him through the daughter's eyes.

Ma'tcha' clapped her hands. A slave brought a stool. She put it at Ptahshepses right side, slightly behind him, and sat, silent, for the rest of that evening.

Ptahshepses fondled his dancing girl, shouted approval at the musician, and helped himself to prodigious quantities of sweets. But it was all for show. How could he feel pleasure, with Shepseskaf sitting behind him like that?

The next night, Ma'tcha' came again, and took her place behind her husband. She wore a new dress of white linen trimmed with silver lotus blossoms, and her long, black wig was adorned with silver beads. They clinked as she walked, making sweet music of her movements. The courtiers smiled at her beauty, and looked harshly at her husband.

That second night, when the musician took a break, Ma'tcha's maid offered the high priest a bowl of dates. He refused to take any. Ma'tcha' came forward, took a date, and placed it in her mouth to show its harmlessness. Still, her husband refused to eat from the dish.

The next night, she brought a dish of jellied, sugared fruits. She offered them to the courtiers, who took and ate. When she had finished her round of the room, she offered the dish to Ptahshepses. There were grumbles and frowns. It was not right for a husband to humiliate his wife in this manner. Dancing girls were one thing. But to refuse to eat her food? It was the same as accusing her of being a poisoner.

Ptahshepses, feeling the increasing disapproval around him, slumped in his chair. This devil woman was beating him down, wearying him. He felt, for the first time since the waters of the river had tried to take him, many, many years ago, that living a long life was perhaps not so wonderful after all. He put the last sweetmeat in his mouth. He tasted sugar and papaya. Nothing else. He chewed tentatively. The texture was correct. He swallowed.

Ma'tcha' beamed. Her plan was going to work after all.

That night, she crept through the darkness to her father's tomb, laid out the offerings, and waited.

Soon, dark figures stole their forms from the darker night and approached. When hands reached out to grab the bread, the meat, the cheese, she put her hands over the plates, protecting them.

"No," she hissed. "First you must grant me something."

The blackness around her whispered and rustled.

"What do you ask of us?" a voice rasped. She could not tell if it was male or female.

"The third night from now, this tomb must be opened," Ma'tcha' said. "I know you know how to do this. You may keep whatever gold you find in the tomb. But you must open it three nights from tonight. The corpse within must walk again."

Ptahshepses saw his own death approaching. He no longer enjoyed his dancing girls. He could not sleep. When in meeting with the priests, he could not concentrate. He gorged himself on honey pastries and roasted lamb, stuffing handfulls of greasy meats and dripping cakes into his mouth, down his throat, growing heavier, more solid, by the minute. As if that would help him. Did not dead men also eat? Why else were loaves of baked bread and jars of wine put in the tomb?

The courtiers who had once smirked at the hapless Ma'tcha' now laughed openly at Ptahshepses, who stumbled, sleepless and ranting and obese, through the palace.

He had taken his revenge of Shepseskaf. Now Ma'tcha' would have hers. She was cunning, Ma'tcha.' She would select a poison from which there was no recovery. A poison without taste, without texture. Without hope.

Each evening, as he sat in his hall and pretended to enjoy his dancing girls and the clowning dwarfs who tumbled over the floor, he tasted from the dish his wife put before him on his little ivory and turquoise table, just enough to still the clacking tongues of the court, just enough to convince himself that the death was not this day, this week. He allowed his wife to kiss his hands, feeling in her moist, full lips the touch of Shepseskaf's dry, thin mouth.

And when Ma'tcha' asked if she might not give a feast in his honor, because husband and wife were reconciled, he tried to move his head sideways in denial, but it only would move up and down, in assent. Shepseskaf, he was certain, held it by the chin and forehead, forcing him to nod. Ptahshepses felt the cold, clammy touch of a rotting, linen-wrapped hand.

The morning of the feast, the high priest considered, only for a moment, putting the funeral stela in its place and completing pharaoh's tomb. If he did not, his heart would soon be weighed against the feather of truth in the hall of demons. He decided that he desired vengeance more than he feared judgment. It was too late to change course.

Ma'tcha' greeted him in the doorway as he entered. She was dressed in new white linen with a celebratory collar of blue and red beads. She kissed him on the eyelids, the mouth, the earlobes. Kisses for the dead. She led him into the feast, gently, by the hand, like a young girl leading her lover to the soft riverbank, to lay together.

"May the grace of Amun be in thy heart! May he grant thee a happy old age and let thee pass they life in joy!" was her greeting. Dream of a thorn. You are being lied to.

She put a sweet-smelling cone of incense on his head, and they ate. Ptahshepses sat heavily on his ivory-inlaid chair and Ma'tcha' supervised a long line of slaves who brought him succulent dish after dish. Ma'tcha' ate from each dish set before her husband, to show all was well, all was safe.

The flute players performed well that night, and the harpist. The dancing girls were more graceful than ever, the singers more sweet-voiced than ever. The court, for the first time since Shepseskaf's death, was happy and at ease.

After the emptied food platters were carried away, the drinking began. Ma'tcha', as custom demanded, brought in a small, carved coffin and passed it around, reminding the feasters that life is short and death long, and that none can return again who has gone hence. She laughed as she did this. It was another lie; they were fools who did not see Shepseskaf standing there, in the darkest corner, pointing his linen-wrapped fingers at them.

She poured red wine into Ptahshepses' new glass goblet. Her priest-husband drank freely, and when he extended his glass to be refilled for the tenth time, she turned sideways so he would not see her emptying the contents of the small cloth into it. Powdered glass and hair, minced finer than dust. The particles floated for a second, a filmy gauze over the wine's red surface, then sank, to mix in with the dregs, which Ptahshepses in his greed always downed.

By early morning, when the other priests were yawning and wishing the high priest would rise so they could go home to their beds, Ptahshepses felt the first pains. A rat begin to gnaw at his guts, trying to eat its way out.

Ptahshepses fell forward, drunk and in pain. He looked up, and in the darkest corner of the room he saw Shepseskaf, wrapped in his burial linen, beckoning. Ma'tcha' stood next to him, her face twisted with hatred and scorn. Outside, the *khamsin* howled and threw sand against the bolted door but only Ptahshepses heard the wind and felt the stinging sand.

It was to have been a long death, filled with exquisite torment. The simplest poisons take the longest to work, and she had counted on this, and on the fact that the physicians would be helpless. There was no antidote for powdered glass and chopped hair. Once it reached the guts it did its job: death by thousands of minute cuts, the leaching of the blood from its accustomed pathways. The damage could be neither repaired not halted.

On the fifth day of his torment, Ma'tcha' visited her dying husband. He was in his bed, writhing, searching for a restful position that would ease the pain. He was incoherent with suffering.

Ma'tcha' bathed his forehead with cool water and propped him up in her arms.

"Now," she whispered, and her voice was like jagged glass, "you will tell me where you have hidden my father's funeral stela."

Ptahshepses came back from his hall of torture and opened his eyes upon the living. He saw his wife, and next to her was silent, pointing Shepseskaf. He signaled to his guards that they should seize the man, but they pretended to see only his wife standing there, and she, they would not touch.

Pain rippled through the high priest, but he had passed fear. He had already seen the faces of the demons of judgment. Let the river take him. He grinned and fell speechless back into his pillows and died without speaking again.

The priests filled his tomb with bread and wine and dates, and statues of dancing girls to keep him company throughout eternity. On the walls of the tomb they inscribed this: "The King Shepseskaf placed Ptahshepses among the royal children; he was more pleasing in the sight of the King than any other child. The King gave him his eldest royal daughter, Ma'tcha', to be his wife, for he preferred her to be with him more than with any other man."

After Ptahshepses's death Ma'tcha' ran through the

court screaming that she had lost her husband too soon, he owed her a last word, a last deed. The court and the priests, impressed by her grief, held her up to the world as a noble example of wifely love.

Secretly, they felt that perhaps she carried her wailing and lamenting a bit too far. When she began to rave that the priests cheated and robbed, they decided that Ma't-cha' should mourn in a more subtle manner and elsewhere.

The priests bound her thin, flailing arms and put her on a barge from whence she was delivered to the priests of Sobek, who worshipped the crocodile. Pharaoh's daughter no more but a nameless madwoman, they first passed her from bed to bed, using her for their pleasure, but not even her beauty could make them forget her raging madness. Then she was trained to feed the sacred crocodiles but the animals hid from her, so she was led to a room in the temple, a room filled with jugs of water and plates of bread and dates. Before they sealed the door shut, one of the oldest priests, in an effort to be kind so that her spirit would forgive him, gave Ma'tcha' the package which had been sent up river with her: her father's funeral stela.

Then the door was shut and sealed. The pharaoh, Shepseskaf, became a dead man locked in the world of the living because of his unfinished tomb, and his daughter, Ma'tcha', possessor now, finally, of the stela, was a living woman locked into the world of the dead.

10

Grey city night. Ancient cobblestones. Emptied streets.

In Athens, Spiros moved through the darkness, his chisel, hammer, and lever thudding against his legs as he walked. A cold wind rushed past, and he made a sign against the evil eye.

The old temple rose up from the grit and litter of the narrow alley. Moonlight washed its blackened marble walls; an eerie bubble of silence surrounded it. Statues missing noses and fingertips stared at Spiros as he entered. Wild grapevines reached for his ankles.

People feared this place. Devils gathered here. The ancient gods still played their cruel games here. The centuries had forgotten this place and left it stranded in the old times, when Christians were thrown to lions and virgins danced around stone phalluses. Spiros made the sign against the evil eye again and moved forward through the treelike columns.

A smell of tomcats rose in the still air. He stumbled in the darkness, and his chisel fell, making a loud clank of metal on marble. He paused, still as one of the cracked, mutilated statues. The abandoned temple would be empty. Still, caution was a virtue. He silently picked up the chisel and thrust it securely into his belt.

Not that Spiros considered himself a thief. He was a Suliot, a Greek, committed to fighting the Sultan and Turkish rule. Of course, that took money and antiquities were popular items in the marketplace where the wealthy foreigners shopped. But if he were discovered at this night's work the most pleasant punishment would be the amputation of his right hand.

Something soft and evil-smelling brushed past him. Spiros flattened himself against the wall and swallowed a scream.

"Father! You almost gave me a heart attack!" he muttered to the old man who stopped and stared at him. An acrid odor of piss rounded the corner.

The old man poked his bony finger into Spiros's chest and cackled.

"At your age, I could hold my wine all night," he boasted through gaping teeth. "And here you are, a young man, looking for a damp corner! Aiii, men aren't men anymore!"

"Go away, father. I'm waiting for someone." Spiros grinned weakly.

"Don't bother. You'll disappoint her. I can tell just by looking at you." But he went away, leaving Spiros alone again with the statues and the old gods. Bats flew overhead.

Spiros moved to the alcove where the panel was. It would be easy work. This panel had not been carved into the stone, but brought from elsewhere and then plastered in place. Five strokes would release it, he estimated.

He reached out to touch the female figure in the panel and say farewell. He traced her swelling thighs and naked breasts, the sweet mouth opened in protest. The Woman Carried Away. That was what his great-grandmother had called her. That was what grandmothers had called the little figure for centuries and centuries. Spiros touched the jackal-headed figure opposite the woman, remembering how, as a child, this figure had frightened him.

When the world was young. That was when this couple was carved, he thought. Now we are old. The world is old. Black figs and bad weather. He would miss her.

He carefully placed the chisel at one angle and struck the first blow.

The next morning, Spiros woke with last night's wine and song lingering on his lips. It is a rare morning when a man wakes to the promise of great wealth, a morning worthy of song and ouzo with the first cup of coffee. He made his way down the narrow, laundry-basket lined stairs to the steaming, soapy kitchen. He allowed himself all three— coffee, ouzo, and song—despite his woman's screeching that he was a drunk, a good-for-nothing, a burden, and other numerous compliments.

To quiet her, he twisted his hand in her rope of black hair and kissed her. She bit him on the lip, drawing blood and resumed her litany of complaint as her arms thrashed in a huge vat of soapy water.

"Bah! You'll see, woman. I made us rich last night. Instead of taking in other women's washing, you'll hire servants to do yours."

"You have a job?" she asked, raising both eyebrows.

"Better." He sipped his cloudy ouzo and pointed to the corner of the kitchen where the stela, wrapped in burlap, leaned against the peeling wall.

"Garbage. More garbage," she sighed. "Why you waste your time on the garbage of the ages I do not understand. It will get you nowhere. It will get you in prison. Or worse."

He poured more ouzo into his glass and took a big gulp. "You know nothing. I will be paid much for it."

After his coffee, he put on his work shirt and made his way though the busy streets of the Plaka, where sandalmakers and poets, manure carriers and jewelers jostled each other in the lavender light of dawn. The roosters of the city had barely begun crowing. The sun was a yellow tease peeking over the horizon.

The sun was almost overhead when Spiros reached the harbor, sweating from the weight of the stone stela he carried on his shoulder. Salty perspiration dripped into his eyes as he tried to find the "Athena." He stopped many times to ask directions of sailors and warehouse workers and was not unduly surprised when a man approached him. Probably he had heard the question and knew where the Athena was docked. A man who asks questions of strangers is often not surprised when strangers, in turn, ask questions of him. Spiros forgot this was the harbor, a place of danger as well as commerce.

"Spiros? The stonecutter?" the stranger asked in passable if heavily accented Greek. He was blackened by the sun and wore a beard as well as mustaches. He could have been Greek. Or Turkish. Or Arabic. Spiros couldn't decide which.

"I am Spiros," he answered, shifting the heavy weight on his shoulder. The stranger's black eyes went to the bundle.

"I will take that now." The stranger's arms lifted, ready to take the stela.

"I am to give it to the captain of the Athena. No one else," Spiros said. "It goes to a buyer in Cairo."

The stranger moved closer to him. "I will take it."

Spiros did not like this. It felt wrong. He tried to back away, balancing the stela on his shoulder.

The knife glinted once before it was buried in Spiros's shoulder. Spiros fell to his knees; the man who had once been Ibrahim's partner relieved Spiros of his burden.

The wharf was busy that morning. It was a long time, long enough for Spiros to relive much of his life, as wounded men do, before anyone in the crowd paused to wonder why he was half-kneeling, half-lying in the dirt, and to do something about the knife still plunged into his shoulder. By then the stranger had made his way through the dense crowd and disappeared, with the stela balanced on his shoulder.

11

D
r. Morello made his way through the narrow, crowded souk of Cairo. Most foreigners stumbled and pushed at the market, gawking at snake handlers and one-armed beggars, sneezing at the dust and calculating the cost of gold charms and rugs in European currency. Morello stared straight ahead. He moved with the sure-footed grace of the Egyptian, despite his arched Roman nose and his Parisian-cut suit. He had spent much time in the Orient. And elsewhere.

He kicked scavenging dogs out of his path and nodded without smiling at the vegetable seller, the brassworker, the rug weaver. He did not stop to buy or complain or discuss the rising of the Nile. He went into the tent of Bahlul, the antiquities seller.

Coffee, just-boiled, was poured into little brass cups; the heavy cloth of the entrance way was pulled closed, shutting out the noise, dust, and light of the day. A servant stood by, deep in a shadowed corner, ready to fetch more coffee, objects as they were mentioned and a weapon, should his master be threatened by an irate customer, as sometimes happened.

The European sipped his coffee in heavy silence. Bahlul, too, kept silent. This European did not appreciate the abandoned flapping of tongues that often accompanied the bargaining. Souvenir buyers wanted drama, a story to tell their friends back home about how they (so they thought) got the better of him, Bahlul. But this man was not a souvenir buyer. He was a collector, with purpose and passion and discrimination. And like other impassioned collectors Bahlul had met, he was without morality. The rich wife who, greedy for jewels, betrayed her husband to acquire yet more, the fanatic Dervish who collected ancient instruments of torture for the bizarre rituals of *melboos* . . . this *farengi* was part of that brotherhood, though in what way Bahlul could not yet say. He was about to learn. He sighed and grimaced. Let it be said that he preferred the foolish souvenir hunters to these collectors possessed by *afreets*.

When coffee was finished, Bahlul clapped his hands and his assistant brought the box that had been set aside.

The European opened it. He picked up its contents, a flaking, ancient piece of papyrus, and turned the scroll in his hands, examining it from all angles for a very long time. He called for a lamp, which was brought. Bahlul could stand the quiet suspense no longer.

"Very, very old. Very, very rare," said the shopkeeper. "From the tomb of a king." He smiled broadly, pleased.

"Everything here is from the tomb of a king, I'm sure," said the European in a tone that cut like a knife.

The shopkeeper's smile shrank from the sarcasm. "Effendi. We are old friends. Yet you do not trust me," he complained, throwing up his hands.

"What king? And what does the inscription say?" The European handed back the scroll. He pushed his chair back from the table and stretched his long legs.

"Who knows? Nobody. The meaning of this scrawl is as dead and buried as the hand that made it. Certainly I do not know its meaning. I am but a poor shopkeeper trying to keep food on his family's table. More coffee, Effendi?"

"Do not waste my time. Where is the stela?"

The shopkeeper covered his eyes and black beard with his two hands and moaned.

"There are complications, Effendi. It has not arrived."

"Complications?" Morello stood and paced back and forth on the exquisite rug under his feet, then stood over the merchant, glaring, Bahlul could feel his hot breath. "I have already paid for it. If you are toying with me to get a higher price, it will not work."

"I tell you, Effendi, I have no wish on earth but to please you. But . . . it is out of my hands. I do not know where it is." Bahlul pulled at his beard and frowned. "My agent was to have to put it on a vessel that arrived this morning. The vessel is here. Not the stela. I am miserable with sorrow."

The European glared and thought. "Others have bid for it?" he finally asked.

"An Englishman. A Frenchman. A Turk," Bahlul muttered.

Elgin. Bonaparte. Selim.

Morello smiled. This stela was a rare object, indeed. Once Catherine realized Selim also sought the stela, she would pay four times what she had already offered. He would never have to collect for others again. And the woman would be his.

In Athens, just about the time Bahlul was pouring the second cup of coffee for his impatient client, Spiros, with the help of a friend, tripped over his doorstep and fell onto the cool stone floor, at his wife's feet. His bound shoulder had stopped bleeding, but the cloth covering it was rusty with old stains, revealing at a glance that things had not gone as Spiros had planned.

"Well? Where have you been?" Her foot tapped. Her voice was not sweet.

Spiros and his friend looked up at her. They were sober, now, but neither wanted to admit to having spent the past three days in a tavern.

"He's been wounded," the other man pointed out.

"I can see that, you fool." She knelt and prodded the wound to see if it had been cauterized properly or if she needed to heat the poker. Spiros winced. "Did you at least get some money for all your trouble?" she asked in a softer voice, already knowing the answer. "Didn't I tell you so? Come to bed, husband."

The small flame flickered and disappeared, leaving Marguerite and Michel, who sat on opposite sides of a packing crate holding fans of playing cards, in gloomy darkness.

"I'll light another one," Michel offered, reaching into his coat pocket where he stored, safe from mice, the candles he had expensively purchased from the guard.

"No. Don't." Marguerite threw her cards down on the table. "I am tired of forfeit, Michel. Besides, you cheat." She stood and stretched.

"No more so than you, my dear. How shall we while away the time?"

"Tell me about Josette."

"Ah. That."

"Yes, that. Was she amusing?" In the dark, Michel could hear the rustle of Marguerite's clothing, the small click her right knee made when she stretched up on tiptoe to extend her cramped legs. He smiled at the familiar sound and considered asking Marguerite to come sit next to him, to show him some kindness and mercy.

"For a while, since you insist upon knowing," he said instead. "Did you know she has taken to writing novels? When I left Switzerland she was working on the fourth volume of a lugubrious work called 'The Temptations of Yvonne.' "

"She would know about temptation. How weak you are, Michel, to have been bewitched by such a creature."

"At this point, Marguerite, you want me to say that she is a monster, so that you may forgive me and hate her, or say that she is irresistibly charming, so that you may forgive her and hate me. I will say neither. You think me contemptible, but allow me some shreds of dignity."

"On the contrary. It is you who have stolen my dignity."

"How? By taking a mistress when it suits me? My dear, I do nothing that the world, whether it admits it or not, does not approve and even encourage. In fact, most wives prefer that their husbands have a mistress or even two. It gives them more time for their own affairs."

"You are contemptible, Michel."

"No, I am not. I have been a good husband and friend to you. But you are not content with that. You would have me be a lap dog, too."

"Enough. Light another candle. Deal the cards. I will not discuss this."

And so husband and wife, reunited, passed the time. Michel judged that he had made some progress in wooing back the recalcitrant Marguerite. She spoke to him now, and the ice had left her voice, to be replaced by hot anger. That was good. It indicated some level of feeling. When they slept, she curled against him for comfort. He found her touch and closeness to be surprisingly moving.

On the sixth day of their imprisonment, a day when neither Michel nor Marguerite felt like speaking or eating, a day when both husband and wife began to wonder what it would feel like to die in Cairo, either of neglect in a dungeon or public execution in the square, Dr. Morello arrived.

His mood matched their own. He was morose and unkempt. Dust filled the creases of his scarlet breeches and ivory waistcoat, and whitened his hair. He did not waste time on smiles and pleasantries.

"The news is not good, I'm afraid," he said, sitting on one of the crates that Marguerite had covered with a cloth and pillow. "Ibrahim is dead."

Marguerite trembled and sighed. Michel rubbed his

face with his hands, pulling it into a grimace that accentuated the slackening chin, the fine lines around the pale eyes.

"And we are still suspected?" Michel asked through the grimace.

"More so than ever, I'm sorry to say." Dr. Morello coughed and would not meet their eyes.

"This has gone too far. How could we?" Marguerite asked, beginning to pace. Twelve steps to the wall. Twelve steps back to where Dr. Morello sat. "I know nothing of poison. Sultans used to poison each other with ground glass and hair, I read that in a book that General Bonaparte passed around on shipboard. Other than that, I cannot tell a poison from simple table salt. How could I have achieved this thing?"

Dr. Morello met her eyes.

"My dear. The physicians believe it was just that, ground glass and hair, that killed Ibrahim."

"I always said that women should not be encouraged to read histories. Let them be amused with novels," Michel muttered. "Marguerite, since when have you become studious?"

"What will happen now?" Marguerite asked in a small voice.

Dr. Morello addressed himself to Michel.

"It is time," he said solemnly, "to explain why you are here in Cairo, Citizen. I have read the written statement of your interrogation, and nowhere is that particular question answered."

Michel took a deep breath. "I am here because Talleyrand asked me to make this particular journey. I was in Switzerland, packing for a voyage to Milan for the opening of the opera season, when a note from Talleyrand arrived at my breakfast table. I was having fresh brioche with English marmalade and a pitcher of chocolate. . . ." Michel's eyes glowed in fond remembrance of the food, not the correspondence. "The note was in reference to an earlier conversation, wherein it had been revealed to me that certain . . . threats . . . had been made against the General. Talleyrand had availed himself of my . . . diplomatic skills . . . on earlier occasions, and thought this particular errand of truth-seeking might suit my abilities."

"He is an agent for the Directory. Before that, an agent for the Girondists," Marguerite clarified. "As for Switzerland, you may believe him. His mistress has a chateau there."

Dr. Morello ignored her last comment. Obviously, that was a source of private contention between husband and wife, nothing that need concern him. As for Michel Verdier being an agent, he had already guessed that much, when he learned that Verdier was connected with Talleyrand. Talleyrand's associates were inevitably of a professional rather than personal nature.

"May I assume that you were sent to investigate? Not to, excuse me, I must ask, facilitate the threats against General Bonaparte?"

"I agree that, given present circumstances, I look disreputable. Bathing from a jug and wearing unpressed shirts does not improve the world's opinion of a man. But I ask you, Dr. Morello, what would be the purpose of such a foolish action? Bonaparte is the darling of France. There is not a man in the country who could win his place or esteem or power. Only a fool would attempt to come between the man and his destiny by an assassination attempt. And such an assassin would never again be welcome in Paris. A place to which I fully intend to return."

Dr. Morello considered this.

"Your argument is a sensible one," he said. "Had you protested innocence I would retort that all murderers make such protestations. As for you, Madame Verdier . . ." for the first time, he looked directly at Marguerite. "I do not think your limited relationship with the general's wife,

Josephine, could compel you to the passion of attempted murder to revenge a husband's wanderings. Nor do I believe women in general capable of the subtle intrigue needed for political assassination."

Marguerite, not certain she was honored by this assessment, said nothing. Michel did not share the doctor's somewhat short-sighted faith in the harmlessness of the gentle sex, but he voiced no correction, realizing that in this instance at least, silence was more to his purpose than refutation.

"Have faith, *mes amis,* I will do what I can for you," Morello promised, rising from his crate. "Meanwhile, we must all give serious thought to the identity of the true poisoner."

"We have had long days thinking of little else," said Michel.

General Bonaparte's last days in Egypt, like his first, were not without incident. No major battles were fought, but there was much to claim his attention. First, there was little Pauline Foures's assertion that she was with child.

Bonaparte was delighted by this news. Neither his wife nor any of his mistresses had announced such glad tidings to the heir-hungry general. While other men had complained and gloated over noisy, bursting nurseries and the expense of wet nurses, he, Bonaparte, had cultivated a hurt, painful silence.

No more. His little blonde Cleopatra was with child. He must divorce Josephine immediately. Legally, that would present no problem. Under the Directory, divorce was scandalously easy to achieve. Morally, there also was no problem. He was totally justified in divorcing a faithless, disloyal wife, as Josephine had proven herself to be.

Yet the thought of divorcing his Creole beauty made him tap his fingers on his mistress's dressing table and crease his brow. He had loved Josephine. So much so that he had considered it impossible to live without her. Youth often enjoys such immoderate passion. And it comes but once, like youth itself. To sever that part of his past was like cutting off one of his limbs.

". . . and what will you name my boy?" Pauline asked, certain he was thinking of *her,* that other one in Paris. She took one of his lank brown curls and twisted it around her finger, pulling his face closer to her own. "I feel certain it will be a boy, my darling. An heir."

But then, in the afternoon, a servant had come, ashen-faced, to the general's private dressing room, holding one hand behind her back. It was a woman hired by Bonaparte to watch over Pauline, secretly, for her protection as well as his. If there were to be more unfaithful women in his life, Bonaparte would be the first to know, not the last.

The servant stood silent and downcast in the doorway. Bonaparte barked a "Yes? What is it?" and she moved closer, bringing out from behind her back something white and lacy. Flounces dangled to the floor in a pretty, dancing manner, frothing and flirtatious against the servant's own darkly striped skirt.

The stain, so fresh it still glistened, spoke all that needed to be said. Bonaparte took the petticoat, shut the door on the woman, and sat down on the packed sea chest, head in his hands.

She had lied. To keep him from leaving her.

He finished packing. When Bonaparte and Pauline met again for their midday meal, she saw her failure in his pitying eyes, his excessive kindness. She wept. She fainted. When revived, she sobbed so heartbreakingly that Dr. Morello was sent for, to give her a calming draught.

Bonaparte, both embarrassed and impressed by her capacity for grief and drama, said it made no difference. He loved her. He had spoken. That was that. She had nought to fear from him, neither neglect nor abandonment. He would still divorce Josephine, the faithless one. He and his

little Cleopatra would be reunited in Paris, when the time
came.

She pretended to believe his declarations.

Pauline was not the only one to forego weeping and
wailing for the departing general. Since, officially, no one
was supposed to know about this departure, no one could
express public chagrin. When Bonaparte called a last-min-
ute meeting of the savants at the Institute, they assembled
as required, with forced smiles and comradely slapping of
shoulders, as though that August day was like any other.

Bonaparte appeared slightly more tense than usual. His
lips stretched into a thin, wolfish grin when he tried to
smile and he spoke too quickly, revealing his preoccupa-
tion. His thoughts were already back in Paris, calculating
and manipulating and creating political order from the
chaos that the Directory had become. It was a new order,
with him at the top, he envisioned.

"Friends and countryman," he began, when the assembly grew quiet and all faces had turned to him. Pausing, he
took a quick and accurate inventory of those present.
Someone was missing. Ah, yes. Madame Verdier. And her
husband. They were still under detention. And would be,
till it was proven they had not contrived to poison him. His
eyes narrowed slightly as he thought of the pretty female
friend now turned would-be assassin. Then his quick
thoughts moved on. Stranger things had happened.
Closer friends had betrayed him. But never twice.

"We heard a most interesting presentation the other
evening, a presentation unfortunately obscured by subsequent events," he continued. He smiled. There was a
quick and superficial frisson of humor in the room.

Berthollet, hearing his lecture spoken of in flattering
terms, beamed. He beamed for another reason, too. His
sea-chest was also packed. Bonaparte had sent surrepti-
tious word that Berthollet was to accompany him back to
France, as was Vivant Denon.

"But this object of which we heard, many for the first time. Does it truly exist? If so, we must add it to the collection of artifacts we carry back to France with us. Let the world know that France discovers that which other nations cannot; France wins that which other nations lose. France, more than any other nation, values the art of the ages."

Vivant Denon steepled his plump fingers in front of his face and closed his eyes. You had to admire the general's directness. And his strategy. How better to effect a secret getaway than by making a great distraction? How better distract savants than by requiring them to find something that may not even exist? Cunning.

Yet, if it did exist . . . The artist's eyes, behind the blue, closed lids, moved quickly up and down, side to side, trying to envision the panel, the carved woman at its center. He had already begun making his own discrete inquiries. The woman . . . Marguerite was still locked in the storeroom . . . Vivant Denon tiptoed out of the room.

Marguerite and Michel, unaware of the great change about to befall the Cairo mission, threw their playing cards on the table in a steady, purposeful rhythm. Michel was stern faced. Marguerite was smiling. She had discovered Michel's system, and was out-cheating him.

"I win again," Marguerite said. "You now owe me four million assignats. As I am generous, I will reduce that debt by half. But no wonder your mistress abandoned you, Michel. You have no luck or skill with cards. You should give up gambling."

She stretched, raising her arms high over her head. Her dressing gown parted slightly, revealing full breasts.

"I, too, am bored." Michel moved closer to her. He put his hand on her knee. "We could amuse ourselves in other ways, my dear wife. Let me comfort you."

"God help me. I am imprisoned with a madman." Marguerite laughed loudly and moved away to a darker corner, a smaller crate, where there was room for only one person to sit. She watched Michel shuffle and reshuffle the cards, and felt both repelled and attracted by him.

"Don't stare at me so. It makes me uncomfortable. Did you push your lieutenant away in that cold manner?"

"I did not."

"Two can play that game, Marguerite. Josette was . . . warm, I assure you."

She was about to retort when Vivant Denon knocked loudly at the door of the storeroom and demanded of the guard outside that he be given admittance.

"And while you're about it, friend, pack your bag and be off. Your services will no longer be needed," he giggled as the door swung open. He had downed two bottles of wine.

"Says who?" the guard demanded.

"Me. Baron Vivant Denon. You need nor will receive other authority. General Bonaparte is gone from Cairo. Let the cells be opened, roll back the rock from the tomb. Amnesty is in the air."

The use of title and religious metaphor so confused the guard, a veteran of the August massacres of 1792 in which he had aided many aristocrats from this world into the next, that he backed off, muttering, and did as instructed. He left the key in the lock and disappeared to find his comrades, to obtain information from a sensible person.

Marguerite, hearing the word amnesty, jumped up and flung her arms around Denon's neck, kissing him.

"This means, of course, that our general has departed the immediate vicinity," Michel guessed.

"He will, soon. On his way to France and greater glory. He's taking me with him." Denon said, tottering about on his little feet and seeking something stable to hold onto. His arm found Marguerite's waist and happily settled there. "I for one see no reason why you should spend more time in these unpleasant accommodations. Since the accuser is gone and no one else really believes you guilty of the crime, I hereby grant you freedom. Of a sort. On condition, that is." Vivant swept a lace handkerchief from a pocket and wiped his cherubic, sweating face. The night was stiflingly hot and still. His clothes, and those of Marguerite, he noticed, stuck in damp, dark patches.

"Of a sort?" Marguerite raised one eyebrow and pushed away the trespassing arm.

"Ahem. Since amnesty has not been given and you do still stand accused, albeit informally . . ."

"You are permitting us to escape. Not giving us freedom," Michel finished.

"Precisely expressed." Denon staggered again, then pulled on his waistcoat to regain a modicum of composure.

"We must leave the Institute," added Marguerite.

"For your own safety, I would assess. Did you know that we have been armed, in case of attack? Can you imagine, Monge is strutting about with a pistol in his belt! I estimate they'll be shooting at each other before dawn. And since you have already been deemed of a violent nature, you would be one of the first targets of our nervous scholars. I, for one, enjoy your company greatly and will miss your talents. Hic. So much unfinished work. Perhaps you might take some with you? But since this is not amnesty it would be in questionable taste, even dangerous, to remain."

Exhausted from the effort of this explanation, Denon wiped the perspiration from his forehead and leaned heavily against the opened door.

"Have you any suggestions for our future accommodations?" Michel was not pleased with this situation. He had assumed that when release came, so would acquittal of the crime of which they were suspected but not formally charged. Now it seemed release meant wandering the countryside, still under suspicion.

"Dr. Morello has a country home at Giza. It is outside

the city gates, so no guards will question you. He has offered you the use of this house for the time being."

Marguerite and Michel looked at each other, thinking
the same thoughts. Without guards, the house would be
safe in some respects, dangerous in others. They were
farengi, foreigners in a hostile country. Should there be
civil unrest and uprisings, as there most definitely would
be, with Bonaparte gone, they would be in great danger,
isolated in that solitary, unguarded house.

On the other hand, how safe would they be if they remained here, locked in a storeroom, scapegoats for an attempted crime against a too-powerful general, deemed
violent, unarmed while nervous, armed savants prowled
the vicinity looking for targets?

"We accept Dr. Morello's opportune invitation,"
Michel answered. "Have no fear, Marguerite, dearest. I
will take care of you. As I always have."

Marguerite stared at him. It was a very long time since
she had trusted Michel. She was not of a mind to start trust-
ing him now. But she could think of no alternative.

Bonaparte ended this meeting quickly and without for-
mality. Farewells were made, final instructions were given
to Kleber, who would now head the Egyptian campaign.

In the evening Bonaparte left his Cairo headquarters
and traveled north, turning his face to France and his back
on Cairo. An air of desolation settled over the French com-
pound. The savants shuffled aimlessly through the large
rooms of the palace, pistols indeed stuck in their belts, as
Denon had predicted. After midnight someone nervously
fired at a stray cat that had knocked over a flower pot on
the terrace, but Marguerite and Michel, covered in black
habaras, left Quassim Bey's palace secretly and without incident.

12

After Ma'tcha' died in her sealed prison, the priests performed the rites of embalmment, sealed her mouth, and placed her linen-wrapped remains placed next to her father's, in the unfinished tomb.

Fatherless, husbandless Ma'tcha' was mourned only by the embalmer, who had ample opportunity to study her cold face as he pulled the brains out through her nostrils with his wire forceps and then poured in the wax and embalming fluid. She was beautiful in death, smooth as marble, free of passion and strife and regret. In homage, the embalmer secretly took for himself the object her dead eyes had been fixed upon when he had discovered her: a stela for a tomb.

The embalmer ran his fingers over the lithe figure of Hathor trying to resist death, wondering what the dead woman, Ma'tcha', had been like in life.

The stela was placed in the embalmer's garden. A white ibis came and rested on it, and the embalmer was pleased. On that same day, every year, an ibis came, then flew off.

Years passed, decades passed, generations passed, and Hathor's carved legs and arms grew smooth with time. The village and the children of the village where a pharaoh named Shepseskaf had been buried, where stories of the restless, unholy dead had been whispered, disappeared.

The great pyramids became ancient and the knowledge that built them died so that the desert people began to say the pyramids were natural rock formations. Entire peoples were born and lived and died. The garden around the stela was taken over by swamp reeds. Water buffalo grazed there.

A thousand years later a small boy, bare-legged and black-eyed, found his pet hawk dead on the stela. His father, who had been praying for years for just such a find, brought the stela to his home and cleaned it of moss. It was, he judged very old, and created when man still had the secret knowledge of life and death and immortality.

He sent the stela to Khaemwase, son of Ramses the Great. Khaemwase, a High Priest of Ptah, was a discontented man who found no pleasure in the rising and setting of the sun, or in women or wine. He was possessed by that which he could not possess: the lost book of the god of Thoth, whose ancient secrets would let him make the sun rise in the west, control the rising of the Nile, the flight of birds, and eternity itself. The stela was not the book of Thoth, but it was from the old time, the magic time, and he was pleased to accept it. He sent a tax collector to the stonecutter, and the seals were taken from his storeroom. Never again did the stonecutter pay taxes.

Khaemwase eventually found the book of Thoth, but only in a dream which faded at dawn. The sun continued to rise in the east and set in the west and birds flew as they wished.

Another thousand years passed, time for the Nile to rise and fall a thousand times, time for stone to turn to dust, time for a hundred kings to be born and die and be buried with all their ambitions.

The Persian, Cambyses, came to conquer Egypt in his turn, and because god was against him, he turned against god, tearing down all the old temples, the monuments, killing priest and farmer alike, till Egypt was filled with wailing and weeping.

One priest who survived the slaughter and razing crawled through the dung heap left by the Persian army outside what had once been a village, near what had once been a summer palace of Khaemwase. The priest paused, bleeding and exhausted, to rest his head on something hard and cool, so he could gather strength to pull the arrow from his thigh. It was the stela. The priest was a god of Ra, the sun god, but he recognized the older gods, Anubis and Hathor. He considered this a good omen and, indeed, his only daughter found him there the next day, resting against the stela, smiling, cold, and not quite dead.

Soon after that, as Herodotus records, "The Persians . . . had reached about halfway . . . when, as they were at their midday meal, a wind arose from the south, strong and deadly, bringing with it vast columns of whirling sand which entirely covered up the troops, and caused them wholly to disappear." Fifty thousand troops disappeared. And eventually, the Persians themselves disappeared from Egypt.

The Nile rose and fell. Men were born and died. Armies triumphed and were defeated. The desert sands shifted so much they stayed the same.

Then came Alexander, called the Great, who brought a new army, and new gods to the land of the Nile, and Egypt became for a while part of an empire that all empire-builders, including a Corsican general named Bonaparte, would dream about the way less ambitious mortals dream of salvation or love or their mother's breast.

Alexander found the stela, or perhaps it found him, and he brought it to his new palace on Lochias point in the new city on the Mediterranean, a city that would bear his name for two thousand years or much longer: that part of the story isn't finished yet. He left the stela with his general Ptolemy Lagus, and long after Alexander died and was buried and was returned to dust, the Ptolemies ruled Egypt.

The last Ptolemy was a woman called Cleopatra, who had a daughter named Selene. . . .

Mauretania
3 A.D.

Selene had her mother's green eyes, olive skin, and arching nose, the features of the Greek Ptolemies. She had also inherited her mother's unfortunate taste in men. Or was it something in their face or destiny, that made husbands run from them?

She brooded over this question. Heat shimmered in the late afternoon air and bright sun glinted like knives in the reflecting pool. With a minimum of movement, she reached into a basket by her side and tossed a piece of roasted meat to a crocodile hunkering by her chair. The creature's long snout slowly revolved up into the air and caught the meat with a fierce and precise snapping of jaws. The creature was already three feet long. Soon, she would have to send the beast to a temple, to be cared for by priests. Meanwhile, she enjoyed keeping it at her side, well leashed and well-fed like a lap dog. It kept the courtiers at bay and shortened the long line of petitioners that appeared each day at the palace to complain of this and that. And it reminded her of Juba's love.

Juba had given her the beast for her last name day as well as an elephant, several camels and an entire flock of ibis, all from Egypt, the country she could never see again, the home to which she could never return. The crocodile most pleased her because while the other beasts could be found in other places, only Egypt had the crocodile.

Looking at the crocodile, she remembered the snake pit outside her mother's house in Alexandria. As a small child she had leaned on the precariously soft lip of that pit and gazed into its hissing blackness. A slave had always accompanied her whenever she stepped out of doors, for protection from Romans and Egyptians alike, as well as to make certain she didn't play with the city children, who had lice and cursed like sailors. The slave had always stood behind her as she leaned over the pit and because the slaves quite openly hated their masters, that had provided another thrill of terror: to lean precariously over a black hole filled with sinuous death as someone who hated you stood at your back. That was how the child, Selene, had learned of courage.

And now, half a century later, a deeper, darker, even more dangerous snake pit stood before her and the rest of her days. She must kneel. Look into it. Listen to the hissing, feel the hatred behind her, and then rise, smiling.

Juba, her husband, was leaving her.

Temporarily, he said. Unwillingly, he said. Just till the research for his latest book was finished, he said.

They had never been separated before, not since the day of their wedding vows, made twenty-four years before. She did not like this separation. It reminded her of too many things she wished not to remember. The snake pit. Her father leaving her mother. Temporarily, he had said. Hah! He had left them, returned to Rome, and married a Roman woman.

Selene caught up the little bronze mirror resting on the table and glowered into it. Had her mother's eyes faded in this manner? She didn't remember them fading, but maybe children don't remember such things, and she had been a small child when her mother's eyes had last looked upon her.

Did Archelaus, King of Cappadocia, who would soon be host to her husband, have a daughter? Was she young and appealing?

With one sweep of her arm, Selene swept the remainder

of the roasted duck, stewed vegetables, and wine off the table. The priceless glass plates and wine glass shattered into a hundred prisms, a hundred hard, sparkling tears.

Juba, shut into his writing room, heard the noise and paused, stylus in hand. Better not to go and ask what it was. He wanted no more blame and recriminations this evening. He loved Selene. He had been a kind and faithful husband. What more did the woman want of him? To stay. That was her desire.

He must go. He would go. Not even Selene would stand in his way.

"Not even Selene." That was harsh. He had married for love as well as advancement. He could not complain of a wife thrust upon him, a wife unable to please him, as the Roman men so often did. Those evenings at Ovid's . . . the men lounging by twos and threes on the sofas, drinking sweet Cyprus wine, reading their poems . . . complaining of their wives, boasting of their mistresses. Even then, as a youth writing his first love sonnets, he had loved the beautiful, sullen, Egyptian girl, Selene, brought to Rome as a captive, as he himself, son of King Juba of Mauretania, had also been. They had that in common: the Romans had taken everything from them. He had promised to never harm her, not even in his thoughts.

Now, a quarter of a century later, he locked his door against her to get some deserved afternoon peace. He hid from her the anticipation he felt for this journey. She would not understand.

Women, his father had told him long ago, were best dealt with in large numbers or not at all. Stick to one female and she'll dull your senses and turn you into a lapdog. His father had been a traditionalist and kept a harem. But Juba had lived in Rome too long and found the idea of a harem to be distastefully old-fashioned and barbarian. He did not want other women.

He was not making this journey to find a second wife, as

men of his age so often did, searching for lost time in the smooth, moist flesh of a child-woman. No, that was not his purpose and plan.

Juba was going to sail to the end of the world, past the pillars of Hercules, and see what lay there, as his publishers, the Roman Sossi Brothers, boasted. From all he heard, the Sossi Brothers were boasting a bit too much in this effort for notoriety, to increase sales of a book not yet written. Rome was awash with tales of monsters and cannibals, giant sea serpents and flat edges hanging over the ether of nothingness. The book might not prove to be half as fabulous as the rumors already circulating of what Juba would find on this voyage.

In fact, Juba wanted to discover if one could go by ship from the Atlantic to the Indian Ocean. That would be a deed worth boasting of, a father's achievement of which a son would later be proud.

A son. Juba cocked his ear, listening. From a nearby room in the palace he heard a baby's laughter, the sound of a ball falling against the stone floor. His heart expanded with pride and determination. After twenty-four years, Selene had last year given him a boy-child, an heir. Ptolemy. Chubby, brown-eyed Ptolemy, the miracle child, the delight of his mother's and father's coming old age.

Everything had changed the day Ptolemy was born. Juba guarded his west African kingdom, not for himself and the Romans, but for his son. Juba loved the Egyptian woman, Selene, no longer for herself, but for her son. Juba of Mauretania increased his reputation as a scholar and writer, not for posterity but for his son, who would be judged by the father's deeds.

In far-off Rome men of letters would sit together in the evening and discuss the exploits and writings of Juba of Mauretania. Let Ovid write his interminable histories, the very histories he, Juba, had once wished to write. What was the dust of the past, compared to the discoveries of today?

What was poetry, the exploration of old, worn sentiment, compared to the exploration of the world before him?

Sour grapes. As a poet, as a historian, he had been a failure. The travel books had been Selene's idea, a desperate but surprisingly astute suggestion from a wife tired of seeing her poet husband push his dinner away, untasted because the taste of failure tainted everything else. So he turned his hand to travel writing and he was not less surprised than the Sossis when the books turned best-sellers.

But now that they were successful, she wished him to stop his voyaging and stay at home. He would not. For his son's sake.

Juba, newly determined, rose from his desk. He must go see what that noise had been, must comfort Selene. Instead, he paused in the doorway overlooking the garden, enjoying the perfume of roses and bay, his shadow stretching long and black on the marble floor.

Warm breezes moved the curtains. He could hear a musical clinking, distant and coming closer. Selene's headdress. She attached golden discs to her veil so that her every movement was music. It was not a Roman custom. It was one of many things Selene did to remind all that she was daughter of Cleopatra, Queen of Egypt.

He watched her approach. Her movements were graceful, even suggestive, they made him think of the dance she did some nights for him, only for him, in their privacy. Her head was high, held at a queenly angle. But there were tears of frustration in her eyes. He hardened his heart.

"Do not go," she pleaded, opening her arms. "I have had bad dreams. Bad omens."

"I am going. Do not tell me of your dreams."

Husband and wife glared at each other, both angry, both unwilling to swallow the bitter anger.

Juba, as usual, was the first to relent. He took her hand and led her to the couch. She reclined, and he lay next to her, resting his head on her belly. Selene, flat-bellied all her life, now after childbirth had a soft mound between navel and pubic hair. It was here that Juba most liked to pillow his head, listening to the secret underworld fountains and rivers that had produced his son.

"I will come back to you, Selene," he sighed.

13

Letters rested in a silver bowl, on a claw-footed black table in the ochre-papered hall. The bowl was one of the few new appointments in the hall, impetuously purchased during one of Lord Elgin's trips abroad. Its side handles were finished with sphinx heads and these Mary handled quite gingerly, greatly disliking sphinx heads. One letter, addressed to her, had been opened. After an apparently hasty reading, it had been flung back into the bowl on top of the thumbed but unopened correspondence.

Mary looked over her shoulder while reaching into the bowl, then unfolded and read it as quickly as her education, centered on drawing room skills rather than literary chores, allowed.

She frowned. She returned the letter to the bowl, stiffened her shoulders, picked up the bowl, and marched to Elgin's study.

Lady Elgin was not welcome in the study. He had made that clear on numerous occasions with gentle and infuriating suggestions that his tender wife, his gentle Pol, should busy herself with women's chores and leave the tedious details of running one of Scotland's largest estates, whilst also planning a major and protracted journey, to Himself, Lord of the Manor.

Despite all that, perhaps because of it, she flung his study door open, carried in the bowl as if it were a platter with John the Baptist's head on it, and placed the bowl directly on the ledger Elgin studied. He had no choice but to cease his labors and look up into his wife's eyes. His expression was not benign.

"Dearest. You have not yet opened the day's post, except for one piece," Mary said. The courage to accuse him, to state, "You have opened my private correspondence and I will not suffer you to do that," was not yet within her. "You know I have been awaiting receipt from my dressmaker in London, along with other messages that must be attended to promptly. In case you have forgotten, Eggy, we set sail at the end of this month."

"I have not forgotten, Pol." Elgin, who had till this interruption been warming his feet before the fire and finishing a good bottle of port, cleared his throat and rearranged his expression from one of bothered husband to harried landowner. "So much to attend to." His hand fluttered over his paper and folio covered mahogany desk and then slyly slid one large folio under a pile of papers. It was a collection of prints of ancient Athens over which he had been daydreaming.

"I will open the correspondence today, dearest Eggy. Let me be of use to you."

While she had placed the bowl on his ledger, she had not released her white but surprisingly strong hands from its rim. A tug of war, small in gesture but large in significance now ensued between husband and wife, both of whom claimed the bowl of correspondence. Mary, standing, had the advantage of better leverage over the seated Elgin. She won the bowl, and with subdued glee took it to a large, leather chair, where she sat and dumped the mail into her own lap.

Modern husbands, Lady Elgin thought, treat their wives like children. She would have none of that. Having just finished the volume of letters her namesake, Lady Mary Wortley Montagu had written from Constantinople ninety years earlier, she was determined to follow in that resolute lady's footsteps. She would have her say, enjoy her share of responsibility and liberty.

Elgin gnashed his teeth. Why wasn't Pol in the stillroom, making sure that his medicines and tinctures were properly distilled and packed? Modern women, he thought. They have none of the diffidence, the sense of place, of the classical wives. The Romans knew how to treat wives. They beat them quite freely. Not that he wanted to beat Pol, though the thought had some merit.

"Aha. See, here it is," exclaimed Mary triumphantly, holding up the previously opened letter in a manner that suggested she had just now opened it for the first time. "From 'My Lady's Boudoir' of Bond Street. And there is a problem. The lace from Valenciennes has not arrived."

"My love," Elgin said between clenched teeth. "We are at war with France. You should not be purchasing imported lace in the first place. Is not the Irish good enough?" His voice rose in angry crescendo, with "enough" ending on a very high note that the servants, in group discussion on the morrow, would describe as a shriek.

"Eggy, do not shout. You have been cross all day. Tell me why. Is it something to do with the correspondence?" She held the bowl a little higher, as if presenting evidence in a court. "Tell me, so I will understand."

Elgin squinted suspiciously at his wife. How had she guessed that, the cunning vixen?

"I am expecting a piece of correspondence from the Sublime Porte," he conceded. "It has not yet arrived. I was given to understand that it would be here by now." Eggy tugged at his waistcoat and screwed his mouth from side to side so that his side whiskers jumped a bit. "Pry no further."

"It has to do with an artwork," she guessed. "I can't begin to imagine where we are going to put all those dusty old things. . . ."

"Enough!" Eggy pounced to his feet and taking his wife by the elbow, assisted her rather hurriedly out of his study and slammed the door. Mary stood on the wrong side of it, fuming for some minutes, before she quietly retreated to the back of the house, to the stillroom, where the other women of the manor, high and low, were gathered.

Alone again, Lord Elgin sat brooding by the fire, thinking of The Woman Carried Away. He had made several inquiries already, going through antique dealers in Constantinople, agents in Athens, archeologists, and commercial travelers in Alexandria. He had heard nothing.

She had started to haunt his daydreams and nightdreams, this woman. The passion to possess, to claim, grew stronger within him each time he thought of her.

One of Herodotus's students wrote of the stela that it contained ample room to inscribe a name on it. He, Thomas, Lord Elgin, would put his name on the stela.

A log in the hearth broke in two and sent up a crackling shower of sparks. Lord Elgin, lost in thought, had forgotten that he originally wanted the stela for his friend and teacher, Hill, and this once insouciant search for an object that might not even exist had become increasingly important. Indeed, it now seemed a predictor of the results of his entire Oriental expedition, a symbol of the way in which the glorious English nation, represented by Himself, would be feted and honored by the mysterious, and inferior, Orient. He would write to the Sublime Port once again, pointedly mentioning his interest in the piece. Acquiring it for him was a small enough reward to ask of the Ottomans.

In Cairo, home of Druze and Coptic, Muslim and Dervish, where placating gifts were thrown into the rising river and white cocks were sacrificed in front of the Sphinx to honor Hermes and Agathodaemon, who are mere genii now, not mighty gods, a man tore at his beard, and wept and clouded his thoughts with bitter "if onlys." If only he had not let Ibrahim journey to Constantinople! He would not have met Atiyah, and Hamid could not help but think that somehow Atiyah was to blame for this tragedy. Atiyah and the Franks.

Never marry a red-haired woman. She will bring as a marriage portion only trouble and sorrow. He had told his nephew that. Who hath bewitched you, that you should not obey the truth?

Hamid al Shackoui hesitated in the curtained doorway of his nephew's chamber, trying to count the warnings he had given Ibrahim. Ibrahim was not there. Ibrahim was dead. But the angels of death, Monkir and Nekir, were still there in his room. Hamid could feel their wings stirring the air, their breath hot and dry on the back of his neck.

He forced himself to go through the doorway, to enter the room where, the day before, his beloved Ibrahim had given him one last pleading look as the blood bubbled at the corners of his mouth and his spirit wound its painful way out, out, up and out of the pained, dying body.

It must be done. His clothes must be gathered up and given to the poor, his prayer shawl must be sent to his mother. Hamid pushed aside Monkir and Nekir and went into the dark room.

From a distant corner of his house, Hamid could hear the women weeping. They had not had to hire professional mourners for Ibrahim. The women of his house had wept and shrieked as they washed him. They wept and shrieked as he was buried. They wept and shrieked still, listening to the silence that would never again contain Ibrahim's voice, Ibrahim's footsteps. Atiyah wept and shrieked the loudest of all. She tore her hair and smeared ashes on her face and refused food. Ibrahim did not trust her grief. Who hath bewitched you, that you should not obey the truth?

Ibrahim's last words had been for Atiyah. Protect the woman carried away. Hide her, he had pleaded. Atiyah.

At the bottom of Ibrahim's trunk, Hamid found the embroidered shirt that seven-year-old Ibrahim had worn for his circumcision; there was a small dot of blood on it. Ibrahim had not cried when the knife touched him. He had not flinched. The old women still talked of how brave he had been. Hamid folded the shirt and put it aside. It would be sent to his mother.

Under the shirt he found other reminders of the boy and man Ibrahim had been: a slingshot, a little bridle worn by his first pony, a woman's embroidered veil, probably given as a secret love token. At the bottom of the trunk he found a book, spine broken and crumbling with age. *Book of Buried Pearls and of the Precious Mystery, Giving Indications Regarding the Hiding Places of Finds and Treasures* the moldy cover read.

Why? Hamid had wealth enough and in time, all that Hamid owned would have been Ibrahim's: this pleasant house in Cairo with its fountains and gardens, the farms on the Nile, the jewels and necklaces kept stored away because the prophet did not approve the wearing of gold and silver. It would have been enough. But Ibrahim had wanted more. And so he had dabbled in the trade of thieves and cheats selling antiquities. That profession, like Atiyah, had been acquired in Constantinople. Hamid threw the book onto the pile of things that would be given to the poor.

Who hath bewitched you that you should not obey the truth?

Later, when the evening pilaf was brought to him in a steaming bowl, Hamid motioned for the other women to sit at the far end of the *hareem* and for Atiyah to serve him.

Her eyes opened wide. Blue eyes, with black lashes made

blacker by kohl. Eyes like a *farengi,* like a Frank. She was of the same ancient, troublesome race as the Franks. She wore her veil even indoors, when surrounded only by her family, because she knew her husband's uncle disliked her hair. But there was insolence even in that gesture. Red curls escaped the veil and fell over white cheeks. From inside the veil came the sweet music of glass beads swinging against each other. Atiyah had torn at her hair in grief, but had not yet removed all the beads sewn into the braids.

Galatians. Long ago, so long ago that the names were obliterated and only the deed remained, a Phrygian king had imported wild Gauls into the land that later became part of the Ottoman empire to guard his borders. The red-haired barbarians soon became part of the land and could not be gotten rid of. The Phrygians learned this the hard way, because the Galatians were so troublesome that they soon wished with all their hearts to be rid of them. Even the Christian who preached forgiveness and leniency, Paul, had not thought well of them. "Oh foolish Galatians, who hath bewitched you, that ye should not obey the truth?"

Hamid ate slowly and frugally, by habit not yet broken leaving the tenderest pieces of lamb for Ibrahim. He and Atiyah eyed each other in silence as she poured his water and offered him different dishes. He had no appetite, so with his plate still heaped with rice and lamb, he signalled for the meal to be taken away and his pipe brought.

"Atiyah, sit next to me."

"You honor me." Eyes downcast, she gracefully lowered herself onto the cushions, tucking her little slippered feet under the folds of her silk pantaloons.

Hamid cleared his throat and would not look into her eyes.

"When my beloved nephew came home in disgrace, I did not preach to him," he began. "Young men often get in trouble if they are allowed too much freedom. When he lost the wealth his father had left him by betting on bad horses, I did not scorn him or humiliate him, though it was within my rights. When he married a woman from Galatia instead of the bride I had chosen, I prepared the feast and celebrated with him, though my heart was heavy. But now my beloved Ibrahim is dead. I must know why."

Atiyah swallowed the truth, though it was bitter poison, though it would kill her.

"He drank poison meant for another," she answered.

"Did he? Did my Ibrahim die so that this French general might live?"

"Send me home to my father," Atiyah whispered. "I do not want to stay here. You hate me. The other women hate me. Send me home!" She bowed her head to the ground, a supplicant, a grieving wife.

Hamid, watching, grew pale. Thus had his first wife begged, many years before, when she had proven barren. He remembered that Ibrahim had taken this woman and cherished her above all others, that he had promised to protect her from all harm.

"I am stern," he said. "But not without heart. You will stay here. It was Ibrahim's wish. It is my wish." His arms started to rise of their own accord, to go about the slender, girlish shoulders. He forced them back to his sides. He would not touch this woman. "I will be as your father."

Atiyah rose to leave. She hesitated for a moment. She had not really wanted to go back to her father, who beat her. She was glad to stay in this house, even if the women did hate her. Here, she would be protected from the *farengi* who had followed her to this place. After one last look at Hamid, a puzzling glance filled with pity, Atiyah left him and went to sit with the other women.

Hamid sat smoking his pipe for a long while, thinking. The matter of Atiyah was resolved. She would stay among them. Ibrahim's things would be sent away. Hamid would mourn. And then, there was the final matter to attend to. Vengeance.

General Bonaparte was gone. Kleber was now commander of the Army of the Orient. The army was half its original size and running out of both supplies and cash. The plague epidemic had lost some of its virulence but still crept through the bivouacs and quarters like a murdering thief. The Egyptians, even those who had seemed friendly a week before, were hostile.

Kleber was not pleased. For consolation, Bonaparte had sent him a note saying: "If by next May you have received neither help nor news from France and if, in the coming year, despite all precautions, the plague should kill more than 1,500 men . . . you are authorized to make peace with the Ottoman Porte, even if the evacuation of Egypt should be the principal condition." In other words, surrender, and may the disgrace be on you. Not me.

Kleber roused himself from these angry thoughts and rang for an orderly. So many loose ends. Which to attempt to ravel up first? The easiest. The couple in the dungeon.

"Remove Monsieur and Madame Verdier to the Citadel," he told the orderly. "They will be held there till a trial can be arranged."

Minutes later the orderly returned, ashen-faced.

"They are gone," he said.

"Gone? Gone where?"

"I do not know. But the door is open and the storeroom empty of captives."

"Well. We must find them. But do not waste good soldiers on this. They will turn up eventually. French cannot hide for long among the natives. The Egyptians will let us know where they are."

He shuffled papers on his desk, looking for a task that might actually be accomplished.

———————

"Kleber would most definitely wish Bonaparte dead," said Marguerite. She half-reclined on a silken couch and her lips were stained with pomegranate juice. Michel stared at this odalisque who was his wife, in wonder. Since arriving at Morello's house the evening before, she had adopted Oriental clothes, loose trousers, and a long vest and shirt. They well suited her. They were, he saw, a style of female clothing that would best adorn the pregnant female, making of her swollen body a beautiful temple rather than a barricaded, secreted dungeon, as European clothes did. He wished he had once, just once, seen Marguerite thick and heavy-breasted carrying his child. But no use thinking of that, not now. . . . To the matter at hand . . .

"That is not sensible, Marguerite. If Bonaparte had died from the poison, it would cause the same effect as this apparent desertion of Bonaparte. He is gone, and General Kleber is in charge, a situation which seems not to appeal to Kleber. No, Kleber is not the attempted assassin."

"Expressed in that manner, it would seem that the same people who wish Bonaparte dead would also wish him to remain alive. Including, of course, Madame Foure," Marguerite wiped her mouth with the back of her hand. Michel felt an urge to lick away the juice still staining the corner of her mouth, but he kept to his place on the opposite side of the room. "She will undoubtedly wish revenge of some nature, but what is the point of taking a powerful personage as lover, if he dies before his power can better her own condition? We may then eliminate Madame Foure as well."

"And Eugene Beauharnais," Michel said. "He would not wish his stepfather dead before his mother could amend her precarious situation with him."

"Poor Josephine. I wonder if she knows yet *HE* is on his way back to France. What a scene there will be." Marguerite frowned, but there was a suggestion of glee in her eyes.

Josephine had caused her much trouble by taking her paramours to Marguerite's rooms.

As frightening as the dungeon had been, the midnight journey through Cairo, to this village, had been even worse. They had traveled many miles on foot, dressed in cumbersome black robes. At the Nile, they had had to find a ferryman willing to take them across at that late hour and this had been no easy task. The river was brown and angry, and even crossing in daylight was not without hazard. The ferryman had lightened their purse considerably. Cairo, with its four hundred minarets piercing the moonlit sky, the Institute, the bazaars, the mosques, fell behind them. Before them was the vast, empty, flat horizon of the ochre desert, broken here and there with muddy ribbons of the overflowing Nile.

Between the two lay the village of Giza, a small cluster of mud-colored houses arranged on narrow, sandy paths. In the near distance, the Great Pyramid and its smaller sisters loomed, and closer yet was the Sphinx, partially buried in sand, its gaze as passive, as eternal as the desert despite its missing nose, which had been used by Turks as target practice.

They had continued on foot, disheartened and uncertain, until in Giza they found Morello's home, sand-colored, two-story, a blue handprint painted on the door for protection against the evil eye, just like all the other village houses, except this one had a mounting block in front of the door and a tall, thick wall enclosing the back.

A Nubian man-servant, tall, thin, black, in red and black striped robes that flowed to the floor, opened the door to them.

"You will be Monsieur and Madame Verdier," he said in accented but clear French. "Welcome. Dr. Morello has spoken to me of your arrival."

Michel, speechless with relief, took his wife's hand and lead her through the carved doorway, putting behind them the dungeon, the city, the river, and the night. Safety.

This morning, Marguerite was already in much better spirits. She had regained some of her bravado.

"I shall never get the sand out of my hair," she complained, brushing through it with her fingers.

"You have beautiful hair," Michel said. "Remember when I used to send away your maid and brush it for you? You said I was more gentle than she."

"You must be thinking of one of your mistresses. I am certain I never said that," Marguerite said.

"You did. And when I am with you, I never think of others. You fill my vision. You are all I desire."

"Just until temptation crosses your path once again." But this time she laughed. He had gone on his knees to her and put his hand over his heart.

Husband and wife smiled at each other, each remembering what they had first loved about the other: Marguerite's tireless devotion, Michel's equally elusive charm. Memories of what they also disliked about each other soon followed: Marguerite's tiresome devotion, Michel's slippery charm.

Michel, uncomfortable in the too-suddenly adopted kneeling posture and obviously rejected despite his wife's smile, rose and made a tour of the room in a businesslike manner. Aside from the expected divans and cushions and brass tables, it contained anomalies which identified it as a European residence, including a liquor cabinet, stoutly locked. He would have to check to see if the servant had the key and could be persuaded to relinquish it. There was a large bookcase, filled, it appeared at a quick examination, with histories and travel books of the Orient. A writing table, shut but not locked. Obviously, the doctor had no secrets.

"It was good of Dr. Morello to let us have the use of his

house. Why did he, do you think?" Michel wondered aloud.

"Perhaps as a kindness to Citizen Denon who, as you may have noticed, is fond of me. He and Denon are fast friends. They both have an interest in rarities and spent many evenings this past year discussing oddities."

"Oddities?"

"Denon's collection of bones and relics. The Etruscan vase collection he sold to Citizen Capet. The reproductions he made of various Vatican treasures. Things of that nature."

"Dr. Morello is a collector?"

"It would appear from his conversation, but not from his home. Aside from books and carpets it is singularly bare." Marguerite stretched on the divan then sleepily rested her chin on her arm.

Michel, admiring the curve of that arm and knowing he would not yet be permitted to caress it, looked away.

"We shall have to be inventive and find ways to amuse ourselves," he said.

"Now is the time to catch up on your reading," she suggested, eyes closed.

He reached for a book from the case. His random selection was a well-thumbed copy of the ancient *Book of Buried Pearls and of the Precious Mystery, Giving Indications Regarding the Hiding Places of Finds and Treasures.*

Marguerite, comfortable and relaxed for the first time in a long while, slept all afternoon, her head resting in Michel's lap as he leafed through the *Book of Buried Pearls.* With Marguerite asleep and Michel concentrating on the printed word, there was peace between them. When the setting sun slipped through a shuttered window and cast a shaft of yellow light onto Marguerite's face, Michel put down the book and, with a pang, realized how much he had missed his wife's trust and affection.

14

S elene sat alone, watching the gold sun descend into
its white-capped, turquoise bed. Behind her, she
could hear slaves giggling and whispering. In front
of her, stretching beyond her new, red-roofed city of Caes-
area with its green gardens and grey streets, was the ocean.
And somewhere on that ocean, already several days away,
was Juba.

Juba the Wise, Juba the Good, had become Juba the Ambitious, Juba the Wanderer. Cleopatra had bitterly warned
her once, long ago, this can happen to men in their middle years. They look back over their shoulders, or into the
depths of a disquieting dream, and something they see or
fail to see shames them, spurs them into the future by way
of a different course, a different and more dangerous
pace.

Juba, lately, reminded Selene of the horse riders who
put thorns under their saddles, hoping the pain would
spur the horse to victory before trampling the rider. Juba
had acquired the despair of the middle years, the chagrin
of the racer who always comes in second.

Selene dipped her hand into the sun-warmed pool. Its
waters were so calm she could see the little silver fish dart-
ing past her fingers. She thought of the Nile during the
Inundation, the frothing, brown, ambitious waters that

were as much to be feared as admired. The Nile, unlike this tame pond, could be greedy, taking more than its share, or it could be sullen and withholding.

Maybe Juba's problem was one of greed. He always wanted more. All he owned was never enough. When Juba had been a child and a prisoner of Caesar, it had been enough for him to live, to not be imprisoned, to not be in pain. Surviving childhood, his plea to the gods had been: Don't let them treat me like a slave. Though, of course, as a captured son of a conquered king, he was just that. And, he was brown skinned, a true African, with mauve fingertips and crisp black hair that did not let him blend safely into the Roman multitude, as other sons of other conquered kings sometimes could. "There goes Juba!" people pointed and shouted, even those who had never met him but knew his description.

After having gained Caesar's favor, Juba, the young man of Rome who wore the ring of the freeman, had wanted only Selene and poetry. They had been the same thing to him. She was his moon, his Nile, his sapphire-eyed queen.

Looking back on it, perhaps the poetry wasn't that stirring after all. Certainly, no one else had enjoyed it as much as she had. He could claim a coveted place at Ovid's exclusive banquets any evening he chose, as he had earned a reputation for scholarliness and learned conversation. But the Romans would not buy his poetry, so the Sossi Brothers would not publish it.

Juba went on to other goals, other pursuits. A kingdom to rule, courtesy of Augustus, who had decided to nominally return ungovernable, unprofitable Numidia to the son of its dead king. Histories to write which, like his poetry, had not sold. A child, finally, after years and years. The gods had certainly dragged their feet on that one.

And now, alive, free, king (in name at least) of his father's kingdom, husband of his beloved, father of his heir, the man still was not satisfied. His kingdom was not enough. His wealth was not enough. His palace filled with art and arcane collections, of green statuary and muddy herbal concoctions, shelves of scrolls and drawers of builders' plans, Phoenician vases, Egyptian funeral masks, toy wooden farms complete with flocks of sheep and miniscule shepherds playing minute pipes, once collected for little Ptolemy to play with, now stored away with the other rarities . . . was not enough.

Ask too much and the capricious gods are liable to take back what they have already granted. Why must Juba now pursue literary success? Why make this long, expensive, dangerous journey, leaving his queen behind?

Selene sighed and withdrew her hand from the marble-sided pool. Her fingertips felt slimy. The basin needed to be cleaned again. Those worthless slaves. They did nothing right or when they were supposed to. Had Cleopatra been plagued with lazy, stealing slaves? She couldn't remember.

Disgusted, she turned her back on the weedy pool and unkempt garden and went back into the palace. The crocodile, sleepy from its dinner of three fowl, lumbered beside her, pulled along by its golden chain. Soon it would be too large for her to keep as a companion. They would have to build a bigger pool. Juba had promised that the architect would make the pool an exact copy of the one where the sacred crocodiles of Arsinoe were kept in Egypt. But how would she know if it was accurate or not? She, daughter of the queen of Egypt, had not set foot in her own country in almost four decades. Her memories of it were blurred and incomplete. Sometimes she found herself trying to recollect something, her mother's carved chest in the dressing room, the menagerie where the baby lions were kept, and find the memory was gone, stolen by time as surely as the palace slaves now stole her Roman lamps and pots of unguents.

The last rays of the vanished sun disappeared from the

sky and quickly falling night folded her into its cold, unwelcome embrace. Now would come bats and clouds of
mosquitoes and all the abominations of the dark. She rose
and turned her back on the sea, which had turned from
bright turquoise to the color of ink in the pot on Juba's
writing table.

This was the time of day when Selene was overcome by a
vast emptiness. A lethargy would fall over her, robbing her
of strength and filling her mouth with the taste of dust.
She remembered the golden color of her mother's bare
arms, and how dark the asp had looked against those arms.
She remembered the child, Selene, who watched her
mother leave her, not as a captive of Caesar but as a willing
guest of death, who more gently carried her away than the
Romans would.

Tonight, left alone again, Selene recognized that what
she thought was emptiness was actually a great yearning.
Don't leave me. She had swallowed those words as she
watched her mother die because bravery was expected of a
queen's daughter. Lean over the snake pit with a slave at
your back.

She had swallowed those words when Juba had made his
formal farewell to the court because pleading and tears
would have been a sign of weakness.

But every bone, every drop of blood in her, sang those
words over and over. Don't leave me.

With the crocodile lumbering at her side, she walked
listlessly through a long dark arcade. The lamps had not
been lighted, although she had ordered they be lighted
immediately at sunset. In the darkness, untamed vines
reached for her through the latticing.

Juba had left her.

Alone, she presided over the nightly rituals of the court:
the feast, the petitions, the gossip. She pretended to eat,
pretended to listen, pretended not to see that people were
talking behind their hands as they watched her. The peo-

ple of Caesaria were friendlier than those of Numidia, their first home after leaving Rome, but even the Caesarians made her feel unwelcome. To them, she was a Roman, one of the conquerors. And to the Romans, she was Egyptian, one of the conquered.

Mauretania and its newly built city (which in later years would be called Algiers) had been Augustus's wedding present to them. The new city's name was meant to show gratitude to Augustus, but she sometimes found it difficult to feel and demonstrate the expected gratitude. Why had Augustus given her Mauretania? Why not Egypt? Why not return Egypt to Selene, daughter of Cleopatra?

Because Cleopatra had been beloved by the Egyptians, and far too clever for Rome's comfort. What if her daughter proved similar? Rome needed Egypt, its grains, its taxes, its trade routes. Rome decreed there would be no more troublesome Ptolomies on the throne of Egypt.

Later, alone in the big bed she shared with Juba, Selene clung to one side of it, fearful of touching the middle and knowing with her fingers, her legs, her belly, that Juba was gone. Selene the child had done the same thing: clung to the side, leaving plenty of room for the mother who was not there.

The ink-colored ocean roared in the distance and she closed her eyes, praying for Juba's safety, for Juba's loyalty. Long after all the lights of the palace and city had been doused she tossed in bed, yearning for Juba and for something else she dared not say aloud.

She wanted to go home. To where she had started. Not Octavia's house on the Palatine in Rome or the scorpion-infested palace of Cirta or even this beautiful white palace in Caesara. To Egypt. Alexandria. The home she had last seen on the day her mother, Cleopatra, sent her to the snake pit to fetch an asp so that she, Cleopatra, would not have to march in chains through Rome. As the daughter had, in the mother's place.

This trip was forbidden. Augustus would hardly approve of her, Selene, marching through Egypt proclaiming: "I am Cleopatra's daughter. I am your lost queen!" There would be riots. Perhaps battles. For a second, Selene let herself think about war with Rome, about taking back the throne that her mother had lost. But the thought, she knew, was not worth pursuing. Rome was a giant, a god, an octopus, its tentacles reaching and ruling everywhere. No one could win a war against Rome.

She could not go to Egypt as Cleopatra's daughter. But she could go as Selene, a Roman wife, a citizen.

Water rustled and splashed and she heard the crocodile, the gift from her beloved husband, lumber into its shallow pool. In the darkness she imagined it loglike, grinning, blinking back the ancient, beginning-of-the-world secrets that tried to tumble out of its eyes.

She would return to Egypt.

And she would bring out of Egypt a gift for Juba, a proof of love so complete he would never leave her again. She would bring him The Woman Carried Away.

15

Atiyah did not blame the women of Hamid's house for their hostility towards her. And though the Prophet valued hospitality, she did not blame them for their lack of kindness. She was a stranger among them, a foreign woman from the land of the conquerors, and she had known other ways than the ways of this house.

She did not blame them. But sometimes she wished that they would be struck mute, or that their tongues would cleave to the roofs of their mouths.

"A gift from a lover! And Ibrahim dead only seven days! Ayeeee! The woman is heartless!" Hamid's eldest daughter shrieked when the basket of figs arrived.

"It is not from a lover. It is from a friend of my father's," Atiyah lied, grabbing the basket from the woman's arms. She took the basket and went into Hamid's garden, into the shaded corner reserved for the women. She sat on the bench she had claimed for herself and stared for a long time at the basket of figs. Then, she shoved her hand among the fruits, stirring them, half expecting to feel the quick, sharp dart of an asp secreted among the figs. Instead, she found the note, with a place and time, but no words of comfort. He, of course, would not mind that Ibrahim was dead. He would rejoice.

She sat there for the rest of the morning, barely moving,

trying to decide the exact moment when this course had been set, when it had been written, that Ibrahim must die and she must mourn him. For mourn him she did, with all her heart and being, though these stupid women of Hamid's house did not have eyes to see her grief.

When was it written? When Ibrahim had first brought her home and lied to his uncle, said that he had brought his foreign bride out of her father's harem and had lifted her veil only on their wedding day?

A *hareem*, her, Atiyah? A virginal veil? A protective father? Hah! Her father had sold her when she was ten and refused to marry the cotton weaver's son. Luckily, she had been sold to a keeper of *almas*, not a slaver, and so she had been taught to sing and dance and recite love poetry to rich men who sighed over her but did not abuse her. Luckily, she was beautiful, despite her *farengi* eyes.

Istanbul, far from her father's village, had delighted her with its nerve-jarring commotion, thick city smells, tall, sun-blocking houses, and rude, loud-voiced merchants. No one there knew that her father was a cotton-picker with seven half-naked daughters, that her mother could not write her own name, that she herself had run away from both father and bridegroom. Strangers looked at her and saw merely another stranger.

Mother Halima, who kept the *almas*, gave her new clothes every year, a dancing instructor, a Frenchman to teach her the *farengi* language so that she could sing to them in their own strange tongue, a maid to dress her, the services of a stable boy to clean and fetch her donkey when she wished to shop at the souks. In exchange, Atiyah had only to sing prettily, dance gracefully, never give offense, and never, never allow a customer to be alone with her. Even an *alma* must stay within the law.

Then one day two men parted the beaded curtain of Mother Halima's music room. They arrived separately and sat at opposite ends of the room, strangers to each other.

One was young, Arabic, with black eyes and a black beard and striped breeches tucked into highly polished riding boots. He smelled of horses and sand and attar of roses. The other was a Frank with brown hair, brown eyes, and colorless clothes which gave off the smell of books and the acrid sting of a surgeon's room.

Atiyah sang and danced and poured cool sherbets for them while the sweeper's daughter fetched plates of sweetmeats. By the end of an hour her life at Mother Halima's, which had been getting a little boring, was changed. Because she was sly as well as beautiful, and no believer in a *kismet* stronger than her own will, she found ways to be with both men. Her afternoons with the Arab passed slowly and sweetly, in a smoke-filled haze of love poems and gentle caresses. The Frank was different: always in a hurry, impatient, seething with barely disguised, ancient angers that added a touch of cruelty to his lovemaking. The two men were like night and day, and Atiyah delighted in both.

One of Mother Halima's other girls soon guessed what was going on.

"I do not blame you for your Arab lover. He is beautiful and from a good family. But this Frank is no good," she whispered to Atiyah in the baths.

"You know nothing," Atiyah hissed back.

"Don't I? You think you are his first woman? You think the day he came for you was the first day he came to Mother Halima's?" The girl's eyes grew larger. "I tell you, he is an *afreet*. He wanted to brand me, like a donkey. I will say no more. You have ears, you have heard. If he asks you to stay with him, to be just for him, he will mark you, the way the cowherds mark their cows and then, when you are too old to be an *alma,* Mother Halima will not even find a sweeper willing to take you as wife."

Atiyah was headstrong and reckless, but not witless. After that, she started to notice things about her Frank— she continued to call him that, she never used his name,

Morello. His rooms, where she visited, were filled with statues, paintings, jeweled boxes, and painted screens. The rosewood cabinet of jeweled snuff boxes delighted her; some of them had belonged to the dead French queen, Marie Antoinette and were, he told her, in great demand among English and Austrian collectors, though the French disdained them. He let her keep one, a gaudy little bauble of gold enameled with green and pink roses, with a tiny ruby at the center of each rose.

But other curiosities in his room confused her. Who would want Greek death masks which still had the mold of the grave on them? Who would buy the box of reliquaries, the white bones, hanks of hair and squares of frayed cloth, taken from desert anchorites? "The less one believes in God the more one wants to touch, be close to those who believed completely, and this is a Godless age. Do you believe, Atiyah? Maybe someday there will be a curiosity case filled with your white bones."

Some objects would be there one week and not the next. Others, the ones in the cases at his bedside, could not be touched. He caned her hand one day when she reached for a clever little bronze rider seated on a carved ivory horse. "It was my mother's. You are never, never, to foul it with your touch." That was the day her passion for him began to wither and die.

He knew the names of the unsavory people in the city, the ones never allowed inside Mother Halima's: mountain bandits and grave robbers and smugglers, dangerous men who lived outside the law or barely balanced on its knife-sharp edge.

He never smiled, though sometimes he would laugh. Once the heat of passion no longer dulled her brain, she saw he was a man to be feared.

One day he shouted that he was angry with her because she still sang and danced for Mother Halima's other customers. He wanted to shut her away, make her be only for him. She laughed and pretended it was a jest; she pouted and said that was impossible, she had a contract with Mother Halima. But the Frank only grew angrier and more insistent.

The next day, her Arabic lover, Ibrahim, offered marriage. Atiyah sat still and listened to the boy's love poetry but saw in her mind the *hareem* he would shut her in, the stern religious family she would have to serve, and would not answer him. For the first time in years she thought of her father and the village and the weaver's son, and wondered how they were.

When next she saw the Frank, he threatened her, saying that she must stay with him, be only for him. He would buy the contract back from Mother Halima. She must be his alone, he would have it no other way. His hands left indigo bruises on her throat.

Atiyah, the girl who would be free at any cost, including her family's honor, saw that her days of freedom were over.

She took her savings—silver and gold coins hidden under her mattress—left half for Mother Halima, as partial payment for the broken contract, and sewed the other half into her belt. She and Ibrahim fled Istanbul. If I must give myself to a man, she had reasoned, I will give myself to the gentle poet. I would never sleep peacefully by the other's side.

But now, her gentle Ibrahim was dead. And she had a message from the Frank.

Atiyah rose from her reverie and went to the courtyard, where she knew Hamid would be. She would need his permission to go to the souk, but she knew she would win that easily, even though he disliked her. Hamid was not a suspicious man.

Hamid frowned and pulled at his beard as he listened to his nephew's widow. Atiyah asked permission to go out, alone, to the baths. And he must allow her this. He,

Atiyah's protector now, could keep her from her own mother and father if necessary, but not from self-purification. No man could prevent a woman of his household from going to the baths without ruining his own reputation as a man of honor.

She was clever, coming up with the one excuse for appearing in public that could not be denied her. Hamid had heard complaints of Atiyah's basket of figs. He wondered what the secret message had said.

"You must take a woman servant with you," Hamid decreed.

"I do not need a servant, uncle."

"A woman of good family does not go out without a servant," he informed her. "I do not know your family and what it was, but now you are a woman of a good family. You must remember this."

Atiyah raised her huge, pale eyes to him. "My family was poor and uneducated. We did not have servants. I think you have already guessed this much. Should I tell you more?" Her voice was hard.

"No. Tell me no more, Atiyah. You were Ibrahim's choice. I need know no more. It was his last wish that I should protect you. So, go to the baths, but take Isme with you."

Atiyah could not suppress a smile of satisfaction. Isme was the oldest servant in the house, bowed, near-sighted and half deaf. She would make a more than satisfactory chaperone.

"I will take Isme," she agreed too readily.

Hamid nodded. And Salik will follow and keep his eye on both you and Isme, Hamid did not say. Hide the woman carried away, Ibrahim had told him. He could not hide Atiyah away against her will, but he would protect her, whether she wished it or not.

The day was hot. Summer's dying breath heated the backs of their necks, the soles of their feet. Akhit, the season of Inundation, was coming to a peak, and the waters in the riverbed, canals, and basins reached dangerously close to the top of the Nilometers. Cairo was a city of ponds and pools, canals and lakes.

If the water did not stop rising soon, there would be disaster. Villages would be flooded, beanfields and olive groves would be washed away. Peasants whose fields in the fertile Fayum outside Cairo were now underwater daily offered images of Hapi, the androgynous Nile God, to the rising waters and their children woke at night, screaming from nightmares of snakes and crocodiles and other evils. The muezzin's voice calling the faithful to prayers seemed especially plaintive.

Atiyah rode a donkey and kept a snail's pace, for the sake of old Isme, who walked at her side, and more times than they could count they had to detour and walk a long way round a pond or canal so close to overflowing that the street was unsafe.

Atiyah did not mind. She was not in a hurry to complete this errand. She could have ignored the Frank's summons, but she guessed that blackmail would not be beneath him. The truth had almost been spoken this morning, when she was with Hamid. But he was not ready yet to hear it. Nor she to speak it. But with Ibrahim dead, unspoken truth weighed heavily on her shoulders; she would gladly be rid of the burden, even if it further reduced her in Hamid's eyes.

The noise and confusion of the markets bubbled around her, the tides of people parted like the Red Sea before Atiyah on her pretty white donkey. She no longer hated the all-concealing black veil that covered her from head to toe, though she had cried for days when Ibrahim first told her she would have to wear one in public, to please his uncle. Now, she felt the freedom of the privacy that moved as she moved, that kept her secret from men's eyes. As an *alma* she had walked outside the way European women do, with their faces uncovered and the shape of their bodies revealed by their clothing, so that all men might see and assess. And they did. The weight of their constant judgment had been heavier than the veil.

The entrance to the baths was not crowded. He was there, waiting, his shadow lean and longer than the shadows of the other men, the head flattened by his brimmed hat, rather than elevated and elongated, as turbaned heads were.

A servant of the baths, a woman with four chins and arms as large around as roasted lambs, stormed out of the bath doors brandishing a horsetail switch. She chased away a cluster of men lingering purposefully too close to her establishment. But this man she left alone. He was European and he did not laugh like the others did when she flapped her switch in his face.

"Isme, I have forgotten my oils. Go back home and fetch them," Atiyah whispered.

Isme glared. "They have oils in the bath. Use those."

"I want my own. Do as I tell you or I will have you whipped."

"Hamid told me I am not to leave you."

"See. I am inside the bath. Nothing can happen to me." Atiyah stepped over the threshold. "Go now and bring me my oil. No. Instead, go back to the market and buy new ones. Here is money." She half-emptied a purse of coins into Isme's hand. It was much more than was needed to simply buy oil. Isme made a sound halfway between a chuckle and a snort and left.

The bath doorkeeper, who had been watching this, made a little bow to Atiyah. Atiyah poured coins into the doorkeeper's hand and stepped back over the threshold, into the dusty street.

He took her hand and pulled her into the shadows of a nearby silk merchant's tent. The merchant and Atiyah watched as the Frank took dropped three Louis d'ors into the brass vase that served as cash box. When the vase stopped ringing from the weight of the coins, the merchant bowed slightly and left, dropping the heavy flap door behind. Atiyah and the Frank were alone.

This had happened before, but not here in Cairo. In Istanbul, when he had been her lover. Now, Atiyah pulled her *abaya* close and hid even her hands inside its folds. She could not stand the touch of him.

"It has been a long time," he said, looking down at her. His eyes were cold, snakelike. "You left without a farewell. And I had been so kind to you. So generous."

She stared down at the tips of her slippers. The merchant had piled his floor with carpet upon carpet; she felt as if she were standing on soft, shifting sand.

"Ibrahim is dead," she whispered.

"I know. He drank poison meant for another. Do you think I should grieve, Atiyah? He stole my treasure." He leaned closer. His breath was hot on her face.

"I was not your treasure. I was your dancing girl. Free to come and go."

"Free? Tell that to Mother Halima. When she finds out where you are, she will have you whipped all the way back to Istanbul. You will be her new floor-sweeper, Atiyah. Or you could come away with me."

"Come away with you?" she repeated, stunned, looking up.

"I will forgive you."

His hands lifted the smaller veil covering her face and then searched inside the long, black *abaya*, touching belly, waist, breasts. His hands found hers. He gripped them tightly and kissed them through the veil.

Atiyah wanted to spit in his face, but there was danger here, inside this man.

"I cannot come away with you," she answered.

"You must. You will. And you will bring me the stela that Ibrahim stole from me."

"What stela? I know nothing of this," she lied.

"Ibrahim stole twice from me. First you, then the stela. I will have both."

You will not, she wanted to say. But she did not have the courage to say it aloud.

Isme was waiting for her when she returned to the baths.

"What is wrong, Atiyah? Where have you been?"

"Nothing. Nowhere. Say nothing to my uncle." But her teeth clicked against each other as if she had been naked in the cold night air, not in the hot, steamy baths. And when the masseur tried to oil and pummel her into a more relaxed state, she complained that the young woman was so stiff she already felt like a corpse.

Isme, Atiyah, and after them, unseen Salik, arrived back home during the evening call to prayer. Salik knew better than to interrupt Hamid. He waited. When Hamid came to him, Salik saw that prayer had not consoled him that evening.

"Where did she go?"

"To the baths, as she said. But . . . but first she met someone."

"A man." It wasn't a guess, but a statement of Hamid's worst fear. Ibrahim, what trouble have you brought to my house? he thought to himself.

"Yes. A foreigner."

"Did it seem she already knew him?"

"Most definitely."

That night, like the other's since Ibrahim's death, did not bring Hamid the comfort of sleep. Instead, he sat up, wide awake, wondering what Ibrahim's mother and father had done to raise a boy so wild, so reckless that his short life would end in this way. What was he to do with Atiyah? She was young, but part of him said that woman like Atiyah are never young, they are born old. He wished he could care for her, give her his affection, as Ibrahim had wished. But she was a stranger to him. He did not understand her, and the more he learned of her, the less he wished to know. Where was wisdom in this matter? It seemed out of reach, out of sight, as unknowable as God.

In the same darkness, but on the other side of the flooded river, Marguerite, suddenly awake, sat up in a black oppressiveness so suffocating she thought something had been thrown over her head. Heat. Night. Strangeness. Yet one more unfamiliar bed beneath her. Homesickness struck like a blow. She missed Rue de Sevres, her rooms, the familiar things of her own world. She thought of the little porcelain shepherdess her mother had given her, years and years ago. She would give a handful of gold to see it and touch its sweet familiarity.

Where was she? The desert. Dr. Morello's house. The words could not slow the fast pounding of her heart. She pressed her hand to her chest and tried to breathe slowly, but the sensation of suffocating grew worse.

She rose from the cotton mattress. Perspiration dripped between her shoulders. Flies buzzed in the still air and bats twittered in the garden outside. She paced slowly, cautiously, one hand before her, the other pressed still to her heart. A list. She needed a list, something to distract the mind.

Beginning with Jacquette, his mother's seamstress, she thought of all the women her husband had made love to. He had never even been faithful to his mistresses. There had been Sylvie, blonde mistress of the publisher, Charles-Roux; Anne-Marie Claire, lady-in-waiting to the ci-devant queen; Julie, lady's maid to the English ambassador; Frau Sophie, wife of the Austrian ambassador; the tall English brunette . . . what was her name? The list grew more egalitarian after 1789, when ambassadors and good society grew in short supply in Paris: there had been bakers' wives and cobblers' daughters.

As a young wife she had pretended to not notice the

long hairs clinging to his jacket, the smell of other
women's perfume in his hair. It was the way men were,
older friends advised. Did he not always came home to
her? He claimed to love her. To be devoted to her. He had
arranged matters so that she had not been socially humiliated by them. He had been . . . gracious.

She heard a movement in the dark and turned towards
it.

"Marguerite?"

"Here, Michel."

"What are you doing?"

"Pacing. And remembering."

"A bad combination. It will give you indigestion, Marguerite. Come back to bed. Why is it so bloody dark?"

"It is a moonless night and the shutters are drawn."

"Then open them. I feel like I'm in a coffin."

The sound of metal sliding, wood creaking. A gust of
fresh air, hot but scented with hibiscus, entered the room
with a sound of angels' wings. The stars gave enough light
that Michel could now see his wife silhouetted against the
open window.

Her shoulders drooped, her head was low. There was
bitterness in her voice when she spoke to him. Michel, in
the dark Egyptian night, saw that this was not about forgiveness, about being welcomed back to the marital embrace. She had surrendered to hopelessness and now was
slipping away from him. The gulf between them was wider
than the flooded river. Soon, if this continued, he would
lose her completely because she would have lost so much
of what was precious to her. She would become one of
those Parisian matrons he both pitied and detested, a
woman with a cutting voice turned metallic from bitterness, who wore too much jewelry, each new bauble repre-
senting an act of contrition from her wandering husband,
a woman whose bright eyes had turned dull, whose conversation was heavy with malice and envy.

And he would have made her that creature.

He rolled onto his back and tried to recall what had been so alluring about Josette that he had left his wife behind in Paris. Her voice? Her eyes? Her little hands? Her round arms? Indeed, there was nothing special about her. Yet there had been that craving to possess, to conquer. And he had.

He was becoming one of those paunch-bellied middle-aged boors who pinch maids and wink at young women over their dinner plate.

What a couple he and Marguerite would soon be.

He wanted a different future. He wanted to change course, to go back to a time when promises meant something and his wife could believe in him and he in her.

"Come back to bed," he said softly.

"Why? I cannot sleep." But she left the window and sat next to him.

"I missed you very much, Marguerite. When you left I thought. . . ."

"What, Michel? What did you think?"

"That I might never see you again."

"And did that matter?"

"More than I have ever told you. Why did you never believe me when I said the others did not matter?"

"Then why were they there, between us?"

He pressed her close and inhaled the strange, exotic perfume of her hair. Underneath the perfume was her own smell, a scent of grass and salt water, autumn and ripe pears, a scent he had known for years.

"I wanted to love you. I meant to love you," he said. "It will be different, Marguerite."

Marguerite stretched beside him. "It would have been different, if there had been a child," she said.

After a few minutes her head on his shoulder grew heavier, and she slept. He tried to imagine her as a mother, with a baby at her breast. It made a pretty picture. To bad it had not been in their cards.

When Michel awoke again, sun blazed through the open shutter, making a slanting pool of yellow on the stone floor. The call to prayer sounded, its chanted notes floating in with the sun. The muezzin's voice was wistful and insistent enough that Michel remembered being a small boy kneeling in his father's chapel. He wished he remembered how to pray.

Marguerite stirred and there was a shuffling noise in the corridor outside the door. Morello's dragoman, the tall Nubian who had opened the door to them upon their arrival and waited silently upon them ever since, came in, carrying a tray with coffee and fresh figs.

Marguerite, standing now and modestly covered in a black robe, took the tray from him and said a few words in Arabic. The servant smiled, bowed, and backed out of the room.

"What did you say to him?" Michel asked, piqued that his wife now knew words in a language of which he had no understanding.

"Simply, thank you. It is a lovely morning. The necessities of courtesy. We will be dependent on him while we are here, so it is best to try to win his approval."

"Does he disapprove of us?"

"Most certainly. We are unbelievers. In his eyes, we are lower than he is, though he is only a servant."

Michel, somewhat sullenly, poured and drank the sweet, thick coffee, trying to regain the threads of thought he'd revealed in that moment of clarity that comes all too briefly between the first stirrings of consciousness and the opening of the eyes onto the new day.

"The pieces do not fit," he said finally.

"What pieces?"

"The assassination attempt."

"We thoroughly have discussed the events of that evening many, many times," Marguerite pointed out with a sigh.

"Not thoroughly enough. It was too clumsy. Too amateurish. Something is not right. Pieces are missing. Something else happened that we did not notice."

"I want to return to Paris. It is getting hard to breath here. The dust."

"Soon," he said, distracted, still thinking and frowning. "I hope. How will we ever regain Bonaparte's favor? Without it, life in Paris will not be overly comfortable, I'm afraid. We might end up on my father's farm in Brittany."

Marguerite groaned. "I was thinking more of my old apartments. The opera. Balls at dawn."

"Too bad you feel that way. You would make a lovely dairy maid."

"Michel, do not jest about such serious matters. Bonaparte said he would like that old Egyptian stela as a reminder of his victories here, didn't he? Find that, and we will be welcomed in Paris."

"I have already tried, my darling."

"You have?" She sighed again, disliking this new habit of reporting things to each other as if they were strangers.

"The stela has stirred interest in many places. England. Russia. Constantinople. Now, France. Naturally, Talleyrand would also be interested. All this fuss over something that probably does not even exist. Talleyrand has spent half a year's income trying to track it down."

"To what purpose, Michel? Why?"

"I would assume simply because others seek it."

"I do not understand. Are we never to be satisfied with what we have? Must we always desire more?"

"You, my jealous one, may answer that question as well as I," he said.

16

In the vast Egyptian desert, surrounded by sand and cast-off dreams, stands the great temple of Dendera. Its thick columns are as numerous as trees in a primevil forest and atop each column is a carved image of Hathor, goddess of joy. Its tall ceiling is painted with the signs of the zodiac and other talismans of arcane knowledge.

It was to this temple that Cleopatra and her two children traveled in 36 B.C., the year that Mark Antony left her to return to Rome and marry Octavia.

Antony was, at best, indecisive. It was not a fault shared by the Queen of Egypt. Determined to bring him back to her by any method within her means, she decided to enlist the aid of the gods themselves, and so journeyed with the stela up the Nile, to the great temple, to make appropriate sacrifices, prayers, and threats if all else failed.

On a barge adorned with gold and pearls she made her progress up the Nile, past green fields and brick villages, gray ruins and painted temples. The reeds on the river's edge swayed in the breeze of her passing, and their dance reminded her of her own longing for the man who had left.

At Cleopatra's side, enthroned like a fellow queen, was the funerary stela carved with Hathor's image. It had been given to the Ptolemies by Alexander and had been part of their great collection for generations. The ancient goddess had spoken to Cleopatra in a dream, and promised that Mark Antony would return, if the stela was placed in the goddess's temple.

Six months after Cleopatra made her prayers and sacrifices before its tall, limestone pylons and presented the sacred stela to the priests of the temple, Antony left Octavia and returned to Egypt, to his queen.

So it was to this same temple, this same place of miracles that Selene decided to make pilgrimage. It had worked for her mother. It would work for her.

Unlike her mother, who had traveled as a goddess, as the living form of Isis, Selene traveled as a mere Roman matron, with kohl-rimmed eyes and a simple, pleated linen gown. Her small caravan rode on donkeys and slept under the stars, not in the rooms of the palaces along the way where a queen would have been welcomed.

The only concession she made to her now-secret station, to her past decades of wealth and habit, was to include her beloved crocodile in this caravan. It was a gift from Juba, the adored. It would not be left behind. The crocodile, grinning and heavy-lidded, was carried in a box the size and shape of a mummy case, painted in gold and azure with stories of the goddess Hathor, whom the Greeks had renamed Aphrodite. Four slaves bore the bier on their shoulders.

The crocodile's diamond bracelets and necklaces were left behind in the treasure room, along with Selene's crowns and scepters and heavy rings. Selene felt lighter, younger.

The caravan moved north in a long, scraggling line to the Mediterranean. There, Selene hired boats to carry them to Egypt. On shipboard, she leaned into the wind, eyes closed, and let her husband's mistress, adventure, stroke her face. The crocodile terrified the sailors, who walked in large circles around him whenever he and Selene were on deck.

After many weeks of travel they landed at Alexandria, and Selene set foot on Egyptian soil for the first time since she had left it as a child, as a captive of Rome, as Cleopatra's and Mark Antony's orphan. She was both jubilant and sad.

Alexandria was filled with memories. On foot, followed by only a handful of slaves and guards, Selene passed the royal palace at Lochias where she had spent her brief years of childhood; the Roman governor lived in it now and Roman sentinels were at its gates. She went to the Soma and dropped a bouquet of water lilies on her mother's ill-kempt grave, unsuccessfully trying to ignore the graffiti on the tombstone. Egyptian whore. Only a Roman would have written that. She went to the island of Pharos, where she had played with her father, Mark Antony, but Roman children played there now. She went to the snake pit, where she had bought the asp her mother requested, that last day in Alexandria. The snake pit seemed unchanged; nothing could alter the eerie hissing and sliding noises that escaped that black pit.

Everywhere were signs of Roman dominion. Latin names were painted over Egyptian signs, Roman togas were worn over Egyptian trousers, the men who stood in the squares of the city calling out the news shouted first in Latin, then Greek, and lastly Egyptian. The food in the public places was a bad imitation of Roman food and over-seasoned with cheap fish sauce. The bread, bread for which Egypt had been famous, was grey and gritty. The best wheat was sent to Rome.

The people of Alexandria, however, seemed much as Selene remembered them: city people, filled with hurry and bustle and high spirits, eager to make the day's profit, cook the day's meal, then sleep briefly and start all over. But there was something in their eyes she did not remember from childhood, a hint of suspicion, doubt, fear. The merchants in the bazaar would not bargain with her, a stranger with a Roman accent. The landlady at her inn was polite but not friendly to Selene, the Roman matron.

Alexandria had become a foreign country to her. Caesar had accomplished his purpose all too well.

Her footsteps grew heavier as she walked the streets of this unknown Alexandria. Her sense of homecoming, jubilant at first, turned into a fear of discovery. The city was not hers; she no longer belonged to it. She inhaled its strangeness with each breath.

Uneasy, Selene spent a mere three days in Alexandria, then hired a felluca to sail up the Nile. There was one place, one memory, even Caesar himself could not obliterate: the Temple at Dendereh, built by her ancestors to honor the goddess Hathor.

Without Juba, all color was fled from the world and she thought and dreamed in black and white . . . a black asp on her mother's white arm, her husband's black legs entwined in her own white ones . . . she would not be abandoned again.

Juba loved her. Juba was faithful. But Juba was being eaten by ambition beyond his powers, as Mark Antony had been, and such ambition leads to disasters. She would go to Dendera and pray for his return.

On a distant isle, where the scent of wild thyme filled the night and the music of gentle waves lapped at the shore, Juba was not thinking of his wife Selene.

Stars shone overhead in the blue sky canopy and he sat back in his lounge, inhaling deeply, smiling. Glaphyra's small boys, Tigranes and Alexander, played marbles at his feet, occasionally sending a wayward marble careening over Juba's toes.

"Darlings, do not disturb our guest with your silly

game,'' Glaphyra reprimanded them. ''Juba, should I send them to bed?''

Her voice, as always, was silky, soothing, her arms, as she ushered the children towards their nurse, were white and shapely. Juba eyed those arms greedily. Glaphyra, the young widow, daughter of King Archelaus of Cappadocia, had filled his eyes, his thoughts, his dreams, for a month now. He should have left this little island weeks ago; he could not. His feet were of lead; his heart was already anchored. He had forgotten the rest of the voyage he was to make, the book he was to write, his ambition, his way back home to Selene. He was bewitched.

''Let them be,'' Juba said, smiling up at Glaphyra, delighting in her beauty, her youth. She made the world young again. ''I enjoy their games. They remind me of my son, Ptolemy. He is about Tigranes's height and age.''

Glaphyra and Archelaus exchanged quick glances. Then, she lowered her head and a curtain of black hair hid her face momentarily. She did not like to hear Juba speak of Ptolemy or the boy's mother, Selene.

''It is time for them to be in bed,'' she said, giving each boy a quick kiss on the forehead. They made polite bows, a nightly ritual that pleased Juba, who feared that he and Selene were allowing Ptolemy to become a little willful, a little bad-mannered.

''It is hard to be away from home, alone,'' Glaphyra said when the boys' laughter could no longer be heard. ''Do you wish me to dance for you, or sing, to shorten the night?''

''The night is already too short,'' said Juba.

Guiltily, he looked at Archelaus. He had given away their secret. What would the king of Cappadoccia do, knowing that his guest had so abused his hospitality? Force him to leave? Demand compensation? His life?

It didn't seem to matter. He had arrived at the island ill and weary from his travels. He was, he had realized during this voyage, no longer young. Black-eyed, white-skinned Glaphyra had nursed him back to health, and made him feel young, at least for a few moments a day. The young, lonely widow had comforted him in every way a woman can comfort a man, with her hands, her voice, her glance, her breath, her body. The ease with which he kept Selene out of his thoughts no longer troubled him.

Archelaus pretended not to hear Juba's slip, not to know that these two were lovers. Secretly, he was pleased by this. Juba was rich and powerful; he had high connections in Rome and there wasn't a king in the world who would not feel safer, having such a . . . friend.

"Did you see the artist, Aristide, today?" Archelaus said. Time to speak of things other than the night or the guest might become ill at ease. He plainly was not used to affairs of this sort. Perhaps he had restricted himself to slaves, ignoring the charms of high-born ladies. All the better for my purpose, thought Archelaus.

"I did. His work is promising. I have bought two statues he recently completed." Juba, searching for excuses to stay on the island, had decided to purchase statuary to bring back to Mauretania, to adorn the theatre Selene had built there.

"He is not an artist known to hurry. The finishing of the statues may take some time," Glaphyra said. Her voice was musical with contentment.

Father and daughter exchanged glances once again. Juba, sipping wine that tasted of sun and honey, wondered how long he must sit on this terrace, making small talk, before he could claim fatigue and go to his bed, where Glaphyra would soon seek him.

Somewhere in the night was the other, Selene, and she seemed very far away.

17

Seven days after their escape from the Institute to Giza, Marguerite and Michel, on somewhat friendlier terms though not exactly warm with each other, avoided each other's eyes over breakfast. The safety and freedom they had hoped to find outside the Institute had proved an illusion. On the few occasions they had tried to leave Morello's villa, the villagers had gathered and pelted them with stones. They were, again, prisoners.

Marguerite felt confined and frustrated. Michel felt helpless. It did not make for pleasant conversation.

"The poison was not meant for Bonaparte," said Michel, drawing deeply on a long pipe between words. "It could not have been. . . . The whole thing was far too . . . clumsy." Blue smoke circled his head, adding to the oriental look he had acquired since he had, a few days before, exchanged his tight trousers and jacket for looser pants and the long, flowing kaftan of Egypt.

He sat on the carpeted floor in the Egyptian posture used for dining and conversation, taught to him by Marguerite: left leg curled flat on the floor, right knee drawn up to provide balance and a resting place for his elbow.

Marguerite eyed him warily, not certain she approved of Michel dressed up as a sheik. He looked much too attractive. But, when in Rome, he had declared. And the adopted clothing was much more comfortable, much more suitable for the climate.

Still, her eyes were hungry for familiar things, for the embroidered waistcoats and leather boots that reminded her of Paris, not kaftans and red leather slippers.

"Then who was the poison for?" She sat opposite him on a rose-colored pillow, picking at the dish of boiled beans flavored with lime juice brought to them by Morello's dragoman. It was still early in the morning, not much past sunrise, but the house was already filling with heat. The dragoman, silent and stern-faced, padded about the room, filling porous jars with water and setting them in the windows, where they might catch a breeze and provide some coolness.

"Perhaps just anyone. Perhaps there is a madman loose who does not care who is murdered, as long as someone dies. It has happened before. Soldiers taught to love killing, husbands seeking revenge. . . ." His voice trailed off. He took a long pull on the pipe and exhaled a cloud of blue, fragrant smoke.

"Before Ibrahim, Europeans had been murdered. Three, no four bodies were found in the Nile. They had been strangled," Marguerite supplied.

"Are those deaths related? They could be. But maybe not. Does a madman switch murder weapons, from the garrot to poison?"

"I would not know, my dear. And I must admit it is rather chilling to hear you discuss murder in such a dispassionate manner." She rose from the little table and went to one of the latticed windows. "I thought this would be our freedom. We are as imprisoned here as we were at the Institute." Her hand slid between the empty spaces of the carved window screen and rattled it.

Michel considered his wife through the haze of blue smoke. She had grown pale and thin. There were dark circles under her eyes and her fingers had acquired a nervous habit of plucking at her sleeve. He wanted to take care of her, keep her safe. But here, in this foreign place, he did not know how. He was in as much jeopardy as she.

Certainly, until Ibrahim's murderer was discovered, they were prisoners of whatever walls hid them.

"Patience, dearest. I agree that this dismal village is hardly the place for the happiest of reunions, but it is superior to our last lodgings. We are making improvements in our situation."

"No improvement was required until you arrived," Marguerite muttered. "And tell me what you meant when you said you had already searched for the stela."

Michel smiled. It was, he supposed, far better for Marguerite to be angry, and to remain angry till this situation was resolved. Sadness, combined with their danger, would be intolerable.

"Well, enchanting one, I admit that I did perform some duties in other quarters of Cairo, before coming to you at the Institute."

"How many days were you in Egypt before you came for me?"

"Just two, dearest. And I could neither sleep nor eat because of the urge to run to your side."

"Where were you?"

"As I said. There was a slight matter requiring my attention. Letters had been intercepted from the English mission to the Sublime Porte, in which mention had been made of this stela that seems to be the only topic of conversation these days. It seems Lord Elgin has decided to add the stela to his collection of artifacts. Consequently, Talleyrand also grew desirous of possessing the thing."

"And the other letters, the ones saying Bonaparte was to be assassinated?"

"No invention, I assure you. They were received. The stela merely added further impetus to my journey. Think, Marguerite. Would the Directory discharge the expenditures for this journey had I not at least two purposes for it?"

"Three. You have also claimed you came for me. I wonder if I can believe anything you say, Michel, as you leave so much that must be guessed at."

"Believe this. I would not be here, if you were not. Talleyrand could have sent any number of men equally suitable to the tasks. Marguerite, for days now I have been trying to make you see that it is pointless for me to go on without you. You must come back with me. I love you. You are my wife."

She raised her eyebrows. "How disappointed Josette will be," was her arch reply.

"Marguerite, you are the only woman, the only thing, that truly matters to me. Why can you not believe that?"

"Because you have so often been unfaithful, Michel."

"A mistress is a different matter from a wife. And a husband is not a lapdog, a creature who sits at your knees and begs tidbits each night before the fire. A true marriage is more than that."

"Ours, it seems, is less. . . ."

So heated grew this conversation that neither heard the arrival of Madame Beaucaire, who stood in the doorway, grinning and clearing her throat. She waited for Monsieur Verdier's passionate disclaimer to dissolve into silence, then burst into the room in an explosion of perfume and exclamations aimed at Marguerite.

"My dearest friend! Oh, sublime acquaintance! How I have missed you!" she trilled.

"Madame Beaucaire," answered Marguerite, stunned. Her voice evoked surprise, but little enthusiasm.

"Madame." Michel made her a polite little bow.

Silence.

"I have interrupted and come at an unfortunate time," guessed Madame, looking from Marguerite to Michel. She rubbed her hands with glee. "It has been so dreadful at the Institute," she began, seating herself on the red divan and helping herself from a bowl of sweetmeats.

Michel, smiling with a little more enthusiasm than either he or Marguerite had shown a moment before, sat next to her.

"Tell us," he said with forced politeness. "How are matters at the Institute? And however did you find us, my dear Madame Beaucaire?"

"That naughty little Vivant Denon. Immediately before he left . . . he has flown the coop, along with Bonaparte, you know . . . I took him aside and begged, absolutely begged, to discover the whereabouts of my friend, Marguerite. . . ."

Marguerite felt a jab of regret. Her sponsor was on his way back to France. She could have traveled with him. At the Institute there had been that very brief moment when she could have left Michel's side and gone to Vivant's. She had, for reasons she did not understand, chosen to stay with Michel.

She looked at her husband and saw from his expression that he had guessed her thoughts. There was gratitude in his face. And something else. Devotion? From Michel? How very strange. Her husband looked back at the huffing Madame Beaucaire who was red-faced from the heat and her journey to this little house and his expression became closed once again.

"The Institute?" he repeated.

"Well. I must have a password simply to go from room to room. Madame Foures wanders about in a hussar's tunic and trousers and walking hat, weeping. General Kleber is livid, as you can imagine, left to pick up all the little pieces and find a way to get the remainder of the army back to France. . . ."

"Who left with General Bonaparte?" Michel asked.

"Let me see. Monsieur Monge and Berthollet. Vivant Denon. Young Beauharnais, the stepson and three other aides-de-camp—Duroc, Lavalette, and Merlin, I believe. The secretary, Bourienne. And the Mameluke bodyguard, Roustan. . . ."

Madame Beaucaire paused and fanned herself even more briskly. "They say," she said, grinning gleefully, "that you tried to poison General Bonaparte. I don't blame you. Such an alarming little man. Do tell me about it."

"We did no such thing," Marguerite protested.

"General Kleber has been left in charge, now that Bonaparte has gone, and he says. . . ."

"He probably is sorry we did not make better use of our supposed opportunity to assassinate," Michel guessed.

"Well. I am not one to repeat words carelessly said, but that is exactly what he said, when he learned that you were no longer at the Institute," Madame Beaucaire admitted.

"And does Kleber know where we are?" Marguerite asked. "Is he looking for us?"

"My lips are sealed," said Madame Beaucaire.

Marguerite and Michel exchanged glances. It was simply a matter of time.

Madame Beaucaire, having gone to the expense of hiring a donkey and dragoman to make this visit to Michel and Marguerite, stayed for lunch, for afternoon tea, and for dinner, returning to her own abode only when the sun began to set. She stayed on when Michel and Marguerite, yawning, intimated they wished a nap; she stayed on when Michel and Marguerite, pacing, indicated they wished to speak privately. She stayed on until she felt she had wrenched all the amusement and gossip possible and then, only then, did she depart.

"The day is gone and we have made no progress," Marguerite commented when they were alone again.

"There has been progress, but I admit it has not been the kind we seek. Kleber will soon know where we are. My sense of him was that he is a man attentive to duty and fine points of the law. He will return us for trial."

"Do you think they will hang us or shoot us? They have not yet got a guillotine in Cairo."

"That is a question not worth dwelling upon, Marguerite. Put it from your mind." Michel used a patronizing tone of voice which, in the past, had done much to irritate his wife. This evening it did not.

Instead, it reminded her of other dangers she had shared with this man: the Paris riots in '89, the Committee for Public Safety and its bloody Place de Greves, the summer night in '92 when they had been arrested and charged with being enemies of the republic. Michel had always found a way out for them. He was cunning and manipulative and sly. She had forgotten how very endearing those qualities could be when one's life hung in the balance.

She had also forgotten how pleasantly blue his eyes were at twilight.

Sheik Hamid, sitting in his private courtyard under the August stars, also thought of blue eyes . . . the eyes of the strange woman who had stolen his nephew. A young man's heart is a dangerous and uncivilized place, a garden overgrown with impossible exotic flowers and wild animals, lions and crocodiles ready to maim. Hamid was not so old he couldn't remember the thrill of dangerous love. But to marry that dangerous woman and bring her home . . . it was beyond comprehension.

And now, this.

Next to Hamid, on his right side, was his pipe, cold and unused. On his left was the stela of Hathor confronting Anubis. It had just been delivered to his house by a messenger who kept his face hidden under a dirty shawl, who offered neither greeting nor explanation, except to say, "This is for Ibrahim, who lives here. He awaits it. I have dispatched my debt."

Apparently, the messenger had not known that Ibrahim was dead.

Hamid had removed the cloth wrappings from the heavy stone, and traced with his trembling fingers this carved blasphemy, these ancient, heathen figures who mocked the Creator's own work. Ibrahim had promised he was done with this trade. He had promised he would deal no more in antiquities, too many of which were stolen or blasphemous or both, nor have contact with the men who dealt in such things, the *farengi* who honored neither the law nor the people of the land.

Yet here was this stela, heathen, smelling of graves and more time than man should be conscious of, smelling of money and hidden negotiations and greed.

Why had Ibrahim turned to greed? Had he not all that a man could honestly desire in this life? Perhaps it was the woman's fault. Perhaps she had wanted gold bracelets and more slaves. Beware the strange woman who is not known in her town.

Hamid clapped his hands and the doorkeeper, who had been napping on a stone bench, came running, his blue shirt flapping about his knees.

"Shall I light your pipe? Bring you sherbet?" he asked in a sleepy, placating voice.

"No. Bring the widow, Atiyah, here," Hamid ordered.

The doorkeeper nodded then backed away, bowing repeatedly, pressing thumbs to forehead, frightened by the storm in his master's eyes.

Atiyah appeared just moments later. She looked small and young. Her eyes were downcast, her shoulders under her voluminous veil curled forward and down, like an oft-beaten servant. The doorkeeper had warned her of Hamid's anger.

Hamid breathed deeply and said a prayer before speaking. It would do not good to frighten her. She must speak freely.

"Tell me of this," he finally ordered, pointing to the stela.

Atiyah looked down at the stone and her pale eyes flickered once with surprise and joy, then grew masklike. Hamid could not see the rest of her face. She had veiled herself, as she usually did when meeting with Hamid, who was not a blood relative. Hamid, at that moment, wished she was not so prudent with the commandments. He wished to see her face, to trace that emotion that had started in her eyes and traveled, he was certain, to the hidden mouth.

"It is a carved stone," she answered in her deep, melodious voice. The emotion had not traveled as far as her heart, her breast. He heard in her voice that he would get no truth from this woman.

"This much I have seen for myself. Why is it here? What does it have to do with Ibrahim? You were the choice of his heart, Atiyah. He must have told you things he did not tell me. And I wish to understand. I wish to know."

Hamid's voice had grown soft with pleading, his eyes were moist with loss. Atiyah would have been invincible against his anger, but not against this grief. She dropped to her knees and touched her forehead to the ground in the traditional posture of supplication for mercy and forgiveness.

"I will not harm you," Hamid said. "But I must know the truth."

Atiyah lifted her face to him. "Ibrahim needed money. More than you gave," she whispered. "He agreed to find and purchase this stela for a buyer," she said.

She did not say that the money was needed to pay off the rest of her contract with Mother Halima, who had traced her to Cairo and threatened to throw the two of them in jail, if they did not buy the contract.

"Is this why Ibrahim died?"

"I do not know. Perhaps." Fear kept her from saying

more. Ibrahim had learned of the stela from her, Atiyah. It was for Atiyah he had traced it and found buyers for it. But they had stolen it from someone else.

"You hide more than you tell," Hamid said, dissatisfied. "I will get to the truth of this. And if I discover that Ibrahim was murdered for this carved blasphemy . . ." He did not finish. But Atiyah knew his meaning. If it was murder, blood revenge was required.

Atiyah did not sleep well that night. In her dreams, Ibrahim came to her and he was weeping and angry. He roared for vengeance, and wept for the grief he had caused his uncle. "For the love I gave you, my Atiyah, you must make this right," he told her.

Lord Elgin, almost hidden by a thick curtain of riding coats, dressing gowns, and starched shirts, wiped the dust from a pair of black riding boots and handed them to his waiting serving man, who sneezed robustly.

The ground work for the embassy to Constantinople was finished: all the required correspondence had been sent and received, gifts for the Turks—chandeliers, telescopes, watches—had been purchased and sent ahead to the Phaeton which awaited them in Portsmouth harbor, a doctor, secretary, and minister had been hired for his party, his orders and salary had been fixed. Grenville, the Foreign Secretary, had been miserly with both, and Elgin strongly suspected Grenville's hand in the matter of the inferior Privy Councillor honor he had been given, instead of the Order of Chivalry, which he had wanted. The Order of Chivalry included a star and ribbon he could have worn in the Sultan's presence. Oh well. One must make do.

But the worst, the largest disappointment came from Grenville's attitude towards the antiquities Elgin planned to collect for the glory of England. "Knickknacks," Grenville had been overhead muttering in his club. "Dust collectors. Not a shilling will Elgin get for that ridiculous plan." The official rejection had been phrased in more gentlemanly manner: The Foreign Office had not the funds to support such a plan. Furthermore, the Society of Antiquaries, the Dilettanti Society and other individuals had collected quite enough "art," thank you.

"Pack them," His Lordship directed to the servant, wishing he referred to the London bureaucrats, not the boots.

The lord's and lady's dressing rooms of Broomhall were being transferred from drawer and closet to travel trunks, a long row of which already stood in the great hall, lined up like servants awaiting their Christmas tuppence.

Mary, standing outside the lord's closet, wrung her hands. The packing was not going as she had planned. Elgin had taken it over completely, tearing up her lists, countermanding her orders to the servants and telling her unceasingly in his most patronizing voice, "Pol, my dear, leave everything to me. Go rest. Go read Lady Mary Wortley Montague's letters from Turkey."

Pol did not want to rest. She did not want to reread the letters, though some were particularly instructive, especially the ones about harem life. Pol felt fine, despite her condition, despite the unexpectedly damp late summer weather. Pol wanted to take over her duties, and those, as her mother had explained, included taking charge for their material disembarkation.

But here was Eggy, charging through dressing rooms as though he were after the fox, undermining her in front of the servants, treating her like a child, though she carried his.

"Eggy, must you bring all this old gear? I had hoped to buy new leathers in Italy. They are supposed to be so well made there, and we will be stopping in Naples, you know."

"Naples. Ha. Italian leather is not so fine as good English stock." He reached deeper into the shelves, searching for a certain pair of gloves.

Pol refrained from stamping her feet. She was quickly learning that the practiced, coquettish gestures that had made her the belle of Edinburgh did not elicit the desired response from her spouse. When she sulked he roared. When she prattled he ignored her. When she showed temper he mocked her. This left her few weapons other than truth and reasoning, and she was becoming practiced at both.

"Eggy, that is unwise," she said in her most reasonable voice. "You are trying to avoid a meeting with Lady Hamilton. Oh, don't look like that. I know you disapprove of her. Everyone does. I insist we stop in Naples, Eggy, I really do. To not stop, after he has invited us, would be a slight to Admiral Nelson."

Lord Elgin stopped rummaging long enough to scratch his chin and consider. Pol had a point.

"The deuce, I suppose we must stop, since we are invited. Lord Nelson is far too important a person to snub, despite the muck he's made of his private life. But I'll not have you speaking alone with Lady Hamilton. The devil only knows what kind of ideas that woman might put in your head. Do you understand?"

"Of course, Eggy. Anything you say. And I'll have my riding boots backed, too. No need for new ones." One battle a day. One victory a day. That was Pol's new goal. She had won the victory of the visit to the infamous Lady Hamilton. She would be content with her old boots.

Outside in the dark hall, she placed her hand over her belly and hesitated. Would the child be like his father? Frowning, she turned her back on the lord's dressing room and returned to the kitchen.

Alone again, Elgin began to hum to himself as he worked, to raise his spirits. Why couldn't Pol do as she was told? She had been such a diffident bride, although there had been that scene at the altar when she had collapsed and the ceremony had to be held up some minutes. He had felt the fool, then, standing there in that ridiculous groom's get-up, alone at the altar, waiting, smiling sheepishly. Pol had come back, smiling, to finish the ceremony, but never explained that interruption.

And now, pregnant, she seemed to be growing willful. He would not stand for it.

Elgin, humming and frowning at the same time, felt a ringing in his ears and a tingle in his nose that would, in time, turn to syphilitic disfigurement and dementia. But that evening the disease was no more than a headache and certain dankness of thought, which he blamed on the Order of Chivalry, which he did not get, and his bride, Mary Hamilton Nisbet, whom he did get.

One thought cheered him. The awaited letter had finally turned up, and it bore good news, indeed. His man in Constantinople reported that the hints, direct and otherwise, to the Sublime Porte, had paid off and Selim was, at that very moment, gathering together the gifts that Lord Elgin would receive at their first meeting. If "The Woman Carried Away" could be had, then Lord Elgin would have her, courtesy of the grateful Selim II.

Selim, half a world away, where the night was hot and sticky and filled with the cry of peacocks and the soft, sad singing of the harem, listened, eyes closed, as the secretary droned on and on.

Aimee, the Queen Mother, was waiting for him, but he would not be able to visit her until this chore was finished. He must feign some interest in the English embassy, in this Lord Elgin. He was tired of foreigners. The other, Bonaparte, was gone, but had left his army behind in Egypt. Selim, who had never ridden into battle, wondered briefly what it was like to be thirsty and hungry, to be burned by the sun, to see the punishing sun glinting off scimitars raised to kill. The thought seemed not worth pursuing.

Behind his heavy, closed eyelids he saw, instead of battles, Aimee, the French woman, his uncle's widow, with her high forehead shortened by the little cap she wore low on her head, her heavy pearl necklace hanging down to the knees of her trousers. She made other women look like cows.

"Eight trays of fine Berlin china. A coffee service of Dresden china. An Indian shawl embroidered with gold. A dozen jars of perfume . . ." the secretary read from the long list of items that were to be presented to Lord and Lady Elgin upon their arrival.

Selim yawned. Bored beyond reason, he let his thoughts wander. Isaac Bey, a man both well traveled and well read, had told him of a philosopher, Socrates, who, standing at the opening of a great bazaar, had said "How much there is in the world that I do not want!" There seemed to be much in the world that the Englishman did want.

Selim raised his hand. The reading stopped. The room was silent until Selim spoke from his throne.

"This Elgin, this English lord, wishes statuary. Do not read to me of coffee services and shawls. Have you found the stela he desires?"

The secretaries looked at their assistants. The assistants turned around and glared at the messengers. The messengers kicked their servants. The servants scurried in circles and whispered futilely.

Isaac Bey, standing as protocol required but leaning intimately against the Sultan's throne, laughed.

"It would seem the answer is no," he said.

Selim laughed too. Then he kicked the secretary standing closest to him. "Give the kick to your neighbor," he said. "A hard kick. And a slap for good measure."

The secretary turned and kicked, then slapped the next secretary, who turned and kicked the next, until the punishment had been passed all the way down the line.

Isaac Bey was laughing so hard he had to hold his stomach. Selim did not not laugh again after his initial burst, but sat stone-faced, waiting. When the court was calm again, and the red-faced secretaries, messengers, and servants stood in orderly rows again, Selim rose.

"Find the stela," he said. "Or you will lose much." He turned and left, walking in the direction of the Queen Mother's rooms, his private guard hurrying to keep up. There was silence even from the peacocks in the garden. Only the fountains continued to speak and what they said was meaningless.

But then the peacocks started to call again, and the women, hidden behind thick walls, started to sing, and the palace filled with the seductive songs of brides who await their lord.

18

Marguerite pulled the heavy black robe over her head and then adjusted the white veil that hung under her eyes. If she pulled the folds of the robe forward, not even her eyes would show clearly.

"Well?" she asked Saladin, Morello's dragoman.

He stood kingly straight in his loose, striped robe, a broom in one hand and a cat, about to be cast out of the kitchen, in the other as he studied her.

"The veil is not straight," he said. Marguerite straightened it.

"It will do," he then pronounced gravely, thrusting the cat out the door and resting the broom against the wall.

Marguerite poured coins from her purse into her hand. Saladin picked out a three and held them up so she could see them clearly. "This much. No more," he said. "If you let them cheat you, they will know you are a *farengi*, and there will be trouble."

Marguerite nodded, took a deep breath, and left Morello's house, joining the stream of village women headed towards the market.

It was a fair, late summer morning and the sky, as always in Egypt, was blue and cloudless. The mud-colored cluster of houses and small square of the village seemed smaller than when they had arrived; the river had moved even closer, the floodwaters had claimed even more land. Some palms had been engulfed by the rushing water and their brown trunks and green fronds rose desolately from the overpowering river. The night before, two houseboats had been swept away by the current. The bereft families who had lost home and possessions now crouched by the river, wailing and cursing and ignored by the other villagers, who had worries of their own. It was *Akhit,* the Time of Inundation, the dangerous time. If the Nile continued to rise, the western-most houses would soon be flooded.

Perhaps that was why the village women either did not notice her, or simply ignored her, the stranger among them. The river was of more importance, it claimed all the thoughts not dedicated to their daily tasks.

She was able to move freely from table to table, admiring leeks and cabbages, piles of beans and baskets of fruit, half-carcasses of lambs and sheep and glassy-eyed, plucked chickens. She stopped at the melon seller's table, studied the fruit, pointed to one and thumped her coins onto the table.

The man started to bargain vehemently, shouting incomprehensible promises and threats, as Saladin had warned he would. Marguerite shook her head, snatched away the coins and turned to leave. But before she had taken one step, the seller's voice changed. He smiled and pleaded. She returned the coins to the table, took the melon and left without ever uttering a word.

Success. They could leave the villa.

Michel was still asleep when she returned. She pulled the covers away from his face and sat down on the bed, still wearing the robe and veil. Michel opened one eye. A strange, exotic woman sat on his bed. He opened the second eye. He sat up.

"How strange you look, Marguerite. I hardly recognized you," he said, only when he was absolutely certain it was indeed his wife. Was there a hint of disappointment in his voice? Had he hoped to savor the more intimate joys of Egypt and its women? Marguerite, still pleased with the morning adventure, decided to push that thought aside and consider it later.

"Saladin has robes for you, also. We can go out, Michel. I've done it. Voilà." She held up the melon. "From the market."

"Go where?"

"To the bazaar, if nowhere else. I cannot stand this confinement. If only Josephine could see me. How envious she would be of this costume." Marguerite rose and turned slowly around. She looked like a black column, stern and secretive and unapproachable.

"She has other things on her mind, believe me. I should imagine she is seeing her lawyers and friends for advice just about now. Or fleeing to the country, as Bonaparte gets closer to Paris. You look like a nun, Marguerite. I would not adopt that costume in Paris, if I were you."

Michel rose from the bed and poured water and essence of rose into the wash basin. "But this is an excellent thought, Marguerite. Go out, we shall. We will solve nothing here, going over and over facts that will mean nothing till more pieces are added to the puzzle. I, for one, would appreciate a chance to speak with Ibrahim's widow."

"Atiyah? For what purpose?" she asked suspiciously, watching as he bathed his face and shoulders and prepared to shave.

"To find out more about Ibrahim. Ibrahim, my dear, was a smuggler. A very good one. Half the mummies now on display in Europe were acquired through his services."

"I didn't know you had resorted to mummy powder, Michel. Is it as potent an aphrodisiac as they say?" She teased, but the old, possessive edge was in her voice.

"I have not resorted to mummy powder, dear wife. But others have. They shall be unnamed, don't press me, and yes, I have had dealings with Ibrahim myself through a very long string of intermediaries. Some months ago, Talleyrand decided to acquire a death mask from one of the pharaoh's tombs. Perhaps he wished it as a congratulatory reminder of ridding France of Bonaparte for the moment. Ibrahim procured a fine death mask for me. After a delay and expense that almost ruined me, I might add."

"And did Talleyrand like the pharaoh's death mask you procured?"

"Not much. He said it reminded him, unfortunately, of a certain young and very ambitious general from Corsica, the same one he had recently been rid of. Something about the eyes and cheekbones. I did not pay undue attention. My employer can be capricious."

"The young general from Corsica finds him capricious, too. Why did Talleyrand not send peace emissaries to the Sublime Porte to help pave the way for Bonaparte in Egypt, as he had promised to do? Instead of assistance from Selim, Bonaparte ended up with a war with the Turks because of Talleyrand's capriciousness."

"Talleyrand, and the others in Paris, are less than enamored of our general, I'm certain. He's too cunning and too popular with the people by half. Quite a few of the old guard would like nothing more than to see Bonaparte trip over his own feet. Of course, Josephine may have changed that somewhat. Other men often feel sympathy for the deceived husband. She may have done him more good than harm."

Marguerite frowned. She was tired of hearing about Josephine and deceived husbands. Wives were just as easily deceived.

"Perhaps Ibrahim was, after all, the assassin's target," Marguerite said. "He was murdered by a Frank, I think. One of us. Not an Arab. Not a Turk. Not a Mameluke. An Arab would have done the deed in private; a Turk would have used a silk bowstring around the neck; a Mameluke would have left no doubts as to the purpose of the execution. This murder was by poison, publicly administered, for no easily discernible purpose."

"You are becoming far too knowledgeable about murder, my darling wife. It makes a husband nervous. But why would one of 'us,' whomever that means, want Ibrahim dead? Maybe Atiyah has an answer to that."

Michel washed away the last of the soap and combed back his hair. Marguerite, instructed by Saladin, showed him how to place the close-fitting tarboosh on his head and then wind a turban around it. Because Michel was beardless, Saladin had procured a black turban, sign of the Copt, because sometimes men of that Christian sect did not grow their beards, as the Prophet ordered. The rest of his habilement consisted of a white shirt, short cotton trousers, striped silk robe, and red leather shoes.

"It will do," Marguerite said when he was completely robed. "You look splendid, Michel." Was it his imagination or had her eyes grown soft and inviting when she said that? The moment passed.

"I feel ludicrous," he protested. "Wasn't it Pascal who said 'We both conceal and disguise ourselves from ourselves?' Is this pantomime necessary?"

Marguerite decided not to supply specific details about the bastinado, the caning of the soles of the feet that left the victim crippled for months. Instead, she simply said, "If we are discovered by any of the Mameluke soldiery we will be beaten, most likely. They enjoy beating foreigners. We are safer this way. Now come, it is almost noon and we should cross the river before the ferryman goes home for his meal."

Dressed in their concealing robes, they left both villa and village, and recrossed the swollen river to Cairo. Once safely arrived at the other side, Marguerite sent a message to Atiyah, at the home of Sheik Hamid al Shackoui, asking if she would, for friendship's sake meet with them.

Hamid had already been up many hours when the messenger arrived. In Egypt, dawn comes quickly. Devout men must be careful to waken before the day, to be alert for that moment when greyness is dispelled and they can first tell the red threads from the black ones in the cloth that will wrap their heads. This is the time for the first prayers, and the time when truth seems closest at hand. And the truth distressed Hamid, for it revealed to him a task he had never done before: take another man's life. Ibrahim cried out to him for vengeance. A life for a life. Soon, the time of mourning would be over. The time of action would arrive.

After prayers he called for coffee and his pipe, but no food. He sat and thought for a long while in his garden. On the other side of the thick wall he could hear the snarling of camels being led to the market, the softer, complaining voices of small boys on their way to the mosque for instruction, and the bawdy songs of the street sweepers.

His thoughts scattered like loose leaves driven before those sweepers' brooms. His grief formed itself into something hard and metallic, like a copper worker's vase still blackened inside from the fire and ashes which had formed it. Hamid knew, as surely as he discerned red threads from black ones in the clear light of dawn, that Ibrahim's death had not been an accident. Ibrahim had been murdered and his murderer must be found and punished. Atiyah was the key. Beware the strange woman in your town.

In early afternoon Selik came to him with news: Atiyah had received another message.

"Hidden in figs?" Hamid asked angrily. Did the woman have no end of secrets?

"No. On paper. A proper message," Selik said. "But the women's chambers are in an uproar. Things have been broken. They are screaming at her for being cold-hearted and disrespectful. They say she never loved her husband. They call her many things."

"I know the words they will have used. Perhaps they are right, Selik. I do not know who this Atiyah is. Or what."

"I will follow her."

"No. This time, I will follow her. It is my duty. I must see what shame she brings to my house and my nephew's memory. Maybe it is not too late to prevent a greater shame."

Hamid thought of the package brought to his house, the package that smelled of the ages, of theft. Ibrahim was dead and what trouble was Atiyah in?

When Hamid had been a very small child, his father Mustafa had bought him to the great souk of Cairo to see the Frank, Fanny Spencer. The Englishwoman was there, with her maids and bodyguards, sketching a cake seller. She was surrounded by pointing and jeering Cairenes but she sat serenely on her folding chair, sketchbook in lap, concentrating so that the hand might capture what her eyes found. Her blue gown, low in front and very full beneath the waist, overflowed the chair. She looked like a tent pushed down by the khamsin, with a sphinx sitting on top of it.

It was the first time Hamid had seen an unveiled woman, other than his mother and sisters and slaves. Her pale hair was piled high on her head and dusted with white powder, her skin was the color of white sand, parched like fields in the Time of Insufficiency. Her eyes were so light the boy cried in fear.

"It is only a poor crazy heathen woman," his father had consoled him, laughing. "Her Frank family does not know what to do with her. They have sent her to us." Had Fanny Spencer overheard this assessment of her situation, she might well have agreed. A spinster of thirty-five with no prospects, her family had not in the least objected when she proposed to use her small income for travel. Then, at least, she would not be wearing her riding habit to formal dinners, or bringing her entire troupe of King George spaniels to Sunday service, or causing those hundreds of other minute but painful embarrassments to the family. And she was well aware that in Egypt she was considered crazy, and therefore protected by God and all his children. No harm came to the crazy Frank lady in Egypt till the day she felt the first warning lump of pain in her throat that presaged plague.

But the child Hamid's sleep was stalked by troubling dreams after the day in the souk, when he had watched the unveiled Frank put on paper the forbidden image of a man. She stood for the unknown, the dangerous, the foolish. And lately, in his sleep, she had come to him again and put her pale, skinny arms about Atiyah.

Fanny Spencer. Hamid had heard, years later, when the Frank died, that her home in Alexandria was filled with objects she had found in the desert, or bought from merchants who did not use their given names: mummified birds from Siout, little carved bulls from Memphis, statuettes of Hathor from Dendera, papyri from Beni-hassan, mothy camel blankets and Roman coins and other useless things. Her home had been filled with things; there had barely been room to carry the stretcher in and out to fetch forth the body.

Others had followed the poor crazy Frank woman, and more were to come, with their spades and chisels and wallets. Egypt was being carried away, piece by piece.

Hamid thought of his courtyard, with its fountain and pots of mint and soft pillows, its openness, its serenity. He looked about, and saw that all he needed was there, complete. Except for Ibrahim, who was dead.

In her *hareem,* where the searching sun passed through the latticed window to draw boxes of light and shadow on the tiled floor, Atiyah dressed calmly, forcing a composure she did not feel. The other women screamed and pulled at her veil, but she ignored them. She would go to Marguerite. And not just for friendship's sake. But first she would go to see Bahlul.

Isme followed her, close as a shadow, through the narrow streets of the souk. At the street of the rug sellers she paused before a heavy cloth door and looked over her shoulder before entering. When Isme tried to follow, she pushed her back outside, into the glaring sun.

"Leave me alone, old woman," she said. "Or I will tell Hamid who has been stealing from the purse of coins he keeps to give to the beggars."

Isme's eyes, over the veil, grew large with fear and she did as she was told.

Bahlul the merchant was not happy to see her. He smiled broadly, offered tea and sweet pastries. But Atiyah could see he was not at all pleased by her visit. He swatted at the flies buzzing over the pastries, fussed with the coffee service and used his eyes for every purpose except to look at her. When she spoke to him he tugged unhappily at his beard and swallowed hard before answering.

"Such a grief! Ay, he was a fine young man, your Ibrahim. Such a tragedy!" he exclaimed over and over, all the while peering over her shoulder, hoping for an interruption.

"You knew him. I know you did. Ibrahim spoke of you," she said calmly. She pulled the veil tightly across her face, making certain only her eyes were exposed, a dutiful widow, a chaste wife.

"Did he? Did he now? I am flattered. I am not worthy." Bahlul tugged unhappily at his beard. He knew the questions that were to come. He decided to taker her off guard, to charge rather than retreat. He knew women like Atiyah. Their own hearts were spotted and torn with histories that could not bear close inspection but once their husband's honor was threatened, they would fight like tigresses.

"Yes, we had occasion to work together. Finders, that's what we were," he admitted.

"Thieves," Atiyah said.

"A harsh word."

"There are harsher words I am ready to say. I think his death was not an accident. Why would someone try to poison the French general?"

Bahlul smiled and poured himself a second cup of coffee. She was only an ignorant woman after all. This would not be as difficult as he had imagined.

"Many nations would try, aside from any personal enemies he might have," Bahlul answered.

"Even so, it is not the fate of the French general that concerns me, but what has happened to Ibrahim. And why. Tell me of your business with my husband."

Her self-righteousness irritated him. Again, he tried to attack.

"Ibrahim was in need of money."

Atiyah would not drop her eyes, though she knew this was now expected. The money was needed to buy back her contract, to buy back her name, which had been the name of a popular dancing girl in Istanbul. Bahlul had tried to shame her. But that shame was an old one. It was the new one, the worse one, that drove her forward.

"You tell me what I already know. Tell me about the stela, The Woman Carried Away."

Bahlul sat forward. His fingertips twitched so he brought them both to his nose in a little steeple, to hid his nervousness.

"A legend. A false dream pursued by many men."

"Not a legend. I have it in my house, Bahlul. Tell me of these men who seek it."

Bahlul closed tea-colored eyelids over black eyes. It was the only way to hide his surprise, his joy. The stela was found. Now, he could finish this business. He chuckled. Ibrahim had been clever. He had outwitted Bahlul himself.

"A worthless piece of stone. As a favor, I will buy it from you and take it off your hands."

"And sell it to who, Bahlul? At what profit?"

"You know I cannot tell you that. You learned enough of Ibrahim's commerce to know that such names are not freely given or discussed lightly."

"A European," she said.

Bahlul did not answer.

"A collector. A man who also finds things for others. For profit," she continued. "A man who arrived in Cairo only after we ourselves returned here last year. A man who wears a tall hat, whose eyes are cold, like stone."

Bahlul kept silent and lifted his hands in protest.

"You have told me all I wish to know." Atiyah rose.

"You will not let me buy the stela?" Bahlul asked, miserable now.

"It has another purchaser. You could not pay the price."

She walked back out into the harsh sun. Isme clucked disapprovingly beside her.

"Not a word to Hamid, or I will have your tongue cut out, old woman," Atiyah said. "What is to follow will be on my head. Hamid must be kept free of it. This is as my husband would wish."

Isme clicked her tongue against her teeth and bobbed like a hen. "Ayy! Such words," she complained.

Atiyah did not even pretend to go to the baths. Water would not clean her now. After, she would go to be purified. Instead, she went to the Souk-ek-Guzmah, where the letter writers set up their desks and ink stands, and paid to have a message sent to the French Institute. It was a short message, and the Institute not far away, so the letter writer was puzzled that she did not bother to haggle over the price. He decided she was sending a letter to her lover. But what a curious meeting place she had chosen to name in that letter!

After sending her message, she went to the Souk of the Red Shoes to buy new slippers for all of Hamid's household. She did not know why she wished to do this, except that she felt grateful to them. Their squabbles had been petty, their words, even when intended to wound, harmless. They were good people, they had often tried to be kind to her. And she may not have much time left in which she could show this recognition, at least, of the kindness she would not accept. She did not buy new leather slippers for Hamid. She had a different gift in mind for him.

And then what? Where would she go after her appointment in two days time? Back to Istanbul? To her family? None of those places were possible for her anymore, it was as if they had ceased to exist. Well, whatever it was to be for her, it was already written. But she would miss the soothing sound of the fountain in Hamid's courtyard. She would even miss Hamid's stern, sorrowful face.

After the red shoes had been wrapped and delivery promised that very afternoon, Atiyah went to the last of her errands, to meet Marguerite in the coffee house in Roumelieh Square, near the slave market. Only foreigners went to this coffee house, and the untouchables of the city, the lowest class of men who dressed in dirty, ragged trousers and coarse blue tunics, and women who were so poor they had no pride and did not bother to veil their faces. No one from Hamid's household would see her here.

Inside, the air smelled of sweat, tobacco, dust, and fried chickpeas. There were no cooling water jugs placed in the windows and the heat was stifling. Atiyah paused in the doorway till her searching eyes found Marguerite. The French woman was dressed in the black robe of the Egyptian woman and a white veil rested on the table in front of her. She was with a man Atiyah did not know.

The two woman exchanged courteous but wary greetings. Much had happened since they had last met. They had been friends once, but the changes, the death, and the suspicion and confusion, were a river that had swept away their commonality.

"Look, Atiyah. I still wear the charm you gave me." Marguerite pulled the silver chain and crocodile from the folds of her robe.

Atiyah pushed aside her veil and smiled. She took the amulet and polished it a little with her fingers, then said, "Luck is a funny thing. Just when you think it has run out, it turns good. I think this charm is good for you."

She sat down and a silent but grinning servant brought them waterpipes and small cups of coffee. The smoke was so thick Marguerite had trouble reading the expression in Atiyah's eyes.

"This is where the young women of the city come to meet their lovers," Atiyah said. "The waiter is confused by us. But he will leave us in peace."

"My husband," Marguerite said, tilting her head towards Michel.

Atiyah studied his face with great interest. "Does he beat you?" she asked Marguerite.

"No, he certainly does not."

"That is good. My husband, Ibrahim, he did not beat me either."

"I am sorry about your husband," Michel said.

"It was written," said Atiyah. "But you, too, are in danger. I think it is time for you to leave Cairo. Madame Beaucaire's husband, the rug buyer, has been taken to jail. The imam order it."

"For what reason?" asked Marguerite.

"Because he is French. He is not wanted here anymore. The other Franks are moving into the Citadel or the Institute."

Marguerite and Michel exchanged glances.

"We cannot leave just yet, nor can we move back into the Institute, much as we would like," Michel said.

"They think I poisoned Ibrahim," Marguerite said. "They think that I tried to poison Bonaparte and Ibrahim drank the poison by mistake."

"That is what they are saying," Atiyah agreed.

"It is not true."

Atiyah took one of Marguerite's hands. "The henna has faded," she said. "Your hands are so white, so pale. I think they are not the hands of a murderer. I think I know what has happened. It is not your fault. All the same, you should leave Cairo now."

"May we talk of Ibrahim's death?" Marguerite asked.

"What is there to say? He was a good man. Now he is dead. It was written."

Atiyah's fatalism worried Marguerite. The girl was neither religious nor complacent by nature. She had changed. Something was wrong. Something more than death.

"It matters greatly," said Michel. "We may hang. Tell me about The Woman Carried Away."

A flicker of emotion momentarily darkened Atiyah's blue eyes. Then: "An old wive's tale. It does not exist," she protested vehemently. "Take home a mummy if it amuses you, but do not search after a mirage." She had her own plans for The Woman Carried Away. She would not let these Franks rob her of it. She would sell it to the highest bidder . . . she already knew who that was . . . and buy back her contract from Mother Halima, as Ibrahim had wished. She would no longer be the property of another or a runaway. She would be a free woman. She would do all that Ibrahim wished her to do. Make it right.

"Too many people believe in it and are searching for it for me to believe it does not exist," Michel insisted.

Atiyah put on the smile she had used when she was an alma. These two must not interfere.

"In three days' time the period of mourning for Ibrahim will be over and Hamid will seek vengeance against those who have killed him. But in two days' time, it will be ended. I will leave. You should leave, too."

Atiyah rose to leave.

"You must pay the waiter," she told Michel. "I have no more money."

Outside, Hamid, who had followed Atiyah from souk to letter writer to coffee house, frowned and pulled on his beard, waiting for her to pass by and then precede him through the thick crowd. His pause allowed him to see who left the coffee house immediately after Atiyah. The French woman and her husband.

The French at the Institute said that this couple had tried to poison Bonaparte, and Ibrahim had died instead. He had not believed it, but Atiyah had led him to the truth. He did not believe in coincidence.

It would be hard enough to take the man's life. Must the woman die too?

19

He should leave now. But he could not.

He could not kill the woman and she said she would die if he abandoned her. He believed her. He felt he would die without her.

The King of Cappadocia has a daughter. Where had he first heard that? In a tavern, where the sailors wink over their cups? The words had meant nothing. And then Juba had come to Cappadocia, and been taken prisoner by that king's daughter. Her white, tender woman's arms were stronger than Caesar's chains.

There was a woman named Selene, whom he had once loved. But not like this. She was in a distant place and his heart did not remember her. His years with her were like so much dust gathered on a shelf. Wiped away with one touch of Glaphyra's hand.

People cannot change, Selene had told him once. We are like boats on the Nile, with the wind either carrying us in one direction or the currents carrying us in the other. Destiny takes us where it will. She had always sounded pleased as she said this. It was, Juba thought, because losers blame their failures on destiny, just as winners take victory as their full due. He was neither rudderless nor sailless. He guided his own course. And this past month he had realized what that course must now be. He would take Glaphyra as wife. He would divorce Selene.

Juba looked out his window to the harbor, to where his ship rocked gently in the swell. She sat low in the water, weighted with marble statues and bronze figures made by the finest artists in Athens.

Originally, he had intended to take that fine collection back to Mauretania, back to the palace he shared with Selene. But the king of Cappadocia was also an art lover and he had come to pay a visit. And the king of Cappadocia had a daughter.

Glaphyra, he knew now, was what he had been looking for these past years. She had been the source of the restlessness that made him sleepless, that made him turn away from Selene, that made him work harder and harder, publishing as often as possible, seeking fame. He had wanted Glaphyra, daughter of Archelaus, daughter-in-law of Herod of Judea, to know his name. He had been seeking her, wanting her love and admiration, and he hadn't even known of her existence.

Juba, dressed for his wedding, turned away from the window and from his memories. He parted the curtains of his chamber and walked down the jasmine-scented path to the little altar, where Glaphyra waited. It would be a small, private ceremony, as was suitable for a widow. He would place a gold ring on her finger, words would be said, documents signed, and his life would be changed. It seemed simple. But there would be a price.

His footsteps faltered as he thought of that price. A message had been sent to the Roman senate: he had divorced his wife, Selene, the message said. He was taking a new wife, Glaphyra of Cappadocia. A similar message had been sent to Selene. It had been brief and formal and cold. When he thought of Selene reading that message he was tempted to turn back, to return to his rooms, tell his slaves to pack, and leave, secretly and quickly.

He had promised her over and over he would never do what Antony had done to Cleopatra. And here he was, abandoning Selene and marrying another, leaving her with a small child to raise by herself, making her the cause of cheap and dirty jokes in the Roman forum. Just as Antony had done to her mother.

Could he do this? If he did not, he would never again hold Glaphyra close to his breast. Glaphyra made life new. Life with Selene was stale and filled with a shared bitterness for all they had suffered, both together and separately. Glaphyra was like the dawn, new and unused, a goddess who loves and is loved, gives birth and yet remains virginal. Young.

Juba's steps down the cobbled garden path were slow but determined. He studied each cobble his feet touched, and each one seemed a milestone, an important marker into the future he desired.

At the end of the path, Glaphyra greeted him. She wore white linen and her hair was arranged in the six braids that brides wore only on the wedding day. A girdle with a knot of Hercules was about her waist. Later, Juba would undo that knot and the girdle and gown would fall.

He wanted Glaphyra more than he feared Selene's curses. He would have her. He pushed away the memory of what had been said by the Romans about Selene's mother, Cleopatra. That she was a witch. That she cast spells that imprisoned men and stole their souls.

Juba walked forward to his new bride. He would be wed before Selene even heard about it. There was nothing she could do.

20

It was Saturday; it was twilight. Dr. Morello knew he would not be disturbed. The Egyptians began days at sunset of the day before, not at sunrise, so for them it was already Sunday. And Sunday, for them, because it was the Christian holy day, was an accursed day filled with bad luck and evil jinn. It was not a day to go wandering through old tombs as Dr. Morello intended to do.

The Tombs of the Khalifas, north of the Citadel where the French soldiery still drilled and paraded—though surely, Morello thought, they knew their cause was lost—rose up from the sandy expanse of desert on the east side of the Nile, just at the foot of the Mokattam Hills. The sun, in a burst of dying glory, cast long shadows behind the Tombs onto the barren hillside. The shadows of the spires and minarets of the ancient Muslim cemetery twisted and whirled into fantastic shapes.

Slowly but perceptively the shadows disappeared as night fell and the world became a place of blackness pierced by lantern beams and noises. Morello, a man neither easily impressed nor easily frightened, continued on his way.

He wished he had the book with him. The passage had been memorized, but the book itself had become like a talisman, guiding, reassuring, promising. This cemetery had been new when the book was written but the author, a visionary who interpreted the future as surely as he tracked the past, had thought to include it in the list of treasures anyway. *The legend states that the tomb of the pharaoh is hidden beneath the tallest minaret,* the book said. *This earlier tomb has been here since history was recorded, but none sought it, because it was invisible to the eye.*

Ptahshepses had succeeded. The tomb of Shepseskaf was unmarked, unknown. The name of Shepseskaf was dead to history. Not even the legend makers knew of him.

All the markings of the tomb had disappeared under centuries of sand. It was, Morello reflected, probably a mastaba-style tomb, built of mud brick that, vulnerable to cutting sandstorm and dispersing wind, had been eroded away till nothing was left but the underground burial vault. And then, the Muslims, unsuspecting of the buried secret, had built over it.

For a second, Morello felt glee, the kind of glee he had felt in childhood when he saw a silk-stockinged aristocrat slip into the slimy mire of a Parisian spring street, or in a London park when a haughty, blue-blooded rider fell from his costly horse. Lo, how the mighty are fallen. Fallen, too, was this nameless king who, greedy with the greed of the rich, had sought wealth in death as well as life. His tomb had disappeared from human sight; he had disappeared from history. The boy's glee disappeared and was replaced by the man's calmer, crueler satisfaction.

Morello stopped at the narrow marble steps of the first minaret and struck flint to tinder, lighting the small brass oil lamp he carried. It did not matter if the light was seen from any of the Cairo houses at his back. At dawn perhaps a servant would go to his master, blubbering that the jinn had been walking the old graveyard again. Superstition was useful. He himself was certain that nothing walked or bothered the earth except miserable man. When his father had died Morello had sat by the table he was laid upon for three days waiting for a final curse, a final blow. But death was the final equalizer, rendering all men helpless, hopeless, and finally, permanently, harmless.

Even the king whom ancient treasure seekers said lay buried here would be only dusty bones, empty eye sockets, an ashy hole where the heart once was, though his face be covered with gold, though his fingers be covered with emeralds and rubies. Morello felt warm with joy, thinking of the black nothingness that replaces power and defenselessness, wealth and poverty alike. This was the true joy of the treasure seeker: to stand over the tomb, or in rooms covered with black mourning clothes, and say "I have now what you so prized. It is mine."

Staying within the small circle of light from his lamp, Morello moved cautiously, stepping over rubble of mud brick and marble, kicking away the wild dogs who prowled, progressing to the heart of the Tomb of the Kaliphs where the tallest minaret poked up at the night sky. He reached its staircase, constructed with wide steps and sturdy walled railing so that the blind muezzin who had climbed it would not falter. No muezzin, blind or otherwise, had climbed these steps for centuries. Dust and sand filled all the corners, the stone under his hands was pitted and rough. Yet the stairs were strong, secure. He climbed them and soon was staring down at all the other tombs of the kaliphs. He had reached the tallest spot.

This was where he was to meet her. This was where he was to claim his two stolen treasures.

Morello sat on the sepulchre's railing and gazed out into the dark night. The lamps of Cairo shone from houses and terraces and the little boats that sailed the flooding Nile, bursting through the darkness like a child's wish, like earthbound stars.

A dog bayed, casting splinters of ancient sounds into the imperturbable, inky sky. From a distance, its mate bayed back. Morello, smiling, closed his eyes and imagined how this small spot of earth must have smelled and sounded thousands of years before, when the land was ruled by pharaohs, not Turks, and the fellaheen made sacrifices to a god of death which, he was certain, was the jackal-headed god.

Death should be a dog, lowly and scavenging, lonely, a night creature who feared men, like the wild dogs that prowled the cemeteries and souks of Cairo. And death, in his loneliness, would seek a mate of course, just as the dogs baying at the moon sought mates. A woman, a soft, gentle woman to stroke the forehead, to sing away the long nights, to leave her fragrance on the sheets. He'd had such a woman once. He would have her again. Like his first edition of Winckelmann's *History of the Art of Antiquity,* his Roman bronze vase, his gold ring once worn by Cesare Borgia, his glass vial filled with ashy moldings scraped from the stake where Joan had been burned, the woman was his. He would claim again his woman carried away.

The heat of the day was spent. Rising from the cold balustrade where he sat, Morello took one last look at the old cemetery. Slaves were buried here. They had called themselves kings, but slaves they had been, nonetheless. He now walked over them, alive and free, as far from death as those ashes beneath were from life.

Madame and Monsieur Verdier. Now there was a couple who might well spend time contemplating death. Refuge at his home in Giza had bought them only time, and not much of that. Eventually, Kleber would learn of their whereabouts. And Kleber, a stickler for detail and in a foul humor because of the predicament Bonaparte had left him in—to defend a huge city with a small, ill army, to take a land that was ably held by the Turks and assisted by the English—would not be inclined towards mercy. Assassination, even when it failed, was a capital offense. Too bad the guillotine never made it to Egypt. It was quicker and more merciful than death by hanging.

Sunday. Marguerite rolled in bed, eyes closed, remembering cups of thick hot chocolate, church bells, the smell of lilacs, the coolness of bed linens. Eyes still closed, she smiled despite the fear that gnawed, the certainty that even this small measure of peace would not last long. She could hear Saladin coming with the morning coffee, and she was not alone. These things counted. Someone once asked Talleyrand what he did during the Terror. The question was meant as an insult, for Talleyrand, like many others, had fled the country. But Talleyrand, beyond both insult and assault, had coolly replied, "I stayed alive, madame."

She had stayed alive. She and Michel together. If she had her say, she would stay alive for a much longer time. She did not feel ready to die, especially not on the gallows which, she had heard, was a harder way to die than by guillotine. Nor did she welcome death by bowstring or scimitar, which would be Hamid's choice.

"Michel!" she called, still not opening her eyes. She already knew what she would see. First, the mosquito netting which, no matter how fine, did not prevent new red bites from appearing each night. Then, the tiled floor, the elaborate mosaic walls, the turquoise handprint over the doors, the little green lizard that sunned on the windowsill, the carved wood grill over the window.

"Open your eyes. Wake up, Marguerite, I can't tell if you're dreaming or awake."

"Awake," she said, looking up at him. He was dressed and shaved, and there was a pleasant white smear of talcum behind his right ear.

"Michel, we must do something. I do not want to simply wait till Kleber sends soldiers for us or Sheik al Shackoui sends his own assassin in revenge."

"Agreed," said Michel. "Rest, today. Tonight, we will leave. We have been in more difficult situations and yet we are here, we are together." The last words were whispered, not out of sentiment but because Saladin appeared just then with the tray and Michel could not overcome a gnawing suspicion that the dragoman understood more of what was said than he indicated.

"For how long, this time?" Marguerite asked when Saladin had left.

"Marguerite, I promise I will never leave you again." As Michel said the words, he realized he meant them. The shock of his sincerity was no less stunning to himself than to Marguerite. He repeated the promise, tasting the words and their intent. He took her hands in his. "Believe in me. There will be no more Josettes."

Marguerite tilted her head to one side and studied him. Her unbrushed cloud of black hair fell over one eye and she pushed it aside, wanting to see him clearly, wanting to see beyond the skin, the practiced expression of his eyes, into his thoughts and heart. He seemed earnest. But he was a master of duplicity, she reminded herself.

"When we return, you will spend a week, a month at the longest, playing the devoted husband. Then you will catch some woman's eye, she will return your smile, you will come home late, then not at all. I know this tale too well, Michel. It is not an amusing one."

"I have changed, Marguerite."

"I dare not believe you," she said finally and with great sadness. "But today there are other more important considerations. Where are we to go? Perhaps we would be safer at the Institute, after all. Madame Beaucaire has probably already informed Kleber of her visit. It would look better if we went to him, rather than forcing him to come here."

"Perhaps. But since Morello has offered the shelter of his home, might he have other suggestions? He seems of a mind to provide assistance. I would appreciate the opportunity to speak with him." Michel relinquished her hands but kissed each on the palm first, leaving a small spot of warmth in the midst of their white coolness.

The opportunity arrived later that afternoon, when Morello appeared.

Michel and Marguerite had spent the day pacing and thinking and finding no answer to their situation. They had both fallen into a dark mood by twilight, when Saladin came and announced a visitor. Half expecting to see Kleber and an armed band of soldiery waiting to greet them, they descended to the main room of the villa, hand in hand and grim faced. Instead, it was the doctor.

"I have been a remiss host," he said jovially, coming forward to greet them. "I have left you alone too long, with no news. Come, sit with me and we will talk. Saladin, bring the pipe and coffee."

Michel and Marguerite, musing and surprised, followed him into the sheltered garden. Saladin brought pillows large as mattresses and arranged them in a three-rayed circle around the water pipe.

"You are well, I see. I am gratified, most gratified," Morello said, sitting on one of the pillows and busying himself with lighting the pipe. "I meant to come before, to see all was in order for you, all to your liking, but, well, things are not as they should be as the moment. Excuse my lapse, please."

"We are grateful for all you have done," said Marguerite, sitting on the pillow between Morello and Michel. "Do not think of doing more. We already have a debt greater than we can repay."

"Nothing, it is nothing," Morello insisted, but his eyes shone with pleasure. "It is a beautiful evening, is it not? It bodes well for the morrow. The vice of the orient," he said, offering the pipe first to Marguerite.

Marguerite accepted the mouthpiece, considered, then returned it to Morello. "Not tonight, thank you. We have too much that demands serious consideration. We fear that our location is known to Kleber, and so must consider where to go.''

Morello frowned. ''Kleber? I think not. I spoke with him just this afternoon. He said nothing of you. In fact, he is quite busy in Cairo, as you can well imagine. You are perfectly safe here.''

''But Madame Beaucaire was here.'' Michel said, frowning. ''Surely all the Institute must know by now.''

''Well, madame must have learned discretion. I assure you, no one else knows you are my guests.''

Uneasy silence. Beyond the garden, a tomcat wailed and a breeze shook the leaves over their heads. Michel and Marguerite looked at each other, at a loss. Their sense of danger had been so complete, so immediate, and now that danger seemed distant. Their silence was broken by the gurgling of the waterpipe as Morello put the mouthpiece between his lips and pulled deeply. He coughed once, then exhaled a cloud of pungent blue smoke.

''It will calm you,'' he promised, offering it again to Marguerite. ''Then we will talk. Then we will strategize.''

The fair, warm night seemed like a reprieve. A thousand stars shone overhead and the air smelled of acacia blossoms. Marguerite, longing for an hour of escape, accepted the pipe, then passed it to her husband. Michel, new to this rite, coughed violently the first time, almost turning the pipe over. Morello smiled and reassured Michel. ''It is like deflowering a virgin. Difficult at first but more pleasant with practice. Try again.''

They passed the pipe for some minutes without speaking, and the heat of the night took on the qualities of a familiar overcoat, heavy and warm and protecting. Stars began to explode overhead, showering them with silver light. Marguerite felt the acacia blossoms reach for her and surround her with fragrance. She felt at ease. Tension slipped away like a garment and she felt herself floating.

The pipe made its rounds again.

Morello exhaled blue smoke. "The Arabs," he began, "have made of this pipe an art form. They mix different herbs into the hashish to produce different results. There is a blend to make the smoker sing, one to make him dance, one that sharpens the intellect, one that causes dreams."

"Which have you brought us?" asked Michel, leaning back on his elbows but keeping his eyes on Morello.

"One to calm. I think you have had enough excitement, have you not?"

"Quite enough." Marguerite laughed.

"I have lived in the Orient many years," Morello continued. "It is where civilization began. It is as old as the world. Bonaparte is right about Europe. It is a molehill. But like Bonaparte, I must soon depart. My future is elsewhere."

Future. Marguerite mused over that word, wondering what it meant. When she had left Michel she had given up the future. She had sought the single day, a long row of them, like stitches on a knitting needle, to be worked then cast off. But Michel had said he loved her, he still wanted her, and now she must think again of the future. Was he part of it? She surrendered to the luxury of letting down her guard, of letting her feelings, dormant for so long, take root and grow. Just for this evening she would enjoy the pretence, let herself believe in him again.

Michel watched Marguerite, wondering what that strange smile meant, wondering what her thoughts were, wondering how he could again claim her.

Saladin came, took the pipe, changed the water which had grown murky and sour, and brought coffee for them.

Morello poured, and they let the embers of the pipe grow dark and cold. The pipe had done its work. They floated free and fragrant as the scent of acacia.

For a long time none of them spoke. They danced in

peaceful solitude among their silent thoughts and Michel wondered if he were awake or asleep.

"You have not seen much of Egypt. It is a shame." Morello finally said. "There is such beauty here. Such age. And you have been locked away from it. Most unfortunate."

"It has not been an ideal visit," Michel agreed.

Under the pipe's influence, Morello felt a sudden good will towards this unfortunate couple. "A shame," he repeated. "All you will never see. The daughters of the desert tattoo their hands. When they stroke you, you are touched by the sun and the moon. And there is an ancient stone idol in the valley that sings at sunset. This is a land of miracles."

Marguerite thought of Atiyah, who had once dyed her hands the color of frost-bitten marigolds. She remembered something Morello had said. When? How long had they been in this garden, bathed in starlight? Ah. He was leaving. Morello, like Bonaparte, was leaving this land of miracles. And what of them?

"Where do you go, when?" she asked. "May we go with you?"

Morello thought carefully before answering. How much could be revealed? Their part in this was accomplished, or soon would be. They had served their purpose. "Tomorrow," he said. "But we must make other plans for you. I meet my own fate in a manner different from yours. Dawn. The Tomb of the Kaliphs. Then, I will send for you. This house will be shut up. I will not return to it."

There was a sudden large explosion outside the garden. The night grew bright with a hundred falling stars, and the explosion repeated itself. Shouting. Running feet. Another explosion.

Michel jumped up, alarmed.

Morello laughed. "Calm yourself, my friend. You do not know what night this is. *Saleeb*. The river is at its greatest height. It will rise no more. The people celebrate with fireworks. Listen.''

The Munadee, who had passed this house each day, passed again, but his voice was jubilant, not heavy with promises of doom. It crackled with triumph like the firecrackers as he shouted the news.

"What is he saying?" Marguerite asked, tilting her head to listen.

"The fortunate Nile of Egypt has taken leave of us in prosperity. In its increase, it has irrigated all the country," Morello translated. Saladin appeared and Morello threw him a bag of coins. "For the Munadee," he said. "And bring us wine. We must celebrate."

"The danger is over," Marguerite said, wondering.

"It is, indeed. I knew this night would bring good news, for it followed good news of the day." Morello smiled benevolently upon them.

21

Selene, haunted by all that no longer was, by people who were no longer with her, fled Alexandria, the ancestral city which was no longer hers.

On a hired barge, she drifted up the Nile, past Babylon where the Roman legions camped, past the sky-piercing pyramids at Memphis and the Sphinx crouched in the sand, past the town of Momenphis where Hathor, now called Aphrodite, was worshipped, past groves of olive trees and beanfields, past vineyards and marshes, past Labyrinthe and Arsinoe, City of Crocodiles where the sacred crocodile, Souchos, was fed by the priests, past Herakles and the City of Dogs where Anubis was worshipped, past Lycos and Ptolemais and Abydos, place of the singing statue.

The journey was not a gentle one. The river which carried her past her own forgotten histories was rough and frothy with inundation. She sat, white-knuckled, holding to the sides of her chair which was lashed to the floor but still rocked dangerously back and forth. The barge was not as large as she would have liked. But a Roman matron would not have hired a boat as Cleopatra and her daughter would: huge, a Sphinx-headed flat vessel rowed by dozens of slaves, its masts gilded with silver and its sails embroidered in green, with singing girls stationed fore and aft.

This one was badly in need of new paint and the wood smelled of rot. The hired rowers were insolent and rude.

So she sat, stiff and lovely as a carved statue, her face its own death mask, only the eyes moving, taking in the muddy water, the inundated villages, the occasional wharves and docks where bystanders gawked and waved at the rich Roman. The land glided by, her own past glided by, and the graceful, swaying reeds made her think of Juba, whom she longed for greatly. She fell asleep each night thinking of the joy in his eyes as she handed him the stela, the token of her love for him, a love he could never relinquish.

At Denderah Selene stepped tentatively onto ground once again. She picked up a handful of sand and let it slip through her fingers. The wind carried it away so that her hand held emptiness, but she refused to read this as prophecy.

She retraced her mother's footsteps to the temple they had visited together forty years before, to the sanctuary of tall pylons adorned with the face of Hathor, the pylons supporting a roof painted with the designs of the heavens themselves.

Cleopatra, celebrating Antony's return to her, had dedicated this temple to Hathor, goddess of love, and Hathor's calm gaze now topped the stone forest of towering columns.

Selene's arrival whipped the hot, summer's-end day into a frenzy. Outside the temple grounds tents were unrolled, stacks drove deeply into the thin soil. Slaves laid rugs, built cooking fires, fetched water and fresh dates.

The priests of the temple stood in the columned porch and watched. They had seen this before, countless times. The temple was a favorite with women. They came to pray for the getting of children, for the return of wandering husbands, to find missing rings and lift household curses.

They looked at Selene and knew without guessing what her prayers were for.

Selene stared shyly back at the priests and awaited a propitious moment for entering the temple.

The priests would have to be well bribed. They would not easily relinquish the stela. She would bargain and cajole, even reveal herself as Cleopatra's daughter, if necessary.

At sunset, after a rest, something like joy stirred her. She had dreamed of Juba, and when she woke her maids were singing a love song. The twilight brought a gentle, reviving coolness. She rose from her pillowed, curtained bed in the rich, cloth-of-silver tent, and dressed in simple white linen. She walked across the slight expanse of sand separating her from the temple, her footsteps making small, delicate marks next to the deeper, swirling wake of the crocodile.

The priests, who had been impassive, now watched in alarm. They held up their palms and blocked her path.

"This temple is sacred to Hathor," they said in unison.

They glared at the crocodile and Selene understood. The priests followed the old rites of Denderah. To them, the crocodile was unholy, part of the evil of the world. She would not be allowed in the temple, because of the leashed crocodile at her side.

"I am the daughter of Cleopatra, Queen of Egypt," Selene protested, fear rising in her and making her incautious.

They did not believe her. She saw it in their closed, cruel faces. Why should they? Selene Cleopatra had been a child when Egypt last saw her, so in the minds of the Egyptians she was still a child. This woman standing before them hid gray hair under her wig. She was middle-aged, growing old. She was a Roman matron, nothing more.

"It does not matter if you are the daughter of Hathor herself," the oldest priest said, smirking. "You are not allowed inside as long as you are tainted by . . . that.'' He pointed with a long, bony finger.

Selene looked down at the crocodile at her side. Its large, triangular snout rested in the sand, its eyes rolled loosely in their sockets, like marbles. When she looked back up, the priests had turned their backs on her and were returning to the shade of the temple.

She had not been so humiliated since Caesar's Egyptian triumph, when she had walked behind the dirtied effigy of her dead mother. She felt cold, despite the remnant of heat that still rose from the ground. She felt small, despite the fact that her Greek lineage made her tower over those small, smirking priests who now, she saw, were talking and laughing. They pointed at her, and the laughter echoed from column to column.

Blood pounded in her ears. Defeated, she returned to the silken, carpeted tent her servants had erected in the sand and hid behind thick curtains.

22

Marguerite dreamed of a hand holding a coffee cup, reaching over the expanse of white tablecloth littered with crumbs, grains of rice, fruit peelings and sauce stains. Another hand reaches out and accepts it. Bonaparte, long-haired, sullen-faced, lifts his ungloved hand. The executioner lifts the blade. No, she says in the dream, the guillotine is taken away. Desert climates do not suit women, Bonaparte says. His hand falls, the blade drops. A hand, holding a coffee cup, again reaches over the expanse of white tablecloth. The hand is sunburned, but between the fingers, where the sun does not reach, the skin is very white. Another hand reaches out to accept the coffee cup. This hand is darker, the fingers both longer and stronger. It is Ibrahim's hand.

She awoke in a cold sweat, the dream fresh in her mind. Even as the dream slipped away into the hot, dusty night, she struggled to recall each detail of it. In the dream, she saw what she had not seen before. She had poured the coffee. But someone else had passed the cup to Ibrahim. There had been a distraction. Someone had had a choking fit. Ah, yes, a moth had flown into Kleber's coffee. When she had looked back at the table, the coffee cup was in Ibrahim's hand. Almost. She had seen the hand passing the cup. The hand of the true assassin.

Fully awake now, she sat up. It was still dark, but there was a stillness to the air that indicated dawn was not far off. She was in the garden, on the mattress Saladin had arranged. Michel was still asleep. Morello was gone.

She shook Michel awake, tenderly brushing back the hair from his eyes, and letting her hand linger on his cheek.

"Marguerite?" muttered Michel, struggling to sit up. "My head is like a piece of wood."

"From the hashish," she said. "Morello is gone. And I have another piece for your puzzle. The one you knew was missing. It will not reassure you. We have been most cleverly used. When coffee was passed around and Kleber choked on that moth, everyone at our table turned to the commotion. But I was sitting at a right angle to Kleber. I had only to turn my head, not my entire body. And as I watched Kleber, I saw a hand reach over for Bonaparte's coffee cup, and pass it to Ibrahim. The same hand that passed coffee to us last night, here, in the garden."

"Morello."

"Our benefactor."

A rooster crowed as Michel, as awake now as Marguerite, ran his hands through his sleep-tousled hair and shook his head vigorously, trying to get rid of the cobwebs.

"Our safety was never his concern. Shifting of blame was his intention," Marguerite whispered. "Morello knew that Bonaparte would not drink his coffee. He, as the general's doctor, had forbidden coffee for Bonaparte's illness. And he knew that Bonaparte's rejected cup would be given to Ibrahim. He had seen Hamid do this other times, at other dinners. He knew Bonaparte would not drink from that cup, but Ibrahim would."

They rose stiffly to their feet. The village outside the walled garden started to come to life. Marguerite could hear children crying, fathers shouting, sheep bleating.

"But why?" she asked, smoothing back her hair and frowning.

"It has to do with the stela. I'm certain. My memory of last night is shaky. Did he not say that today he is leaving Cairo?"

"He had a meeting at the Tomb of the Kaliphs, and then . . ."

"Dress quickly," ordered Michel. "We have an important appointment to keep. It will be our first step back to Paris, to home."

"Home. What a lovely thought."

Home. It would never feel the same to him, now that the Galatian woman had come. There had once been peace here, in this quiet, paved courtyard. Now his home was filled with suspicion and anger.

He did not know if he was pleased that he had followed Atiyah or if he regretted it. Because now he must do something. The time of waiting, of mourning, was over.

This morning, Ibrahim's death would be avenged.

Hamid dressed quickly, not even waiting for the first true light of day, when grey dissolves and colors appear. The feel of the dagger between shirt and skin was unwelcome but necessary. He was glad he would not have many such mornings in this life.

It was not yet the time when a red thread can be told against a black one, when Marguerite and Michel arrived at the river. The ferryman was asleep in his little hut, but they woke him. Marguerite tried to give him a bag of coins but he would not take it. The man screamed and pushed them away.

"What is he saying?" Michel asked.

"The water is dangerous. He will not take us today. At least, I think that is what he is saying."

Michel searched his pocket and found more coins. He poured them into the man's unwilling hands and pointed towards the river, towards Cairo. The ferryman made the sign against the evil eye, sighed, and accepted the money.

Halfway across, he lunged at a rat which had fallen asleep under a torn sail. Expertly, he caught the rat and tossed it into the brown water. The rat sank immediately, carried down by the strong currents of the flood. Strange, Marguerite thought, to drown in the desert.

Cairo was pink and cool with the first light of dawn when they arrived. The city was strangely quiet. They hurried, running through cobbled streets and dusty lanes, to the Tombs of the Kaliphs. Coming from the other direction, hidden from their sight, was Atiyah, rushing to the same appointment. She moved strangely, angles not human jutting from beneath her robe as she struggled with the weight of the stela. Hamid, following, had to force himself to go slowly, to not catch up with her.

But Morello arrived first at the Tombs of the Kaliphas. He climbed the steps of the tallest minaret and awaited the woman and the gift she was bringing him. Soon, both would be his again. He would be complete. He would keep them securely, this time, behind locked doors in private rooms only he would enter. This morning, his final morning in Cairo, he wished that he had a home, a place to take this woman, a place that would be clearly marked, clearly fenced, clearly protected. He would have hounds guarding the grounds, as the English lords did, and eunuchs guarding the house, as the Turks did, and the locks would be big, complex, unbreakable. He would keep, once and for all, all that was his. And the woman.

23

While she hid in her tent, slaves took the crocodile to the river and bathed it. Selene heard the gnashing of the reptile's teeth. The animal was Juba's gift to her. Was this sacrifice possible?

It frightened her that she had forgotten so much of her own country. The simplest, youngest child of the most backward family of Egypt would have known better than to bring the crocodile here. Yet she had forgotten. Years of exile had robbed her of so much she had once known. That had been part of Caesar's plan, Caesar's punishment. To make her a stranger in her own country, an ignorant visitor in the land she should have ruled.

Juba had understood this. She had wanted to make this journey years ago and he had said no, they would travel only to new lands, now. New lands. He was discovering new lands, the future, and she tossed and turned in a stifling tent, in the past. It had been a mistake to come here. She had been humiliated. For what? To fetch some dusty bit of sculpture for her beloved?

She would have the stela. At any cost. It was hers to take, she would not be denied it. When Juba returned to her the stela would be there, in his collection room, waiting for him. And when the rare visitor from Rome came to their distant mountain palace he would point to the new stela and boast of his wife's cunning and bravery.

She would make this sacrifice for Juba.

Her slaves built a platform of stone near the open portico of the temple. A dozen heads of Hathor, perched on top of tall columns, watched, bemused. Selene fed the reptile a bowl of wine doused with the same sleeping draught she had taken the night before.

They half led, half pulled the reptile up the three steps of the platform. Selene called to the priests, to witness.

24

Carefully, Atiyah threaded her way through the rubble of the ancient Tombs of the Kaliphs, stepping over low walls which had once stood high as ten men, balancing on broken steps that had once led to mausoleums as ornate as palaces.

There was no color in the City of the Dead. The sky overhead was greyish white with heat. The ancient cemetery was invading sand, cascading ochre bricks and mud walls. She moved through it, a black shadow, a fury of the night captured in the daylight. There were bodies underfoot. Bodies so old they had mixed their dust with the dust of the desert, but bodies nonetheless. He would not be alone for eternity. She would do him that last act of kindness. Solitary all his life, he would have companions in death at least.

He had chosen the tallest monument for their tryst. Atiyah followed the beckoning shadow of his black hat to an ancient flight of stairs so thick with rubble she had to carefully place her foot in the middle of each step in the small, clear spots where her feet could gain purchase. She moved slowly, struggling to keep her balance. Her arm ached from the weight of The Woman Carried Away.

Overhead, he leaned over a broken stone parapet, smiling. She climbed towards him.

The new, rising sun was at her back, so that a halo seemed to shine around her head. She was veiled and her blue eyes over the veil were unreadable.

She had come back to him. For him. She was breathing quickly and shallowly, tired from the weight of the burden she carried.

She climbed the stairs slowly. Morello thought he would go down and help her, but then thought, No, let her come to me. Time seemed to slow as he watched the way her knees stirred under her dress as she climbed, the gentle arch of her cradling arms.

Atiyah tried to still all her thoughts as she climbed the steps, one by one. There was darkness in her, but a little of the luminous morning remained, too, a corner near her heart where the air was cool and sweet, where the master of the house looked at her thoughtfully, with concern in his kind eyes. Hamid, catching her at the courtyard gate, had asked her not to leave the house. Asked her in the gentle voice he had once used with Ibrahim, not the voice he saved for worthless, silly women.

And then Hamid had said something strange. "Moses and Pharaoh are in thy being. Thou must seek these two adversaries in thyself." Savior and destroyer. Saint and devil. He had been reading the poets and perhaps quoted them carelessly, but his words gave conviction to her own thoughts. She knew what she must do. For Ibrahim and Hamid, both.

At the last step, the Frank extended his long, white hand to help her over the threshold. His head and shoulders appeared over a crumbling wall. His eyes greeted her, then moved greedily to the angular, foreign juttings under the black linen covering. The stela was cradled against her chest, held heavily by the right hand and arm. She let him take her left hand. Her fingers were cold.

"You are late," he said.

"No. I am on time. You were a little early," she countered.

"Have you brought it?"

"It is here." Setting her foot firmly on the last step, she brought the package from under her black robe and presented it to him.

The Frank gave her hand a quick kiss—he did not notice how she flinched away from his touch—then tore the wrappings off the stela.

"Almost there." Michel, four steps ahead of her, turned and extended his hand. "Be brave one more hour, Marguerite."

Marguerite stooped to pick up a handful of loose stones. Those she loosened at an orange, mangy dog that had been sniffing at her heels and hem and showing occasional flashes of teeth.

"Don't bother with him," Michel said. "He is no real threat. They say dogs never go mad in this country."

"But women do. I am verging on it, Michel. I feel it."

"It is only the hashish. I will break you of that habit in Paris. Hurry."

Cairo was behind them, ahead of them was the City of the Dead, the ancient place filled with ancient tombs, the silent place where secret lovers met, the shadowed place where profane and unwitnessed accords were made by those who fled the light. It was a place for the reckless, the desperate.

Tripping over fallen monuments, the past spread at their feet like last year's leaves, they entered the place known as the Tombs of the Kaliphs, a place where many, many centuries before a pharaoh had been buried in an unmarked tomb, where Shepseskaf's dust had merged with the dust of the desert.

In the shadows of the tombs there was a dank coolness

that made Marguerite shiver as they hurried through the cemetery.

Behind them, unseen, Hamid also quickened his pace, following the Frankish man and woman responsible for Ibrahim's death.

Hamid had a sudden, overwhelming urge to know in advance, now, even as he ran towards it, the ending of this day. He was weary from heat, from worry, from having lost both Ibrahim who was murdered and now Atiyah, who rushed away from him, from the familiar, towards the unknown.

He was tempted to turn around and go back home, back to his quiet courtyard, his contemplations, his peace.

Think of the poet, he ordered himself. One of the paradoxes. *Thy thought is about the past* . . . Ibrahim . . . *and the future* . . . Atiyah. . . . *When it gets rid of these two, the difficulty will be solved.* Get rid of the past and the future.

The present is burning sun overhead, sand under my feet, solitude, following a woman's footsteps. I move through this present and it moves with me, faithful and close as my own soul. The present is not a bridge to cross from here to there, not a border guarded by sentries; it is eternal, a chamber separate from the past, the future. It is self-complete and unlimitable.

But his heart grew heavier as he realized the end of the journey these three, Atiyah first and then the Frank woman and her husband, led him to. The crumbling tombs rose from the dust of the old cemetery. A pack of mangy, starving dogs pattered through the narrow alleys of the city of the dead, hunting rats. Even the sun seemed evil in this place. Hamid made the sign to protect himself from the evil eye and continued. He would no longer bother to hide himself from view. It no longer mattered. The pen had written.

———

"He is there," Michel said, stopping before a tall minaret.

"Where?"

"Look up. The top of that tomb. Both of them are there." Past the white, crumbling wall, where blue sky met earthly decay, Marguerite saw the black-veiled form of a woman. Next to her was a taller form, male, wearing the European-style hat that made him even taller while it also partially hid his face. The two forms stood for a moment, looking at each other. Then, the man took a swaddled package from the woman's arms, and the two bent down together, to the ground.

"The stela. She has the stela," Michel said. They were running now, covering the last yards between themselves and the two other figures, running quickly enough that they did not hear the gravely sound of the other, Hamid, also running to catch up.

Beyond them, above them, Dr. Morello knelt on the roof of the tomb and ran his fingers possessively over the cool, white stone of the stela, tracing the sweet curve of Hathor's thighs, the surprised oval of her open mouth. So many people wanted her. And now he had her. He alone.

"It is beautiful," he said to the woman at his side.

Atiyah shrugged her shoulders. "No. It is merely old and rare. They are not the same thing."

He looked up. Her voice was cold and hard, all the sweetness had fled it.

"It is not as beautiful as my Ibrahim was," Atiyah said. Her hands were folded insider her robe. She moved closer to him.

25

Selene lifted her arm. Her robe fell away, revealing whiteness down to her elbow. The polished blade reflected dawn as she plunged the knife down, into the thick skin covering the reptile, into its four-chambered heart. The animal's tail thrashed, then was still. Rich, thick blood dribbled onto the pale sand.

For a moment, Selene felt the worst fear she had ever known, worse than the first time she stared into the snake pit, worse than the time she stood next to her mother and saw her father's dead body on the ground, worse than the time she had seen the black asp white against her mother's arm. She had killed something holy. She had killed Juba's gift.

The priests watched and waited. Hathor's priests. Selene forced her arms to her sides, forced her eyes open. This act restored reason. The furious fear spun around her like a desert devil and then flew away, into nothingness.

She had killed what was abominable to Hathor, offered it up to the goddess, for her husband's sake. A sacrifice for the beloved.

26

A sacrifice for the beloved.

As Morello crouched triumphantly over the stela, Atiyah's arm rose. Her robe fell away, revealing whitness to the elbow, and the dagger gleamed in the early morning sun.

"No!" shrieked Marguerite, black-veiled and standing now at the base of the stairs. She saw only the dagger, not the arm which supported it, not its target. Michel caught Marguerite's arm and stopped her from running up the crumbling steps, stopped her from going to Atiyah.

Hamid, out of breath from running, gasped. Above them in the minaret, a long, sharp knife glinted once in the bright light and then was buried into flesh, into the four-chambered heart.

Morello sighed once as he saw red blood, his, flood over the stone, his blood now an uncontained river. He had the stela. She had brought it to him. And he had the woman. But he could not hold onto them. They were slipping away. . . .

A woman's screams rent the air. It was Atiyah, mourning now, for Ibrahim.

27

S elene had the stela. It was hers. The sacrifice had been accepted.

But at sunset the message came to her that her husband, Juba, had put her aside. He had taken a new wife. He would not be coming back to her. She was dead to him. Her screams filled the night.

The Woman Carried Away stared up at her unpityingly.

28

The Woman Carried Away stared up at them unpityingly. Marguerite and Michel, Hamid and Atiyah,
stood over the fallen stela and Morello, watching
helplessly as life fled him. Morello's face was already grey
as stone, he was turning to stone, hard and unchangeable.

Atiyah's face was distorted with grief. Her hand still held
the dagger, but she had stopped screaming.

"He killed Ibrahim," she said to Marguerite. "He killed
Ibrahim," she said, turning to Hamid. "Now, it is done."

Hamid took the knife from her and wiped it in sand to
clean it. He put it in his robe.

"This was for me to do," he said to the Galatian. And as
he said it, he realized he had meant to kill Marguerite and
Michel Verdier, and he would have shed innocent blood.

"No," Atiyah said. "It was for me to do. And this thing is
why Ibrahim died." She kicked the stela with her foot. Her
voice was heavy with scorn.

It was a long while before Michel could speak. He
looked from Atiyah to Morello, who was wide-eyed but unmoving already dead, lying in a red puddle.

"Now what?" Michel finally asked. And even as he
spoke, he knelt to admire the stela. It was eerily appealing,
this ancient carving of a woman confronting a jackal-faced
monster. He touched the goddess's slender stone thighs,

admiring the lines, the clarity of the chiseled emotion, still
readable after so many centuries. It existed. It was not
mere legend. Many people wanted it. And here it was,
before him, lying in sand and blood.

Atiyah read his expression.

"It is mine," she said. "It will pay an old debt, one that
Ibrahim tried to pay for me."

"No," said Hamid, coming to his senses. "It is cursed.
Leave it here. I will pay your debt. Ibrahim left you for me
to care for. You have paid one debt. I will pay the other."

Hamid and Atiyah exchanged long looks, each for the
first time understanding the other. She smiled. "Uncle, if
that is your wish, I will obey." He knew the meekness in
her voice was a pretence. But that no longer mattered. She
was Galatian. She was the strange woman, the bringer of
trouble. But she had avenged Ibrahim.

"Take it, if you want it," Hamid said to Michel, pointing
to the stela. "I will report this to the governor. You will be
cleared of all suspected crimes." He turned away and
Atiyah followed.

Michel and Marguerite watched them grow smaller and
smaller as they walked out of the Tombs of the Kaliphs, till
finally they were miniature figures on the horizon, one in
black, the other in striped robes.

Michel bent and lifted the stela onto his shoulder.

"Must we take it?" Marguerite asked. "Perhaps Hamid
is right. Perhaps it is cursed."

"This is not the time to grow superstitious," Michel
said. "Of course we will take it. It will restore us to Bonaparte's favor."

"Leave it, please," she pleaded, wringing her hands.
"Something else is going to happen. I feel it." But he already had hoisted the stela onto his shoulder and was making his way carefully down the crumbling steps of the
tomb.

"Tomorrow, I leave Egypt. I return to France, with you

and the stela,'' he insisted. Marguerite, ashen faced and frightened, followed.

At the river, they found the ferryman waiting for them. He complained bitterly in his strange language about the extra weight that the Frank carried, but he allowed them to bring it into the little boat. It is written, he said, making the sign against the evil eye and Marguerite, understanding that one phrase, nodded with resignation.

Halfway across the river, Marguerite's fear grew and took shape. The current was too strong. The boat couldn't navigate it. She clutched the side, rocking and trembling and waiting for what she knew now would happen. The boat struck a log. It overturned and the waters of the Nile closed over her head.

Her heavy black robes pulled her down into the current. She opened her eyes and saw murky opaque brown water, she opened her mouth to scream and bubbles formed but not words. Around and down the current carried her and she felt herself saying goodbye to all she had loved, all she would never hold again, to Michel and her mother's little porcelain shepherdess, to the dancer's hand light on her waist, guiding her through the steps of the dance.

Then, there was pressure on her neck, her last breath was caught off as she was pulled, head snapping back, up and up.

Michel had caught her by the heavy chain she wore, with its crocodile amulet. He was pulling her back to the surface, to life. She gasped, drowning in the air as Michel, clinging to the boat with one arm, clasped her in the other.

He had let the stela find its way to the muddy river bottom. He had saved Marguerite instead. It is written. The choice is made. What is stone, compared to Marguerite's shy smile and knowing eyes? No other woman, not even the stone woman, The Woman Carried Away, would come between them again.

29

Her room at the Institute was just as she had left it. Her slippers were by the bed, her books on the shelf, her gowns hanging on the dressing room hooks. A layer of desert dust covered the book on her little brass night table. A green lizard scurried up the window shutter. It felt like homecoming.

Of course, aside from her personal collection of memorable artifacts and clothing that constitute private possession, much had changed in the time she had been away.

Bonaparte, as far as the Egyptian army knew, was somewhere on the turquoise sea, on his way to France. Near Sardinia, about now, Kleber mused. Kleber, Commander of the Army of the Orient, was angrier than ever. He had had time to study the instructions Bonaparte had left behind for him. They called for the establishment of permanent army fortifications in Egypt, moving the capital from Cairo to Alexandria, building manufactories, hospitals, etc. etc etc. Might as well call for a bridge to the moon or to bring Alexander back from the dead.

The army was in rags and decimated from plague. There was no money with which to pay the remaining French soldiery and most of them were no longer of a mind to even salute a general, much less march and dig for him. Egypt was rebellious, England commanded the seas, and Turkey had an army of 80,000 marching closer, closer, closer.

Kleber put Bonaparte's written orders in a black portfolio at the bottom of a large pile of paper and concentrated his efforts in another area: finding money to pay the soldiers. So it was that when Sheik Hamid al Schackoui arrived late one afternoon to testify to the innocence of Monsieur and Madame Verdier in the recent poisoning at the Institute, the sheik found himself holding, instead of Kleber's hand in a grip of welcome, a new and quite large tax bill.

"This . . . this will ruin me!" Hamid exploded.

"Not quite," said Kleber, who unlike Bonaparte, was tall, teutonic and quite devoid of charm and all the reassuring, if insincere, qualities which encourage good will.

There were no more soirées or entertainments at the Institute. The French were too morose for such diversions and the sheiks were fuming over their tax bills. Kleber dined with a small circle of intimates and those evenings tended to be dominated by coarse and sarcastic jests made at the absent Bonaparte's expense.

Kleber took one act of vengeance that pleased him, one over which he chuckled each night when the wine was poured. Madame Foures was put aboard a ship and returned to France for a surprise reunion with her lover. Bonaparte, who had abandoned both army and mistress, would at least have to answer to the latter.

Kleber was neither happy nor unhappy at the return of Citizen and Citizeness Verdier, who meant nothing to him. But he was relieved to be spared the difficulties of a trial and execution of French citizenry at a time when the Egyptians were most happy to see their conquerors die.

"Morello, you say? All over an artifact?" he said, rubbing his chin. "Bonaparte's own physician. Well, well . . ." followed by a long silence in which the unspoken flitted all too obviously across Kleber's face: too bad the poison hadn't been intended for Bonaparte.

It was agreed that Marguerite could have her old room,

and Michel would share it, until they could arrange transport back to France.

And so, the day after the meeting at the Tombs of the Kaliphs, Marguerite lay in bed, sneezing and chilled from her fall in the river, but quite pleased. She was among the French again, no longer a suspected criminal and soon, soon, she would be on her way to Paris. And . . . Michel, in love again with his wife of ten years, had reverted to the customs of the early days of their marriage. He solicitously arranged shawls over her shoulders, read to her when she grew bored, fetched glasses of sweet tea from the kitchens, declared his undying devotion every hour on the hour.

In fact, such devotion stretched her credulity, but she began to believe that he had truly missed her, that she was important to him, that she mattered. There was a future before them. And futures require plans. Her first plan was this: she threw her arms around him, pulled him down beside her on the bed and said, "Give me a son, Michel. It is not too late." He happily complied to the best of his ability.

Her second plan was more complicated. Their passport back into the ranks of the highest Parisian society lay at the bottom of the Nile. Back at the Institute, safe for the time at least, Marguerite forgot the superstitions and foreboding that made her want to leave the stela behind at the Tombs of the Kaliphs. It was valuable. It could help them. Through a series of intermediaries, she found a group of small boys who dive into the Nile after coins during the festive opening of the canal dams which begins the Season of Sufficiency. The ferryman Michel had hired in Giza was located. And after several long and expensive days, the stela was brought back to the surface, and thence to the Institute, where Marguerite presented it to Michel, who had known nothing of this second plan. He accepted the stela with amazed wonder and, thus inspired, quickly reverted to the first plan, the getting of a son.

"Selene Cleopatra had a son," Marguerite said next day, still in bed, surrounded by frothing bed linen and piles of books. The stela leaned casually against one wall, late morning making seductive shadows in the curves of Hathor's legs and breasts. Curious about the artifact, Marguerite had accumulated all the histories of Egypt she could find in the Institute, and was devouring them, trying to trace the history of the stela.

"Her husband, Juba, divorced her after the son was born. And somewhere in that time, Selene Cleopatra traveled to Egypt, to the Temple of Denderah, to make a sacrifice for his return," she continued.

"Denderah," Michel repeated, putting his arms behind his head and staring up at the ornately carved and painted ceiling. "Perhaps it was a Ptolemaic temple. Perhaps the stela was there. Did the sacrifice work?"

"It would appear so. Within a year of his divorce and remarriage, Juba returned to Selene, and spent the rest of his life with her." She put that book down and picked up another.

"Juba was an art collector," she read. "When he died, he had a large portion of his collection sent to Rome, for public exhibition. But Isocrates said the Romans scorned the collection and dispersed it over the empire."

"I wonder where the stela was sent. And how it was returned to Egypt."

"Well, we have it now," Marguerite gloated.

30

The Dardenelles
October 31, 1799

Lord Elgin, Seventh Earl of the deeply indebted Scottish estate of Broomhall, was not feeling up to par. Never a strong traveler, this voyage had been excruciating, filled with delays and windless days, rollicking waves and a discourteous crew, subjecting his delicate constitution to stiflings and night starvations, nerves and the migraine. His stomach was off and his teeth felt loose, despite the boxes of candied citrus comfits he'd consumed. His evening clothes, still creased from weeks in the clothes' press, felt loose on his sorely afflicted frame.

Worse, he missed Broomhall already.

Mary suffered even worse pains, swollen as she was with her first pregnancy and thoroughly unaccustomed to travel even under the best circumstances, which these most certainly were not. And, being confined with the moaning, complaining Eggy for twenty-four hours a day, weeks at a time, had not enhanced her views of marriage. Pretty Pol looked positively greenish, and her expression was not as sweet as it had been a mere month before. There was a newly determined set to her mouth that Lord Elgin did not care for.

The Turks did not seem to notice. The twelve hundred sailors of the huge Sultan Selim stared at Mary as though they had never before seen an unveiled woman. Perhaps they hadn't. And the oily Captain Pasha, First Lord of the Turkish Admiralty, all but swooned at Mary's hem, so eager was he to kiss her white, trembling hand.

Lord Elgin, newly aboard the Sultan Selim, the largest vessel he'd ever seen, looked uneasily back at the tiny Phaeton, with her meagre thirty-eight guns, which had carried him and Mary to the Dardenelles. For the first time, he suspected that his mission would not be as easy as he had first assumed.

Prince Isaac Bey, resplendent in shimmering silk robes and chains of gold and pearls, interrupted Lord Elgin's dark thoughts with a gentle flick of his hand. Without warning, the Sultan's 132 guns fired a salute to the new English Ambassador to the great Turkish empire. Elgin jumped. Mary gave a little scream, which seemed to delight Isaac Bey. He chuckled, offered Mary his arm, a gesture he'd learned from an Englishman he'd hired as a secretary years before, and led the ambassador and his wife into dinner.

The admiral's cabin was cavernous and elegantly appointed, a palace afloat. It was as large as the largest drawing room of Broomhall and the many sofas were covered with yellow silk, the walls covered with weapons blazing with jewels. Elgin, dropping behind Prince Bey and Mary, discreetly ran a thumb over the edge of a ruby-incrusted sword. It was freshly sharpened. The mother-of-pearl handled pistols, he suspected, were loaded. His mood darkened one more degree.

Mary, appreciative of Prince Bey's gallantry, was smiling coquettishly though, and apparently enjoying herself. Isaac Bey told her the history of the twisting, fantastic candelabras decorating the table, for they were, according to Bey, older even than the English empire. Elgin cleared his throat with displeasure.

But enough of that, Isaac Bey smiled. They must be very, very hungry. With a grand gesture, he helped Mary down onto one of the cushions surrounding an immense carpet. As soon as she was seated, slaves began carrying in dishes: mutton and rice, stuffed figs, calves' heads, grilled fish with shaved coconut, roasted chickens plumped with raisins, almond cakes frosted with silver. The abundance of the Orient was spread before them on, Elgin noted, silver platters much thicker and heavier than those that adorned the royal tables of London.

The rich food and the oriental style of serving made Mary lightheaded. She smiled too often and too intensely at Isaac Bey. He returned her smiles gallantly, all the while thinking that English women had faces like horses, too long and too toothy.

Lord Elgin was not hungry.

The meal was long and very, very spicy. A dozen slaves stood at hand, ready to heap more of the disgusting food on his plate, should Elgin be unwise enough to finish the first serving. Mary could, without offending protocol, limit her meal to the appetizing sherbets and sweets and fruits she craved. But Elgin must partake of everything, from the roasted peacock, which tasted like greasy leather, to the glutinous fish stews, and the obscure, unfamiliar green things which would probably bind his bowels for days.

Isaac Bey smiled benignly as he cajoled Elgin to partake of one more helping of sheep's brains cooked with squid. Elgin pushed his plate away. The meal was finished.

Isaac Bey clapped his hands once, gently, and in a matter of seconds the table was cleared of its litter, and a coffee service of the finest Dresden china brought out.

Elgin's eyes narrowed. The ceremony was beginning. The presenting of the gifts. Soon, in just minutes, The Woman Carried Away would be in his hands. He cleared his throat again, trying to appear indifferent, trying to ignore the slaves and the baskets and chests they were lined up to present.

Issac Bey led Mary to one of the yellow sofas and encouraged her to put her legs up and recline, to rest. Good Edinburgh girl that she was, she rightly refused this improper suggestion and sat stiffly, both feet on the floor and back held straight and six inches away from the pillows, but still smiling in that unfamiliar, coquettish manner which increasingly irked her husband.

Elgin, pulling at his tightly studded collar, was finding it difficult to breathe.

Isaac Bey clapped and coffee was poured by one of the dozen slaves in attendance. Baskets and coffers were fetched. The first basket was handed directly to Mary, who accepted it with a gracious and dignified nod of the head, which was then followed by a very undignified squeal of delight as she unfolded from the basket a shawl embroidered with pearls.

About seventy guineas, Elgin estimated, blinking. This would be even more embarrassing than he had first feared. The most expensive item he had for this Pasha was a pearl-handled pistol, valued at about fifty guineas. But behind the embarrassment was pleasure that The Woman would soon be his.

Subsequent openings of lids revealed crystal vials of perfumes, bolts of silk, boxes of sweets gilded with silver and . . . worst of all . . . a scale model of the Sultan Selim in gold, with its guns and flags done up in diamonds and rubies.

Thousands of guineas, Elgin speculated silently. Absolutely thousands. What boasting. What showing off. Not at all English, these Turks.

The very last chest was presented to Elgin by Isaac Bey himself, not one of the slaves. It was heavy, Elgin could tell by the way it was carried. Quickly, Elgin used the little lever presented to him and pried the wood lid up. Stone, cold and white, glinted in the dark box. The Woman Carried Away. He tore the lid away and reached in. He lifted it into the light, smiling with delight.

His smile froze, then shortened, then disappeared completely. The frieze of stone had been newly restored with bright, garish colors, making its worth as an antiquity negligible. And the subject of the worn carving was not an ancient Egyptian goddess but some temple *houri,* a common prostitute, naked except for a belt around her waste and grinning in a lewd manner at a customer who still hung back. Pornography. Imitation Classical Roman. A tourist bauble, made last year. Elgin almost dropped it.

"It is not the stela you requested, unfortunately," Isaac Bey said, still smiling. "That one is not yet been found, but we will find it for you, be assured. Meanwhile, the Sublime Porte hopes you will accept this substitute . . ."

That was that. Elgin, white faced with disappointment, put the panel in its box and stood to deliver his memorized speech, a speech of gratitude, of delight, of dedication to the goals of the Sublime Porte and eternal friendship between England and Turkey. The words felt like stones in his mouth.

If his speech was tainted with the too apparent disappointment Elgin felt, Isaac Bey pretended not to notice. He cared nothing for this unbeliever's feelings, and what right had he to demand this gift or that? Let him be content with what he has been given. All this search, all this trouble for an old stela that never really existed.

31

Paris
19 November 1802

A freets generally do not like to fly over large bodies of water. But this *afreet*, having been to Scotland and other remote parts of the world, thought it was time to pay a visit to Paris. There was a charming dinner party in progress there—dinner parties in Paris did tend to be charming—and it offered the opportunity to enjoy a reunion with several friends.

Too bad, though, the Grand Galerie of the Louvre was so badly lighted. It was positively dark in the long, cold hall, despite the dozens of candles placed on the table. The *afreet*, half-blinded, bumped into one of the dinner guests. She pulled the shawl tighter about her shoulders and shivered.

"Are you chilled again, Marguerite?" her husband asked with tender solicitude. Monsieur Verdier was the scandal of Paris. For almost two years now he had been absolutely faithful to his wife. He was no longer welcome in several clubs, the members of which were subjected to constant recriminations from their wives: "Why can't you be more like Monsieur Verdier? So devoted! Every night in his own wife's bed!" Of course there were rumors about his activities in Egypt. Perhaps they were true, perhaps he had overwhelmed himself with Oriental pleasures, with *hareems,* and had returned to France, and his wife, to recuperate.

"The air seems a little bracing," his wife complained of the Parisian afternoon. Marguerite was almost always chilled, since leaving Egypt. She had stayed away too long, Talleyrand had told her. Her blood had adapted itself to tropical climes.

But the way husband and wife smiled at each other would have precluded, to outsider's eyes at least, the chance of anything being wrong or causing discomfort. After exchanging extended and ardent gazes, Michel, thinking the tablecloth hid the gesture, reached over and patted his wife's belly, which was rounded as a melon, under her gauzy Empire shift.

Napoleon, who had seen the too *intime* gesture—was there anything in the world he did not see?—cleared his throat in displeasure. Josephine, who had also seen the tender gesture, averted her eyes. Well, one can't be victorious in everything.

She had won back her general. Maybe next year she would give him a son. And then again, maybe not. Don't think of it. She still remembered those appalling weeks of his return from Egypt, when he refused to see her at all. She had hammered at his door, weeping and prostrate, one ear pressed against the keyhole, listening, and knowing that his ear was pressed against the other side because she could hear his breathing. But he would not open. He finally agreed to see Eugene, the stepson he adored, and then, after listening to Eugene's pleas, he agreed to see his estranged wife.

Such timing. Almost a Greek comedy, though it had come close to becoming a tragedy. The day he agreed to an interview was the day her friend Marguerite, looking too thin, too wan, too brown for style, returned from Egypt. She brought a barbaric stone carving and an even stranger tale of it, saying simply at the end of the long afternoon, to the very confused Josephine, "Present him with this. As a token of your enduring love. He will forgive you. And then, tell him that Michel and Marguerite Verdier brought you this.''

Voilà. Napoleon and Josephine were reunited. Monsieur and Madame Verdier were restored to the good graces of the most powerful man in France, soon to be the most powerful man in the world. And Napoleon had, finally, his Woman Carried Away.

The *afreet* paused in front of the stela, which was, at this moment, leaning rather casually against the wall, next to a mummy cartonnage in such bad state of repair that the *afreet*, growing somewhat testy, tipped a bottle of wine from the table to the floor.

"How clumsy of me," said Baron Vivant Denon, wiping at the spill with a lace handkerchief. He smiled cherubically and contentedly, his red-cheeked, high-browed face rising from a froth of lace around his throat. He had reason to be content. He had just published his first volume of *Voyages in Upper and Lower Egypt* and was General Director of the Imperial Museums of the Louvre, thanks to his patron, Napoleon. It was a position from which a man might acquire great wealth, an interesting assortment of artworks for private enjoyment, and also expect to be invited to the best soirees in the capital. Life had not been so satisfying since Louis XVI, rest his soul, had sent him scouring Europe for diamonds for his young wife, Marie Antoinette.

Of course, there was the disappointment of the Egyptian campaign. The bloody English. When the French Army of Egypt surrendered, they'd also been required to turn over most of the artworks they had collected during their tenure in Egypt. Kleber was dead by then, assassinated by an Arab student who used a dagger, not the bowstring or poison. Kleber's successor, Jacques Menou, paunch-bellied and balding, already old at fifty-one, lost several battles and one-third of the already severely reduced French army before coming to the terms with the British.

The best of the artifacts, including the Rosetta Stone, were now in the possession of the English, a situation of which Napoleon did not like to be reminded. He would acquire them again, and with full apologies from the English, he had no doubt. Meanwhile, the few remaining specimens now temporarily lined the walls of the Grande Galeries for this evening's entertainment.

The Woman Carried Away seemed not so sublime, not so desirable, in the Parisian twilight filtering in through the windows of the gallery. But Alexander the Great had tried to acquire this stela and instead Napoleon had. Let history mark this moment. The First Consul, soon to be Emperor, heavier now, his dashing long hair shorn and pulled in thin strands over a high forehead, lifted his glass to the stela.

Too bad, though, the mummy sarcophagus was in such bad shape. Who was this dead king? They would never know. In fact, judging from the condition of the thing, it would soon have to be buried, or the cleaning lady would come in one morning and find nothing but a pile of dust.

The pile of dust was Shepseskaf, resting finally, next to his stela of Hathor, the Goddess of Love and Laughter. While joy may be invisible to the naked eye, the dusty atoms of Shepseskaf were spinning in joy. What are the centuries to the already dead? It was only yesterday that Ptahshepses lifted and kissed the royal foot, only yesterday since Ma'tcha' had unsealed Shepseskaf's tomb so that revenge could be achieved. And tomorrow? It is a dream sent from the Land of Silence.

"It is good to be home," said Marguerite suddenly. It was a statement she made often in company, to remind any who might have forgotten of her adventures in Egypt. "Travel, especially hazardous journeys, are best enjoyed in the memory, not the actual experience. But it is pleasant to look out at grey Paris rain and remember golden Egyptian sun."

"Tell me again of the night they tried to assassinate my dearest husband." Josephine, elbows on the table, eagerly leaned forward.

Napoleon cleared his throat. He did not enjoy this story. What man likes to learn that his private physician is a murderer? "I've told you over and over, it was nothing. I was in no real danger. Let us speak of other matters. That is the past. It is to the future we must look."

All this reminiscing about Egypt. It made him uncomfortable.

"To the future," Napoleon insisted.

"To the future," those at the table agreed.

So much good will quite bored the *afreet,* who decided this journey had not been worth the effort and he would betake himself elsewhere, perhaps to Athens, where the Scot, Elgin, was already devising ways to make off with the best friezes of the Parthenon. These mortals were so predictable.

But that moment, the entree arrived, carried on silver plates by young serving women, one of whom had lively black eyes. She turned those eyes in the direction of Monsieur Verdier, even as she held the plate of Chicken Marengo under Denon's nose. The *afreet* tweaked Monsieur's nose. He looked up. He smiled. Did a message pass between them?

Well, leave well enough alone. Leave Marguerite basking in the warmth of her husband's devotion, Josephine confident that next month will begin the pregnancy she awaits, and Bonaparte thinking of good food, glory, and museums, unaware of his appointment in Waterloo.

The door is closed, the matter is over, the pen is blunt.